JUST DON'T CALL ME YOURS

HEATHER GARVIN

Copyright © 2024 by Heather Garvin

All rights reserved.

No part of this book may be reproduced in any form or by any electronic or mechanical means, including information storage and retrieval systems, without written permission from the author, except for the use of brief quotations in a book review.

Ebook ASIN: B0CQNLNT6Y

Paperback ISBN: 979-8-9885299-1-0

Cover Design: Sam Palencia at Ink and Laurel

Editor: Kristina Haahr

This is a work of fiction. Names, characters, businesses, events, and incidents are the product of the author's imagination.

author's note

Just Don't Call Me Yours contains on page intimate scenes and is intended for mature audiences only.

playlist

Spotify: Just Don't Call Me Yours

Stacy - Quinn XCII
Just my Type - The Vamps
Do I Wanna Know? - Arctic Monkeys
Landslide - Fleetwood Mac
R U Mine? - Arctic Monkeys
Favorite T-Shirt - Jake Scott
My Anxiety - Baby Jake
Don't Blame Me - Taylor Swift
505 - Arctic Monkeys
I Can See You - Taylor Swift
High - Stephen Sanchez
Hits Different - Taylor Swift
Don't You Want Me - Portraits
Dress - Taylor Swift
I Just Wanna Be Yours - Arctic Monkeys

*To the girls who create their own destiny
and make it shimmer*

1
margot

"IF HE DOESN'T KNOCK it off, I'm going to kill him." I glare at the tiled ceiling of my new dorm room as I lie in bed, fighting the urge to check the time again. It's late—a lot later than I care to be awake before the first day of classes. The newly constructed building still smells like fresh paint, and I can vaguely make out my tapestry on the wall next to me. The burnt oranges and yellows of the boho-style sun look gray in the dark against the cool white walls.

I came to the University of South Florida to study journalism, not to be kept up all night. My eyes dart across the room to my best friend, Rae. There's no way she's asleep—she can't be. I followed her all the way here from Indiana, but right now, I'm wondering if that was a colossal mistake. It's not her fault. She didn't pick our neighbors, but she was definitely the ring leader behind this operation. She chose the college and dorm. All I had to do was break up with my boyfriend, pick a major, and tag along.

I thought being hundreds of miles from home would erase the crushing disappointment my parents were radiating before I left, but it's still there, smothering me like a wet blanket. To them, I might as well be a walking hazard. Not only do I disappoint them by wanting to be a reporter instead of a lawyer, but I also broke my poor high school boyfriend's heart.

If I'm being honest, I had wanted to break things off for a while. But he was so *perfect* in everyone else's eyes, and I just couldn't do it. Going to a college far, far away was the perfect excuse to cut ties. It felt less like I was dumping him and more like I was making the best decision for both of us. It doesn't matter, though. I'll always be the villain of that story. Sometimes I think my parents preferred him over me. He's the son of their closest friends. The tangled webs we weave. We were supposed to be the high school sweethearts who ended up together because that's what would have made *them* happy.

It's suffocating.

So, I came to Florida, where I know no one except Rae. We'll take on freshman year together, and we have it all planned out.

But none of my planning prepared me for my neighbors across the hall. We haven't met yet, but I've *heard* them. I've been here for a matter of days and already feel like I know so much about them—their voices, their laughs, their terrible taste in music. It's two guys, and I doubt they just met. I'd usually think it's great they knew each other before coming to college. I'm happy to live with my best friend, but I'm starting to wish they were awkward, quiet strangers.

Awkward, quiet strangers who *don't* play guitar.

It's not relaxing Beatles covers either—I might even enjoy that. The music coming from their dorm is anything but soothing. Even without an amp, the rock music somehow rattles through their four walls, forcing its way under the crack of our door and grating the inside of my ears.

There's no curated playlist. He plays the same song for what feels like hours—over, and over, and over again—until he decides to switch it up, playing an equally obnoxious song for just as long.

I roll over to check the time on my phone again, it's blinding light a beacon in the dark. Groaning, I see another hour of sleep has been stolen from me.

It's almost 2:00 a.m. I let out an exaggerated sigh.

"Margot, I know what you're thinking, but don't do it," Rae says from her twin-sized bed on the other side of the room. It's dark, but I can vaguely make out her blonde hair splayed over her pillowcase.

I don't want to. No one wants to be *that* person, but this is ridiculous. "I have to."

She turns her head toward me. "We're going to live across from them for a *year*. It will just make things weird."

He switches songs, playing harder than he was a minute ago, and I squeeze my eyes shut at the sound. "Tell that to Bon Jovi!"

The dorm has quiet hours after ten—the least he can do is hang it up until tomorrow. He's played for the past three nights, and I didn't let it bother me. We're all new to college, and if homeboy wants to stay up all night pretending he's a rockstar, so be it.

But today is Sunday. Classes start tomorrow, and mine start early. I can't lie here listening to this guy's amateur jam sesh all night.

Rae sighs before fully turning to face me in the dark. "He has classes tomorrow, too. I'm sure he'll go to sleep soon."

As if her words are magic, the racket stops. We both freeze, afraid one false move might ruin what just happened.

I hold my breath, hoping—*praying*—this guy calls it a night.
One.
Two.
The strumming starts again, and I throw the covers off with an aggravated huff.

"Margot!" Rae whisper-yells. "What are you doing?"

I shake my head. "I can't believe this guy."

Rae groans in a feeble attempt to stop me, but she doesn't sit up. Instead, she pulls the blanket up and over her head.

Padding across our tiny room, I look back at her on my way out. "We need to sleep!"

Stepping into the hallway, I squint under the fluorescent lights. The white block walls haven't been decorated yet—probably due to the paint still drying. The sterile scene makes me feel like I could be standing in a hospital, not a college dorm. Well, except for the dark green carpet. Go Bulls.

I was hoping there would be someone else out here, equally bothered by the noise, but our two dorms are at the end of a dead-end hall, practically making up our own island.

Lucky us.

The other people in the building are probably all getting the perfect amount of rest before their first day of classes.

The music stops, and I stare at the heavy, wooden door, hoping he goes to bed.

Hoping I won't have to do this because Rae is right. We're going to live across from them for an entire year.

But before I have time to let the silence sink in, he's back at it, and my fist has no problem finding the door for a few quick beats.

Nothing.

I knock again, this time making sure to pound out some of my frustration.

Still nothing.

The music falls silent, so I go to smack my open palm against the door, but it opens before my hand makes contact. I stumble forward, falling into the person on the other side.

"Whoa." He holds his hand out to steady me but quickly snatches it back like he's not sure he wants to touch me.

His other hand holds a guitar.

He's staring at me with an unreadable expression. His unkempt brown curls barely touch the neckline of his faded black concert T-shirt for The Black Keys. His eyebrows pull together in the most judgmental way I've ever seen, and I get the sudden urge to spray him with a squirt bottle—like trying to discipline an unruly cat. I do my best to ignore that he just acted like I was something about to spill all over him, but I glare at him anyway.

I may not have noticed his eyes at first, but they're easily the only soft thing about him. The rest of him is made up of harsh lines and sharp angles. From the set of his jaw to the bridge of his nose, and finally his lips pressed firmly together. It all contradicts the depth behind those eyes. It's unnerving to have him stare at me, and he's waiting for me to say something.

I'm suddenly overly aware I'm wearing nothing but cotton shorts and an oversized Fleetwood Mac T-shirt and blurt, "I need to sleep."

He frowns. "Well, you can't sleep here."

"No. I—" I'm cut off by a second voice coming from inside the room.

"Who is it?" his roommate asks, and by the grogginess in his voice, I think he was sleeping.

H*ow?*

"I don't know. Some girl. She might be drunk," the guy in the doorway answers over his shoulder, and I gape at him. When he looks back at me, he doesn't apologize. He cocks an eyebrow as if asking, *Well, are you?*

"I am not—ugh. Can you just stop playing the guitar?" This makes him blink, and after holding his attention for longer than comfortable, I prompt, "Please?" Although, that last word comes out through gritted teeth.

Wannabe Rockstar stares at me long and hard. "No."

He shuts the door in my face.

"Seriously?" I say out loud, thinking this must be some kind of joke. *Ha ha! Got you, neighbor. Did you really think I'd do such a thing?*

But there's no punchline.

There's nothing but a damn door in front of me. I pound my fist against it again, but all I get in return is another song I don't want to hear. Once the chorus I, unfortunately, know by heart starts, I turn on my heels and head back into my room, fuming.

"What did he say?" Rae asks, peeking out from behind her blanket.

"No."

"No?" She pulls back the covers to get a better look at me. "Just no?"

Plopping back onto my bed, I turn on my side to face her in the dark. "Just no."

She groans but doesn't say anything else, and I lie awake listening to endless strumming and thinking of all the things I'd like to say to that asshole the next time I see him.

And that's only if I fight the urge to throw something at him.

How am I supposed to live across from someone so . . . inconsiderate and *entitled* for the rest of the year? My parents already think my major is a joke. If I flunk out of college because the jerk across the hall keeps me up all night, I'll never live it down.

2
jackson

MATT SITS up in bed and pulls out one of his earplugs. "What was that about?"

I make my way to my side of the room and sit on the edge of my bed, strumming chords as I answer. "Noise complaint."

His face falls. "Dude, we're stuck living next to these people for the rest of the year."

My fingers pick at the guitar strings like they're on autopilot. "I know. I just have to get through tomorrow."

Matt opens his mouth like he's about to argue, but clamps it shut a moment later, surrendering with a nod. We've known each other since preschool and grew up in the same neighborhood, so he knows more than anyone how important tomorrow's audition is to me.

When I heard one of my favorite Tampa indie rock bands, American Thieves, was looking for someone to play guitar, I couldn't believe it. They're a small, local band, but I've seen them perform multiple times, and the idea of standing on stage with them has taken over my every thought for weeks.

So, as much as I know Matt's right about being nice to the

neighbors, he knows I won't let anything or anyone stand in my way. He knows this might be my golden ticket.

"She was drunk, so she might forget. She almost fell when I opened the door," I add as my fingers start to play one of American Thieves' earlier tracks from their EP—in case it comes up.

"Before the first day of classes?"

I shrug. "Seemed like it."

Matt stares at me. "If she's worried about getting enough sleep before class, I doubt she's drinking tonight."

Matt and his damn logic, always considering every side of the story. His thoughts are organized, encompassing stability. If my brain worked like his, maybe college wouldn't feel like such a drag. Matt thrives in this kind of environment, and even though the work itself isn't hard, I've never been one for standardized tests and multiple-choice quizzes. It bores me—hell, sitting still for too long without a guitar in my hands bores me. The only reason I'm here is because my dad didn't exactly give me an option. He'd love having a son like Matt—a son who actually *wants* to be here.

"She was wearing a Fleetwood Mac shirt."

He frowns. "You have to be drunk to like Fleetwood Mac?"

I seamlessly switch melodies and go into the start of another song. "You should be."

He resigns with a shake of his head. "I don't know, man," he says as he puts his earplugs back in. "Just try not to piss off too many people."

I give him a two-finger salute and keep playing.

There's a good chance I won't make it to class on time. Matt finally threw a pillow at me when I hit snooze on my alarm again. I'm not technically late . . . yet, but the building is still a fifteen-minute walk, and class starts in five. It doesn't help that whoever designed USF's campus built it like a toddler who doesn't want their food to touch.

As soon as the clock strikes eight, I curse under my breath. At least it's the first day. Nothing important happens on the first day.

Thankfully, the professor isn't a dick who likes to make snide comments when her students are late. I sneak in the back and take the first empty seat I find. The auditorium-style room slopes downward to the professor, standing with the syllabus on the projector.

Once I'm in my seat, I take out my notebook even though I have no intention of writing notes. English Comp first thing in the morning probably wasn't my best idea. I feel more creative at night. That's when melodies and songs come to me, so I haven't been a morning person since taking up guitar at the age of thirteen. By the time I got around to registering for classes, this was all that was left—lesson learned.

It's been less than a minute, and I'm already bored. The girl next to me has been shooting daggers at me since I sat down like I've interrupted the secret to life, and the professor is harping on about all the policies we'll be expected to follow while we're in her class.

I finally look over, ready to apologize for whatever the hell I did to ruin her day, but as soon as I open my mouth, I stop. It's the same girl who knocked on my door last night.

She looks rough.

Not only is she still wearing the stupid Fleetwood Mac shirt, but it looks like a bird could nest in the bun on her head, her red hair falling from it in all different directions. Her brown eyes burn into me, and I swear even the freckles on her nose look angry.

"What?" I whisper with a shrug. "I overslept."

Her eyes narrow. "I wonder why," she snaps before facing

the front of the room. Her hand grips the front corner of her notebook, unintentionally bending the pages back, her leg bouncing as she listens to the professor's policy on late work.

My lips twitch into what might be a smile. "Hey," I say, just to get a reaction out of her.

She ignores me, but her cheeks flare.

"Hey," I whisper a second time, and her head snaps my way faster than a jump-scare.

Trying to hide my amusement, I ask, "Can I borrow a pen?"

The girl stares at me, her eyebrows furrowing like she can't tell if I'm serious.

"No."

Before I have the chance to say anything, she's focused on the professor again. I know her clipped answers are in response to last night, and the corner of my mouth quirks. This girl can't stand me, and I don't know if I should find it funny or be offended.

Either way, it's going to be a long year.

3
margot

MY TEETH DIG into my bottom lip as I force my focus back on the professor. She's talking about the final exam? Maybe? My pen silently taps against the notebook in front of me because I can't believe this guy has the audacity to say *he* overslept.

Do you know who else overslept?

Me.

What about the fact that I barely had time to put on pants this morning before running out the door? Whose fault is it?

His.

If he didn't have me up all night listening to him play out his Guitar Hero dreams, I would have gone to bed on time. And if I would have gone to bed on time, there's a 99.9% chance I would have woken up on time.

I could have showered.

And stopped for coffee.

It could have been a great morning, but instead, I'm left wearing the shirt I slept in, and I broke a sweat running to get here. So, he'll just have to deal with the fact that I'm severely under-caffeinated and not in the mood to empathize with him.

"Relax, Red," he mutters, making me look at him.

"What?" I say in a sharp whisper, and as I wait for his response, I'm hit with the infuriating realization that, *of course*, he's hot.

He's hot in this annoyingly underrated way. Maybe it's the way he carries himself—like he doesn't care. Or maybe it's the way his eyes make me feel like he can see too much of me. Maybe it's the subtle smirk—or the way his hair somehow looks messy and styled all at once.

Or maybe I've hit a new level of tired.

Either way, it's safe to say my anger left me partially blind last night because I don't remember him looking like *that*.

His gaze moves to the notebook in my hands, pulling me from my intrusive thoughts. I look down to find I'm squeezing the corner so tightly I'm bending it in half. Quickly releasing it, I do my best to smooth it down, but I know it will never lie flat again.

Just another thing this guy has ruined.

"What's got you so worked up?" he asks with a lift of his annoyingly perfect lips.

He can't be serious. I give him an incredulous look before shaking my head and facing forward again. I'll just pretend he's not here.

The professor, a middle-aged woman in a sleek pencil skirt, carries on about how much our final research paper will count toward our grade, but all I can think about is how many minutes are left until I can get away from this guy. I stopped taking notes as soon as he sat down, but I try to get back on track and make a new heading titled, *Final Paper*.

"Are you seriously taking notes on the syllabus?"

My entire body tenses at the sound of his hushed voice, and I do my best to ignore him.

"You know the syllabus is online, right?"

My grip tightens around my pen, and I pause. Glaring at him, I hiss, "Can you stop talking to me?"

"Anything I can help you two with?" A voice from the front of the room rings out, and I look up to find the professor staring at us, her eyes glazed over like she's already sick of the bullshit.

The guy next to me goes to open his mouth, but I cut him off. "I'm sorry, professor. I'm trying to pay attention, but this guy won't stop asking where I live."

She lifts an eyebrow, her gaze shifting to my neighbor. Letting out a sigh, she says, "Young man, I'm going to have to ask that you don't harass your classmate—or at least do it on your own time." She looks back at me. "The number for campus security is on the last page."

I sigh out a breath. "Thank you."

A few heads turn, but I look down and start diligently writing in my bent notebook to avoid their stares. I can feel guitar-boy staring at me too, but I don't want to look his way either. I'm relieved when he finally finds a pen and starts taking notes like he should have done since the start of class.

The professor lectures on the importance of participating in the online discussion boards, and I take notes accordingly. For the remainder of class, everything feels as it should.

Until he leans over and puts a folded note on my desk.

I stare at it, wishing it would disappear. The unwanted attention makes my heart pound. What sort of terrible thing did he write?

Looking over at him, I mouth, "Really?"

Without a sound, he mouths back, "Really."

I stare at him a moment longer. He doesn't look like a murderer, but then again, do murderers ever look like murderers? I don't know this guy. Maybe I poked the wrong bear. Taking the note, I stuff it in my back pocket and get back to work. I'm not giving this asshole the satisfaction of seeing me react to whatever he wrote.

My cheeks stay hot for the last ten minutes of class until we're finally dismissed, and I feel like I can breathe again. As I gather my things, I keep my head down. Even if we live in the same dorm, he's the last person I want to walk with. Grabbing my bag, I put my notebook and pens away, and by the time I look up, he's gone. My eyebrows pinch as I scan the classroom, but he must have left as soon as the professor finished her last word.

Typical.

Taking a deep breath, I head straight for the campus coffee shop on the way back to my dorm. My next class isn't for a few hours, so I should have plenty of time to load myself up with caffeine and take a shower.

I'm standing in line, about to order my iced hazelnut latte, when I remember the note stuffed in my pocket. Looking around to make sure that guy is nowhere in sight, I pull out the crumpled paper. I don't know what I was expecting, but it wasn't *Low blow, Red* scrawled in sloppy handwriting. After humiliating him, I thought it would be worse—a lot worse.

I'm not even mad until my eyes fall to the PS at the bottom of the page.

Fleetwood Mac sucks.

That son of a bitch.

4
jackson

THANKS TO TAMPA TRAFFIC, the drive takes longer than it should. It doesn't help that I had to walk across campus to get my car after class. Lucky for me, I find a parking spot right away when I finally get to Ybor City. Being late to class is one thing, but I'd never be late for an audition. It's being held at some hole-in-the-wall bar I've never heard of. Growing up about two and a half hours away in Oviedo, this is all new territory.

I have eighteen minutes, but either the Florida heat or my nerves have me sweating as I step out of my Mazda. I don't remember the last time something has meant this much to me, and with how much I want this, I feel like there's a good chance I'll fuck it up.

That's why I've been practicing every hour of every day.

That's why Matt has slept with earplugs ever since we got to campus.

And that's why I hightailed it out of class as soon as I could.

Everything I've done the past few weeks has been with this

audition in mind, and everything I've done musically my entire life has led up to this moment.

I hit the button at the crosswalk and wait for the traffic to clear. The neon OPEN sign across the street calls my name even though it's off. Catching my reflection in the dirty, glass window, I deflate. The guys in this band are all in their mid-twenties to early thirties.

And I still look like I just graduated high school—which I guess is accurate. I'm early, so I wait outside and hear the guy before me nail it. He walks out of the bar ten minutes later with his full beard and aviator sunglasses, looking like he belongs in a band. Swallowing hard, I grip the door handle in one hand, squeezing my guitar case tighter in the other.

Fuck it. Let's do this.

It takes a second for my eyes to adjust to the dimly lit bar. Dave Lutz, the lead singer of a band I've bought tickets to countless times stands in front of me, and nothing could have prepared me for the gut punch that comes with it. American Thieves may not be on American Top 40, and there's a good chance most people have never heard of them, but that's what I love about them. They don't follow the latest trends, their tracks are made with instruments instead of computers, and they aren't sellouts. They're real, and they make real music.

I hold out a hand to Dave and hope he doesn't feel my palm sweating. "Hey, I'm Jackson Phillips."

Dave's dirty blond hair goes to his shoulders, his arms are covered in tattoos, and he's the epitome of a rocker—he's everything I want to be.

And he's eyeing me like I'm a kid at the mall who can't find his mom.

"Shit, man," he says with a chuckle. "Are you even legal?"

The fact that he's relaxed helps to ease some of my nerves, and I let out a breath of laughter. "As of eight months ago."

His mouth cracks into a grin. "Good for you!" He walks

me over to the stage where he takes a seat at a small table, front and center. "Plug in, and let's see what you've got."

Slowly, I make my way up the steps that lead to the small stage of the almost empty bar. I don't even think they're technically open right now. The only person here other than Dave is a bartender cleaning glasses, not paying attention. With shaking hands, I plug into the amp and take a deep breath.

Then I play like my life depends on it.

Because as far as I'm concerned, it does.

5
margot

IT'S amazing what a difference coffee and a shower can make —and a little distance from your obnoxious neighbor. I haven't seen him since we left class this morning, but I'm not complaining. Rae has been in and out of the room between classes, and I spent my downtime earlier getting organized for the semester ahead and working on my blog, Reid About It. The title is a play on my last name, and I started working on it when I was in tenth grade. It's a way for me to express my thoughts and opinions in a way that doesn't feel as stressful as voicing them face to face.

In high school, I loved the anonymity of it. I never wanted the people at school to know it was tied to me, so most of the growth has been organic. One of my goals this year is to share a little more of myself. All of my favorite bloggers pair a face with the words. I know if I want to one day earn money from it, I need to put myself out there more.

Walking back to my room after my US Government class ended early, I open the app on my phone and respond to some of the comments about my most recent post. The fifteen minute walk back to my dorm flies by with the distraction. By the time I make it to my hallway, I've finished responding to the last comment. Halfway down the hall, I lift my head when I hear a few girls laughing and talking through the open door. "I Can See You" by Taylor Swift plays on their speaker, and it makes me pause in their doorway.

"I've been listening to this on repeat." I lean against the door frame and hope I'm not interrupting. Meeting new people has always been a little intimidating, but at least I know I can connect with them on something. She's one of my favorite artists. I couldn't *not* stop.

"Right?" a girl with blonde curls says before jumping to her feet. "It's so good!" She holds out her hand. "I'm Izzy."

"Margot." I smile and hold out my hand to meet hers.

Peering around her, I wave to the other two girls sitting on one of the beds. One has long, brunette hair with the perfect curl at the ends, and the other has short, black hair styled in tight spirals. They both wave back, but before they can introduce themselves, Izzy takes over.

"This is my roommate Jess." She points to the girl with long hair. "And her girlfriend, Imani. She lives off campus."

"She's trying to turn us into Swifties," Imani explains, like playing Taylor's music ever needs an explanation.

"Don't fight it," I say with a shrug. "Lean into it."

Jess laughs. "To be fair, I like a lot of her songs, and I love the 'Swiftie' culture. Empowering women and making everything shimmer? Sign me up." She points her thumb at Imani. "She's the one who needs convincing."

Imani raises both hands in the air in defeat. "All right, fine. I'll *try* to listen." She pauses, eyeing the three of us. "To one album," she adds, holding up a finger.

Izzy and I look at each other in silent debate before collectively saying, "Midnights."

"Midnights Til Dawn," Izzy clarifies, and I nod.

Imani raises an eyebrow. "Yeah. Okay."

My eyes float to the clock on what I'm assuming is Izzy's side of the room. "You have all four album covers?" I take a step forward to get a closer look.

Izzy beams. "It's the only décor I was adamant about getting."

I mostly stream my music, so I haven't paid much attention to the physical albums, but I know she released four of them. Each album has a different picture with different numbers, and if you collect all four, it makes a clock. "I love it," I say with a grin. "This might sound weird, but do you think I can take a picture of it for my blog?" It's probably the first time I've talked about my blog with someone who isn't Rae, but the way Izzy's eyes light up eases some of the fear gripping me.

"You have a blog? Where you talk about Taylor Swift?"

I laugh as I hold up my phone toward her wall. Glancing her way, I check in with her before snapping the picture, and she happily nods.

Angling the shot, I say, "I talk about a lot of things. Music, movies, life." I shrug. "Whatever inspires me."

"I love that," Izzy says whimsically. "You have to tell me where I can find it. I'd love to take a look."

"Yeah?"

She gives a sharp nod. "Definitely."

"Okay." I smile. "I'll write it down for you."

Jess gets to her feet. "I'll get the link from Izzy. I'd love to check it out, too." She turns to Imani, pulling her up. "Come on, I saw some people in the common room and want to meet everyone who lives here."

As she's being pulled out of the room, Imani asks, "Do you two want to come?"

"I'll catch up with you!" Izzy says with a bright smile. "I just want to finish putting some of this stuff away." She points to the top of her desk, littered with knickknacks and keepsakes.

Imani's eyes jump to me, and I say, "Same." I point to my

bag. "I'll put my stuff in my room and then meet you." I had planned on working on a post, but I know I should make more of an effort to meet the other people on the floor. I'm not scheduled to post again for a few days, anyway. I have some time to get things ready.

"It was great meeting you, Margot!" Jess says on her way out, and Imani nods in agreement.

Once the other girls leave, I ask Izzy if she knew Jess before they got to campus.

She shakes her head. "No, but she seems great. I may have lucked out with the random roommate assignment."

"I think you did. Have you met anyone else on the floor yet?"

Izzy nods, still putting her stuff away. "A couple of guys from the other side. I think they live just past the elevator. They seemed nice, though. How about you?"

Just thinking about the guy who lives across the hall has me gripping the strap of my bag tighter. I could tell this practical stranger everything, but I can't bring myself to do it. I want a fresh start—the same fresh start I was supposed to have before that jerk showed up in my class this morning after keeping me up all night.

"Not yet," I say and hope she can't tell I'm lying.

Laughter sounds in the distance, and she straightens, satisfied with her organizational skills. "Well, let's go meet them."

I nod with my best smile and hope whatever-his-name-is is anywhere but the common room.

6
jackson

MATT and I are playing Cards Against Humanity with some of the people who live on the fourth floor with us, but all I can think about is my audition. I can't stop compulsively checking my phone even though Dave said I should hear back in a few weeks. Who knows if he'll even get back to me, but at least I gave it my all. He seemed impressed when he complimented how tight my transitions were, but maybe he's just a nice guy.

"Jackson!" one of the girls at our table cries out. I think her name is Bridget. Or Jaqueline? She ran up to me, introduced herself, and then introduced her girlfriend. I was half paying attention, my mind still reliving the songs Dave asked me to play on that tiny stage. "It's your turn!"

"Shit, sorry." I draw a card.

Matt grabs my shoulder, giving it a shake. "Yeah. Keep up, man," he says with a laugh. He can probably tell I'm overanalyzing how things went today, but he also knows I don't want to tell anyone about it. There's a good chance nothing will come of it, and I'd rather not have to explain what will likely be my biggest disappointment to date.

My face falls as I stare at the card in hand, but I catch

myself before anyone notices, reading it out loud and setting it down on the table.

When your dad pulls you aside to talk about _____ and how it's affecting your _____.

Holy shit. Talk about the shoe fitting. There are too many things I could put in those slots. My dad has an opinion about everything I do, and it's never good.

The door to the common room swings open, and my jaw tenses. Red walks in with another girl, laughing at something she must have said.

She looks different.

She's kind of pretty now that she's taken a shower and isn't wearing a shirt for a shitty band that's two sizes too big. Her red hair is long, falling to her lower back, and I like the way her hips move when she walks.

Too bad she's annoying and tried to make me look like a stalker in front of our entire English class.

Looking over her shoulder at her friend, she says something I can't make out, and both girls laugh in response. Once she's facing forward again, her big, brown eyes scan the room before settling on me and immediately dimming.

My mouth quirks at her reaction.

"Hey!" the perky blonde with her says as she approaches the table, but Red stays quiet.

"Hey," Matt says with a grin. "I don't think we've met yet. Do you two live together?"

"No," the blonde answers. "I'm Izzy. I'm in 416 with Jess." She points to Bridget/Jaqueline who's obviously neither. "I just met Margot a few minutes ago." She looks over at Red as she makes the introduction.

Red, aka Margot, looks at everyone and offers a polite smile.

"Who do you live with?" A guy, whose name I've also forgotten, asks her. He introduced himself thirty minutes ago, but I've got nothing—not even a guess. Just because we live around these people doesn't mean we have to be friends with them . . . but I guess I should at least try to remember their names.

She rubs the side of her arm like having all eyes on her makes her nervous. "Oh, my friend Rae from high school. She's at the library."

"Already?" Matt asks with a furrowed brow. "It's the first day."

Margot lifts her shoulders in a shrug. "One of her textbooks didn't come in on time. I think she went to see if they had a copy."

"Bummer," Matt says with an understanding nod.

"Well, I'm Keith," the guy says, and I vaguely remember him telling me his name now. "Hey, do you want to play?"

Izzy peers at our table, her eyes wide. "Oh, I love this game! Are you sure you don't mind starting a new one?"

"You can take my cards," I offer. "I was planning on sitting the next one out, anyway." I'm used to practicing every day, but while I was preparing for the audition, I kicked it into overdrive. For weeks, I've been practicing nonstop, determined to make sure I'd play flawlessly today. Now that I have nothing to prepare for, my hands don't know how to relax. Even the playing cards are making me fidget. I find myself shuffling for no better reason than to move my fingers.

Izzy looks over at Red. "What about Margot?"

"Don't worry about me," Margot says as she pulls up a chair. "I can just hang out." For the first time since she walked in here, her eyes lock on me, brimming with challenge. "So, what's your name?"

7
margot

HE LOOKS up at me impassively. "Jackson."

That's it. One word.

He focuses on the cards in his hands and starts shuffling. His dismissal makes my blood simmer, but I turn to his roommate and smile. "And yours?"

His roommate gives me a wide grin. His black hair is short and neat, and his brown eyes have a kindness behind them that's impossible to fake. "Matt," he says as he sets his cards down to shake my hand.

So, I guess one word can be friendly.

"Nice to meet you, Matt," I say, genuinely pleasant.

I catch Jackson's eyes drifting up to meet mine for a fraction of a second. The way he looks at me somehow makes me feel analyzed and judged. Every time he looks my way it's like another string inside me snaps.

I fix my eyes on Matt. "Do you play guitar, too?"

Matt tilts his head, his eyes jumping from me to Jackson. I'm tempted to look at him again, but I can't run the risk of being further unraveled. Matt's hands stop mid-shuffle as he puts the pieces together. I have a feeling he knows I'm the one who knocked on his door last night. "Uh, no." He clears his throat. "When it comes to music, I suck at just about everything—played lacrosse in high school, though." He laughs. "Be glad it's Jackson with the guitar."

Despite my better judgment, I look over at Jackson. He casually leans back in his chair, eyeing me like the ball is in my court. I wish I could say his arrogance takes away from his appearance. That asshole smirk may be saying, *Yeah, be glad*, but it doesn't take away from how perfect his stupid face is.

I've met guys like him—guys who think everything they touch is a gift to those around them. Jackson may be used to people fawning over him and his music, but I have no problem being the one to knock him down a peg.

"Oh, I don't know about that," I say thoughtfully with a twist of my lips. "Would you be up all night keeping everyone awake? Or do you have a shred of common decency?" I even have my hand raised with my thumb and forefinger pinched as I say *shred*, and I know I've gone too far.

But he has to know, right? He has to know his roommate is stupidly inconsiderate.

Matt's wide eyes jump to Jackson before he lifts both hands in the air, signaling he wants nothing to do with this.

I can't blame him.

Jackson sits up straight. Resting his elbows on the table across from me, he says, "Let it out, Red. What's your problem?"

The silence that follows his question lets me know I have everyone's attention. The rapt audience makes my pulse quicken, but I cross my arms. "Excuse me for not wanting to be lulled to sleep by the soothing melodies of 'alternative rock.'" My fingers do air quotes as the genre leaves my lips.

He stares at my hands in the air. "What are you doing?" His eyebrows furrow. "Are you implying rock isn't real music?"

This conversation has taken on a force of its own, and at

this point, I feel like I'm no longer in the driver's seat. I'm just along for the ride. Plus, he deserves it. "It's noise." I challenge with a lift of my brow. "And when it's the same half-learned song over and over again at 2:00 a.m., it's shitty noise." Turning to Matt, I add, "Seriously, how do you sleep in the same room as him?"

Matt's mouth opens, but he says nothing.

"Noise? *Shitty* noise?" Jackson says, bringing my attention back to him.

"Yeah," I answer unapologetically.

"What about Nirvana? The Killers? Cage the Elephant? *Shitty noise* doesn't shape the music industry."

I just shrug. "It's not my thing."

"Oh, I *love* Nirvana," Jess says, tossing her long, brunette hair over her shoulder and trying to ease the tension.

Jackson barely looks at her as he nods and says, "Of course, you do." Then he gestures toward her with both hands. "Because that's how you should react when you hear someone say Nirvana!"

The fact that he's getting worked up about this somehow makes it easier for me to stay calm. "I just don't see how jumping around and playing guitar as hard as you can is considered being a musician."

He's at a loss for words, and I have nothing left to say. We glare at each other across the table until Keith says with a nervous laugh, "So, this is going to be a fun year, yeah?"

Out of the corner of my eye, I catch Izzy smiling, but it almost looks pained. She seemed like a nice girl, but I doubt she'll want anything to do with me after this. My cheeks flush, and I wish I could disappear. I need to go back to my room.

I stand, but Jackson does, too. We both freeze. "I'm going back—" he starts to say as I mutter, "I should probably—"

We stop.

Eventually, he lets out a sigh. "Whatever." With a lift of his brow he says, "Can I walk back to my room? Or do you not want me to see where you live?"

I roll my eyes. "I don't care what you do." Turning to the rest of the table, my cheeks heat as I say, "Uh, I guess I'll see you around."

Everyone waves, but it's the most uncomfortable goodbye I've ever experienced. This wasn't exactly a great first impression.

Jackson heads out of the room, already a step ahead of me, and doesn't bother holding the door open on his way out.

"You know," he says over his shoulder as he walks down the hallway. "Say what you want about my music, but it's better than listening to Stevie whine into the mic."

I stop.

When I don't answer right away, he looks back at me. "You'll never be able to unhear it now." He points to his ear. "*That's* shitty noise."

"Um, Stevie Nicks is a *goddess.*"

"Right." He turns back around. "I hate to be the one to tell you this, but you're a little predictable, Red. Let me guess," he says over his shoulder. "You're also obsessed with Taylor Swift, and Paul is your favorite Beatle."

I feel attacked.

My feet find their motion again, and before I know it, I'm marching after him.

"What do you have against Paul?" I demand as I catch up to him.

"Nothing," he says as he rounds the corner without looking at me.

I follow him, practically nipping at his heels. "And how *dare* you mention Taylor Swift's music like it's a bad thing."

He stops in front of his door and gives me a condescending look like I should *know* what's wrong with Taylor Swift.

"You want to know what I think?" I cross my arms.

He rests one hand on the door handle. "Not particularly."

"I think you're just hellbent on not liking anything 'mainstream.' You think you're better than the rest of us because your favorite band has never played on the radio, and if they ever do get popular, you'll turn your back on them. You'll talk about how much you *used to* like them and how good they *used to* be. You know, before they 'sold out.'"

A slight crease forms between his eyebrows.

"Who's predictable now?" I lift my chin, feeling pretty satisfied with myself.

After staring at me long and hard, he opens the door to his dorm. "You don't get it," he says dismissively with a shake of his head.

It's the second time he's shut the door in my face. I yank my own door open, slamming it behind me. I hate feeling like he's somehow won this round.

You don't get it.

What don't I get? I think I was spot on. Hopefully, I never get to know him well enough to find out.

8
jackson

IT'S BEEN TWO WEEKS, and I still haven't heard from Dave about my audition. Focusing on anything school related has been impossible. The first week, I barely thought about it. I knew I wouldn't hear back from him right away. But as soon as the two-week mark rolled around, it's like I've become obsessed. Every time my phone goes off, I nearly have a heart attack until I see it's just my mom or Matt, asking if I've had dinner yet.

Sitting on my bed, I try to finish typing my first English paper, my pent-up anxiety and frustration coming out each time my fingers slam into the keys.

My noise-canceling headphones play "505" by Arctic Monkeys so loud I don't even hear Matt coming into the room until he takes a hard seat on his bed directly across from me. Looping one of the headphones behind my ear, I give him a nod. "Hungry?" I'll take any excuse to stop writing this paper.

"Yeah," he says without looking, still focused on whatever he was doing before he walked in here.

"Cool," I say, closing my laptop. "Where do you want to go?"

"What?" he asks like he's forgotten I'm here.

"To eat," I clarify, eyeing him. "Are you okay?"

He nods. "Yeah." His hand cups the back of his neck as he stares down at the floor of our room, and I cock an eyebrow as I wait for him to say more.

Before he has time to elaborate, movement in the hallway catches my attention. Margot comes into view, stopping when she sees us.

"Hey, Matt." She smiles while she searches for the keys in her bag, and like this, she's unsuspecting. She's cute, friendly, and has an ass I have to consciously remind myself not to stare at.

Matt gives her a nod, but even she can't pull him out of his funk.

Sitting on the edge of my bed, I rest my elbows on my knees and look over at her. "You know, I'm here, too," I say, just to poke her.

She finds her keys. "Oh, I know." Turning her back, she unlocks her door and says over her shoulder, "It's a disappointment I'm faced with every day."

I cock an eyebrow. "Every day? Are you hung up on me, Red?"

She scoffs but says nothing before going into her room, leaving the door open.

"I just need to finish my assignment for Bio and then we can go."

"Yeah." Leaning to the side, I look into Margot's room. She puts her hair up in a bun on her head before taking a seat at her desk and getting out her laptop. "That works because I have to finish my paper."

He nods and gets to work, but as soon as I grab my laptop and look down at the screen in front of me, a distinct voice fills the air. I don't know the name of the song, and I don't have to.

It sounds like all of Fleetwood Mac's other music. Stevie's voice is unfortunately unmistakable.

"Let it go," Matt says in a warning tone.

"Who said I was going to do anything?"

Without looking up from his computer, he shrugs.

Glaring back at my unfinished English paper, I try to focus. It's due tomorrow, and I started it about twenty minutes ago, so the five sentences on the screen aren't giving me much to work with. Plus, the professor has made it clear she has a thing about thesis statements, so if I can't get at least that right, there's a good chance I'm fucked.

The song ends, and "Landslide"—a song I do know—comes on next.

I groan.

"Let. It. Go." This time, Matt looks at me, holding my stare like he needs some type of confirmation I've heard him.

I shake my head and blow out a breath.

Matt's low laughter at least gives me a sense of normalcy, and I manage to put down another sentence during the song.

I've spent the better part of five minutes trying to figure out how many more sentences I'll need to finish this paper until "Landslide" plays *again*.

I lean forward to get a better view. She's still at her desk, quietly singing along as she gently bobs her head and types away like she doesn't have a care in the world. She's probably the type of person who has had her English paper done for at least a week, so I wonder what she's writing. One of the girls on the floor said something about Margot having a blog, and I can only imagine the shit she complains about online.

Her head lifts, and we lock eyes. With a smile that's way too sweet to be genuine, she waves before going back to whatever she's working on. She's doing this out of spite, but I'll let her have her fun.

As long as I can have some fun, too.

I get to my feet and walk over to my stereo. Matt's head snaps up. "What are you doing?"

I shrug. "I want to listen to something." Without turning the volume up too loud, I let the Foo Fighters distract me from Stevie's depressing lullaby next door.

Matt tsks disapprovingly. "She's not going to like that."

I sit back on my bed. "She'll get over it."

The blinking cursor on the screen taunts me, and I rub my hands over my face as I try to get back on track.

Think.

Think.

Think.

There isn't even a break between songs when "Landslide" repeats for the third time, louder than before.

"That's it." I set my laptop aside and stand again.

"We need to get along with them," Matt says with a laugh, but there's a tone of caution in his voice.

Ignoring him, I turn up my stereo speakers until "Landslide" is completely drowned out by Dave Grohl. This time I can't resist looking into the room across the hall, and the sight doesn't disappoint. Red stands in the doorway, and she's straight up *glowering*.

She says something, but her voice gets lost in the music.

With a shrug, I mouth the word "Sorry," and point to my ear. "Can't hear you."

Her eyes flare, and she marches over, pushing past me to get into the room.

"What the hell?" I turn around to find her yanking my stereo plug out of the wall. The silence that fills the room is deafening. She must have turned off her music at some point because there's nothing.

She stands there, holding my stare. I expect her to explode, but she just takes a breath and says, "Have a great day, Matt."

"Yup. You too, Margot," Matt says, his voice clipped and uncomfortable.

Stepping around me, she marches across the hall, and I track her movements as she goes. Turning, she flips me the bird before slamming the door shut.

This girl is a piece of work. She knows she's the one who started this fight, right? How is it my fault my stereo gets louder than her shitty laptop speakers?

"All right," Matt says as he grabs his keys. "Let's go get food before you two burn the place to the ground."

9
margot

ASSHOLE.

He really does bring out the worst in me, and I can't shake the feeling he keeps *winning*.

Winning what? No idea.

But every time he and I go head to head, I walk away feeling like he got the final jab, and it just makes me want to try again. Even today, *I* slammed the door in *his* face. I finally got to be the one to shut him out.

He said nothing.

He *did* nothing.

And somehow his lack of reaction still has me feeling like he got the last word, like he was able to so easily dismiss having his stereo unplugged and a door slammed in his face.

Like he doesn't care.

And somehow, his not caring is the ultimate last jab.

I think he and Matt might have left, but I keep my door shut. Settling at my desk again, I try to get back on track. I stare at my screen where the picture of Izzy's album clock stares back at me with my most recent post draft beneath it.

Networking Through Taylor Swift

College can be a daunting time for anyone. It's a new school, and chances are you've landed in a new city or state. Meeting people can feel like a burden even though we're all in the same boat. We all left old friends to find new ones, so why does walking up to someone on your floor and starting a conversation feel like volunteering as tribute?

I planned on writing about how we can find common ground through music, but as I stare at the words, something doesn't feel right. Sure, I connected with Izzy a few weeks ago over music, but my stereo war with Jackson proves music can drive people apart, too. I hit the delete key until I'm left with a blank screen again. The post was vague, anyway. Back home I used to write about local people, places, events, etc. I plan on doing that for the Tampa area now that I live here, but everything is still too new.

The door flies open and Rae walks in. "Hey."

I glance at her and smile. "Hey, are we still on for Ben&Jerry's? Because I need it after the afternoon I had."

"Sure," she answers with a laugh. "Want to go now?"

Snapping my laptop shut, I jump to my feet. "Please. The only thing that can make me feel better is some Cherry Garcia."

"Yeah, I'm not going to lie, I've been thinking about Half Baked all day." We lock up our dorm, and I'm relieved to see Jackson and Matt's door shut. "So, why was your afternoon so bad?" Rae asks as we walk down the hallway.

I relay the events of my music war with Jackson, and by the time I'm done telling the story, we've reached the Ben&Jerry's on campus.

"Wow . . ." Rae says as she pulls open the door to the shop. "That sounds a little . . . aggressive? I mean why not just keep your music lower? Or shut your door? Or maybe don't play 'Landslide' three times in a row?"

I playfully narrow my gaze. "Whose side are you on?"

She laughs and we pay for our frozen treat before settling at a small table outside.

She takes a bite. "I'm just saying, why does it always have to be war with you two? I mean, it sounds like he wasn't doing anything to bug you before then, right?"

"His existence bugs me," I grumble before I take another spoonful of cherry chocolate goodness.

Rae shakes her head. "Well, I have to tell you something, and you're not going to like it."

My anger dissolves. "Is everything okay?"

She forces a laugh. "Yeah, everything is great—at least *I* think it is."

Sitting up straight, I tilt my head. "Well, if you think it's a good thing, I'm sure I will, too."

She opens her mouth but hesitates, taking another bite and shrugging.

"Out with it." I point to her with my spoon. My heart rate picks up as I wait for her to say what's on her mind. She never keeps things from me.

She lets out a huff and sets her spoon down to put her hair into a low ponytail like she needs to be ready to make a run for it. "Someone asked me out."

I stare at her, waiting for the part I won't like. "And you like him? Or is he a stalker who will murder us in our sleep?"

"I like him," she says with a nod.

My lips turn down. This is our year to do things together, but if she dates someone, we'll have to bring him along with us. It will be different, but not necessarily bad. I don't see Rae liking anyone I wouldn't like. "I'm not seeing a problem here."

Rae grabs a lock of her hair, running her fingers over the tips. She's holding back whatever she wants to say. Eventually, she looks away from her hair and settles her green eyes on me. "There isn't a problem."

"Okay, great," I say with a laugh as I try to figure her out.

"But . . ."

". . . but?"

"Did I mention his roommate plays guitar?" The words come out rushed before she shovels another spoonful of Half Baked into her mouth like it's a coping mechanism.

I freeze. "You did not."

She winces, and we stare at each other, my mind reeling. I've seen Rae and Matt talk sometimes. Just yesterday they were standing between our two doors when I got home from class. He had said something funny to make her head fall back with laughter, but I had no idea she was interested in him.

"It's just a date," she blurts. "There's a good chance it won't turn into anything."

"When?"

Still grimacing, she says, "Later tonight."

My brain is still trying to process the news, and I blink while she's waiting for a response. Keeping my tone casual, I say, "Are you sure dating someone who lives across the hall is a good idea? What if it doesn't work and living across from him gets awkward?"

She gives me a heavy-lidded stare. "It will be fine. You and Jackson have never dated, and look how well that's going."

Okay, fair. "Thank God for that," I mutter.

She rolls her eyes. "He's not that bad. I get that he was playing guitar all night, but he's been respecting the quiet hours since."

Hearing her defend him stirs something inside me. "But he's just so . . ." I struggle to find the right word.

If Rae and Matt get together, there's a good chance we won't only be hanging out with Matt . . . we'll have to hang out with Jackson, too. They're always together.

Which means we'll be around them a lot.

Matt . . . and Jackson.

"Okay," she says, waving a hand. "I know you think Jackson is the worst. Can we talk about my date now?" Her eyes go from annoyed to vulnerable. "Because I'm excited but kind of nervous."

Her comment snaps me out of my haze. "Of course! I'm sorry. I suck. Where are you guys going?"

She shrugs. "He asked me where I wanted to go, so I told him—"

"Rae, if you told him Chili's . . ."

"—I told him Chili's."

"Rae!" Her name leaves my lips with bubbling laughter, but she just shrugs again.

"What? I like it!"

"I know," I say with a rueful shake of my head. "But we're in college now. In another state. Maybe it's time to try some new places." I shovel a few back-to-back bites of ice cream into my mouth, and Rae gives me a concerned look.

"What are you doing?"

"We"—I say between bites—"need to figure out what you're wearing."

Her eyes widen. "I didn't even think of that!" She takes a large bite but gives me a tight-lipped smile through it. "Thank you."

"Hey," I say after licking my spoon. "I will accept your thanks in the form of—"

"Yes, I'll bring you back a molten lava cake," she says without looking at me.

My lips pull into a smile. "This is why we're friends."

10
jackson

MATT DOESN'T SAY a word the whole five-minute drive to Chipotle. He parks, we go inside, and even as we're standing in line, he's lost in thought.

"What are you getting?" I scan my options overhead. I'll get a chicken bowl like I always do, but it gives me something to look at while Matt is busy being weird as fuck.

"Oh, uh . . . probably a bowl. You?"

Rocking back on my heels, I nod. "Same."

Another beat of silence.

We take a few steps forward as the line moves. If there's one thing you can count on, it's that the Chipotle in a college town will always have a line.

"Something on your mind?" I ask, hoping a more direct approach will crack the surface.

Matt blinks. "Why do you say that?"

"Uh, because you're going through the motions like a zombie, and it's starting to freak me out."

He laughs. "No, I'm good. Really good." He steps to the front and tells the girl behind the counter he wants a bowl.

"You and Margot need to figure out your shit, though. It's making everyone on the floor feel weird."

I tell the girl I want the same and step to the side. "What's there to figure out? She sucks."

After ordering his toppings, he shakes his head. "She doesn't suck." He shrugs. "She always waves to me when I see her."

"All I know is I want to see her as little as possible."

We pay and find a table. Matt takes a bite and looks out the window. "She's been hanging around that guy Keith a lot. Maybe he'll keep her busy."

"Poor guy," I say, unconcerned. I take a bite of my food. I'm glad he's finally talking, but I wish he'd stop mentioning Margot. The bossy girl next door isn't exactly my favorite talking point.

"Relationships make people happy, right? Maybe if they date, she'll be in a better mood."

I stop chewing. "I guess?" He goes back to eating, but I can't stop scrutinizing him. Putting down my fork, I say, "All right. What's with you? You don't talk the whole way here, and now you keep talking about Margot of all people? Both are weird."

He frowns, looking down at his food. "Nothing."

"Matt, I've known you since we were four. Something's up with you. Just say it."

"Do you think it's a bad idea to ask out someone on our floor?"

I freeze before taking another bite. "What?"

"Never mind," he says and gets back to eating.

What the hell? His questions about Margot make a lot more sense, and I'm trying not to panic. "Who is it?"

Please don't say Margot.
Please don't say Margot.
Please don't say Margot.

Matt registers the look on my face and laughs. "Would you relax? It's not Margot."

"Thank God," I say with a loose breath. "At the very least, I'd like to be able to pretend I like your girlfriend." I'm about to take another bite, but I stop. "You're not planning on asking out her roommate, are you?"

Matt smiles, but it doesn't reach his eyes, and the reassurance he just gave me disappears.

"No," I groan.

"I'm sorry!" he says, laughing. "You've hung out with us in the common room, so you know she's cool."

"*Why?*" The word drags out of me, and I shake my head. "You're right, dating someone on our floor is stupid. Don't do it."

His mouth quirks because he knows I'm joking.

"You like her?" I ask.

With a casual lift of his shoulder, he says, "I think so."

I know he does. Matt doesn't go into anything without thinking it through.

"Don't think this means I'll hang around Margot more. I'm your friend, but I have to draw the line somewhere."

He forces a laugh. "Understood."

"Okay." I pick up my fork, shoving it back into my bowl. "Ask her out, then."

He grins. "I already have."

11
margot

RAE HAS BEEN on her date with Matt for a couple of hours now. My fingers tap against the keys as I sit on my bed, doing research for my Mass Media class. Faint voices of two girls further down the hallway help to keep me focused, giving me a sense of life around me. If I shut the door, I probably wouldn't hear Jackson playing as much, but it's still early.

He's actually not bad once you hear him play at a decent hour. I'm starting to recognize the different songs he plays even if I don't know the titles or lyrics. He's practicing a few different ones tonight, rotating between four or five songs. One of them has a catchy beginning I always end up bobbing my head to, and I'm just glad his door is shut so he can't see.

Every time I hear voices in the hall, my ears perk, thinking Matt and Rae are back from their date, but the voices always fade in the opposite direction.

I'm on pins and needles, waiting for them to get back. I want her to have fun. She's my best friend, and I love her more than anything, but the selfish part of me is hoping she doesn't like Matt as much as she thought.

Because if she doesn't like Matt, it will be easier to pretend Jackson doesn't exist.

The music stops, and my eyes instinctively jump to the door across the hall. The only time the music stops is when he finally goes to sleep, has to do homework (but usually music still plays on his stereo if that's the case), or he's about to leave the dorm. I stare at the door, waiting for it to open, but it doesn't. The door stays shut, and somehow the silence is eerily more distracting than the constant strum of his guitar. Like the calm before one of us fires a shot.

My eyes fall to my computer again, but it's hard for me to get back on track—especially when the door across the hall finally opens.

Jackson leans against the door frame with no guitar, wearing dark jeans and a Red Hot Chili Peppers shirt. He frowns when he sees me, like the fact that I live next door is an unpleasant surprise he'd forgotten about. "They're not back yet?"

"Nothing gets past you," I mutter and aimlessly scroll on my laptop for the sake of looking busy.

I expect him to scoff or say something snarky, but he just stands there.

Bringing my eyes to his again, I ask, "Is there something you need?"

He points a thumb over his shoulder. "I just . . ." but his words trail off, and he shakes his head. Staring at me with more clarity, he seems to remember who I am, his expression hardening. "Forget it," he says. "I'll just wait for Matt to get back."

"And I'll wait for Rae," I say with a nod.

His frown deepens. "This is going to be weird."

I can't help feeling slightly offended even though I was thinking the same thing. Trying to be the bigger person, I go for a change of subject. "That one song you played tonight didn't suck."

He cocks his head, and my body warms with how intently he's looking at me. "Which one?"

I force a laugh. "I don't know."

"Well, how did it go?"

I know how the song went, but this feels like a trap. He probably just wants to make fun of me when I try to mimic the sound of his guitar. "I don't remember."

Before I can say anything else, he rolls his eyes and goes into his room. I watch, my eyebrows creasing only to have him reemerge a moment later with his guitar in hand.

12
jackson

WHEN I WALK into Margot's room, she's watching me with untrusting eyes, and when I sit on her bed a few feet in front of her, those skeptical brown eyes widen. I look around, taking in her sun-themed posters and orange bedding. By the way she decorates her room, you'd think her disposition was a little more . . . well, sunny.

"What are you doing?" she asks, frozen in place.

I don't know why she's being weird about this. "I want to know what song it was." I position my guitar, but as soon as I'm situated, I realize why she's acting like she has stage fright. I haven't been this close to her since the first day of class, and it's starting to make me uncomfortable, too.

It's like seeing her in HD. From here, I can see a small freckle on her bottom lip I never noticed before, and her eyes are brighter—more captivating than I remember. My heel bounces against the dorm room floor, and I slam it down to stop it.

She snaps her laptop shut. "Okay, fine."

Her hair is up, but a few pieces fall around her face and at the base of her neck. My eyes trail from her neck to where her oversized T-shirt has slipped, exposing her bare shoulder. My gaze snags on the black lace strap of her bra, and I can't tear my eyes away.

It isn't until she clears her throat that I remember why I came here in the first place.

I have a feeling I know which song she's talking about. Of all the songs I've played tonight, one has an opening riff anyone would recognize. It's a great way to open a song, and there's a good chance she's heard it before. Sometimes people notice what subconsciously sounds familiar. As soon as I start strumming the opening chords to Arctic Monkeys' "Do I Wanna Know?" her face lights up.

"How did you know that was the song?"

I let out a breath of laughter. "Because you've heard it before."

She pulls her head back, looking at me with a furrowed brow. "No, I haven't."

I stop playing. "Yes, you have. It's from their most popular album, and that riff has been used everywhere. It's overplayed."

"I've never heard that song before." She speaks slowly like I didn't understand what she said the first time.

Setting my guitar aside, I shrug. "You should hear it with the drum track. It's better than me playing it."

"I'll look it up. What's it called?"

She opens her laptop, but I close it. "You can't listen to it on those shitty speakers." Getting up from her bed, I say, "Come on. I'll put it on, and you can wear my headphones."

Her eyes jump from me to the open door across the hall like it's a terrible place she swore she'd never go. She hesitates before saying, "Sure. Okay," and cautiously gets up to follow me.

After being in Margot's tidy, put-together dorm, I'm blatantly aware of the mess mine is. Matt's side looks like it could be used in a brochure for the college, but mine looks like it should come with caution tape. I'm messy, not dirty—there's a difference. No one will find a half-eaten sandwich under my pile of clean clothes I haven't put away yet.

I quickly shove those clothes off the bed so she can have a place to sit.

She eyes the pile on the floor and then the bed, and with that face, I know she's regretting following me, but I'm too hell-bent on playing her this song to care. Hesitantly taking a seat on the bed, she waits. I get the song ready. I hand her my headphones, and she pauses before slowly putting them over her ears.

I hit play.

Margot's eyes snap to me as soon as the song starts, a smile teasing at the corners of her mouth. "You're right!" she practically yells. I wince but can't help laughing, and she drops her voice before continuing. "The drums take it from good to great." She looks down, her head moving side to side with the sound of the intro, and even though I'm not, I feel like I'm listening to it with her. So, when her eyes widen again, I know it's because Alex Turner started singing. She gasps and whispers, "I love his voice."

My mouth quirks. Of course she does. We lock eyes, and as much as I want to look away from her, I can't. There's something magnetic about the way she looks as she listens to one of my favorite bands, and nothing could have prepared me for it.

"What's going on in here?" Matt says from the doorway, and he already looks like he's enjoying this more than he should.

You'd think the headphones electrocuted Margot with how fast she pulls them off and tosses them on my bed.

Rae stands next to Matt in the doorway, holding a to-go container and staring at Margot with a baffled expression.

"How was the date?" I ask before either of them can say anything annoying about Margot and me sitting here.

Rae and Matt glance at each other before both saying their own version of "It was good." I try to read through the lines, but neither of them gives much away. Rae eyes us with a little too much amusement. "How was *your* night?"

Turning off my stereo, I shrug. "As good as can be expected when you live next to Margot."

Matt laughs and looks at Rae. "And here I thought they were getting along for once."

Margot gets to her feet, and if I didn't know any better, I'd say she looks wounded by what I've said. But that doesn't make sense. This is nothing new between us. This is what we do.

She bounces back quickly enough to come at me with, "I know the only company you keep is Matt, but maybe try cleaning your room for once. God forbid you ever trick a girl into coming back here with you." Her eyes fall onto the pile of clothes on the floor. "She probably won't want to sit on your dirty clothes."

She starts to leave, her hips swaying with each step. "They're clean!" I call after her, but she's already gone into her dorm, shutting the door behind her.

Rae sighs with a shake of her head. Then looking at Matt, she says, "I'll text you." She throws me a wave. "Night, Jackson."

I nod. "Night."

As soon as Matt closes the door behind her, he turns to me. "That was the most fun I've had with a girl. Ever." He runs his hand over his hair. "She likes football, and she's not a Bama fan."

I let out a slow whistle. "Dodged a bullet there. Who's her team?"

"Chicago," he says without losing his smile. "Her family is

originally from there." With a shrug, he adds, "I can get behind the Bears for that. It's the same reason I love LSU."

I've only been on a few first dates, but I've never felt anything close to what he's feeling right now. Hook up with a girl? Sure. Take her out to dinner and talk to her for an hour and a half? Hard pass. I haven't met a girl who would make that sound fun—who knows if I ever will.

"You'll see her again?" I ask, already knowing the answer.

He nods, pulling his phone out of his pocket as he flops onto his bed. He smiles and immediately starts typing a response. Rae must have texted him. With a stupid grin, he answers without looking at me. "Definitely."

"So." I sit on my bed, fidgeting with the headphones I let Margot use. "I got a call while you were out."

This makes him pause. "Like a call from Dave Lutz or a call from your mom?"

My mouth quirks as I coil and uncoil the headphone wire around my finger. "A call from Dave Lutz."

He sits up straight, on the edge of his seat to hear the news I never thought I'd be able to deliver. "And?"

I can't fight my tight-lipped smile as I look at him. "And he wants me to play for American Thieves."

"No shit!" He gapes at me. He pretty much looks exactly how I looked when I got the call. "When do you start? What does this mean?"

"It means my schedule is about to get a whole lot busier," I say as I rub both hands over my face, but even the stress of balancing school and my dream career can't get rid of my smile.

13
margot

WE WERE INVITED to a party off-campus tonight, and even though it's not our first night out since starting college, it will be the first time the four of us hang out together—if Jackson shows. I've been too afraid to ask Rae if he's coming. Just the possibility of him being there has my nerves on high alert. They say you shouldn't live in a constant state of fight or flight, but clearly, *they* never lived across the hall from Jackson.

Parties have never really been my thing—they've never been Rae's thing either, but she suggested we go with Matt and some of the other people on the floor.

"I can't believe you're making me do this." I look myself over in the bathroom mirror after blow-drying my hair. Soft, auburn layers frame my face. Rae bumps me with her hip as she joins me in front of the mirror and unzips her makeup bag.

"No one's making you do anything," she says with a laugh. "Remember when you made me hang out with you and Chris for at least a month so your parents wouldn't get suspicious? That was by force. Tonight will be fun, and you look amazing."

My lips twist. "Well, when you put it that way." My parents

have always been strict. If they found out I was dating anyone, they'd want *all* the details—and I wasn't ready to give them.

They had expectations for me, and when I didn't meet those quotas, to say they were disappointed would be an understatement. Nothing less than straight A's. Must be involved in at least one after-school club and one sport. Earning a scholarship was expected.

I was more like an employee than a child, only appreciated when I performed well. So, when I announced my move to Florida and major in journalism, they weren't thrilled. A degree in journalism doesn't exactly align with the Reid Family's corporate goals. My mother, a lawyer, still thinks I'll follow in her footsteps after undergrad—even though I've told her countless times I won't. My father tries to be supportive, but I can see through his encouraging thumbs up. Deep down, he's wondering where this degree will take me, but I've always loved writing. There's something comforting about being able to craft words in a way that convey what I'm feeling. I like being able to go back and edit. It's a luxury that isn't offered when you talk to someone face to face.

"Keith might be disappointed if you don't show," Rae says with a knowing look as she watches for my reaction in the mirror.

I go back to putting on my mascara. Keith is a nice guy, but that's about as far as my opinion of him goes. He always finds me when I'm in the common room, and he's pleasant to talk to, but I don't see it going anywhere. "But Jackson would love it if I didn't go," I answer dryly.

Rae rolls her eyes. "Who cares what Jackson thinks? I'm not even sure he'll be there. Matt says he's been busy with the band."

He didn't tell me about getting picked for the band, even though I was the one with him that night. That must have been what he was about to say when he first opened his door, but I guess I wasn't worthy of hearing his big news. At first, I was offended, but I guess I can't blame him. If I was looking to celebrate, Jackson would be the last person I'd want to share it with.

It's hard to believe their first date was over a month ago, but at the same time, it feels like they've been together longer. Rae and Matt have this easy way about them that makes you believe in soulmates. When I see them together, it makes me feel like there was a reason we moved in across the hall—as much as I hate to admit it. It's still early, so who knows if I'm right, but I don't think I've ever witnessed a relationship become so solid so soon.

She uncaps her mascara and leans closer to the mirror. Speaking of looking amazing, her jeans, which hug her perfectly, are paired with a light pink flowy tank.

With her lips parted, she coats her long lashes. "Matt will be over soon to drive us."

"He's coming all the way here?" I finish putting on my lipstick and take one last look in the mirror before turning to her. "How chivalrous of him," I tease. My boyfriend-style jeans and olive-green top are flattering enough. The thin straps lead to a scooped back that matches the front. Back home, I'd never be able to wear something like this so close to October, but Florida's heat hasn't lightened up even a little.

Glancing between Rae and myself in the mirror, it's hard not to compare my stick-like frame to her curves. She may complain sometimes, but she has weight in all the right places.

"Ready?" I ask.

She grins back at me in the mirror. "Ready."

We walk back into the room to find Matt and Jackson sitting on our beds, waiting for us.

Jackson is on my bed.

I guess that means the four of us will be going to this party together after all. Dread weighs in my stomach at the thought.

At least it's refreshing to see him without a guitar. He's wearing jeans with a black button-down cuffed just below his elbows, and my eyes drag over the muscles in his forearms.

I blink, forcing myself back to the present.

I haven't seen him much over the past few weeks, but every time I do, he's as unpleasant as ever. He either calls me Red and tries to get under my skin, or he ignores me completely. I thought things would change the night he played me that song I liked so much, but I guess he was just in a good mood after finding out he had gotten the gig.

We had shared a momentary truce. It was nice not feeling like we were at war for a few minutes. It gave me hope, like maybe we could finally find something to keep the peace between us. But, of course, Jackson had to go and fire another shot.

"Shouldn't you be practicing with your band or something?" I ask him as I pick up my shoes.

His gaze is fixed on me, and I'm not sure what to make of it. "Why? You don't want me to come?"

"We both know you don't want me there either." I huff as I slip my other sandal over the back of my heel.

"You know," he says as he leans forward with his elbows on his knees. "I'm surprised you're coming out tonight. I didn't know you were capable of having fun."

I tilt my head. "What do you think I've been doing all the nights you're not here?"

He appraises me with a smug lift of his lips. "I don't think about you when I'm not here."

I'm about to open my mouth, but Rae cuts me off. "Oh my God," she groans, throwing her hands in the air. She looks at Matt. "Do we have to drive with them?"

Matt laughs nervously. "Could you imagine if we weren't here as a buffer? This is them being nice to each other." He shakes his head. "For our sake."

"Yeah," I say to Rae. "If you guys weren't here, I would have said something about how I'll have to wash my sheets again." I gesture to Jackson, sitting on my bed like he's perfectly at home. "Or burn them."

Rae gives me a leveling look, unimpressed with my quick wit. "Let's go," she says as she grabs her phone. "And once we get to the party, you two should stay away from each other."

Jackson gets to his feet. "That's the plan."

"Trust me, we will," I add.

The old, colonial-style house has cars parked all over the front yard. I couldn't imagine inviting this many people to a party. Then again, we don't even know the person hosting it. This has all been word of mouth. Someone on our floor heard about it from a friend of a friend . . . I think.

Most of the people from our dorm left at the same time we did, so now it's just a matter of finding them. Matt takes Rae's hand as we walk up to the house where music blares inside, and I suddenly second-guess coming here. I didn't think about the fact that I'd be on my own now that my best friend has a boyfriend. That small detail slipped my mind completely.

"Come on," Rae says, waving for me to follow them. I do because I have nowhere else to go, but I feel like the third wheel.

As soon as we squeeze into the kitchen, Jackson grabs a bottle of liquor and disappears into the mass of people. Matt doesn't notice his friend slip away as he pours Rae a drink and then hands one to me. The three of us stand in the crowded kitchen, wondering where to go from here.

Relief fills me when Keith and his roommate, Samuel, round the corner. I haven't talked to Samuel much since moving in, but he seems like a good guy. I think the college was playing a game of opposites attract when they roomed them together. Keith's tall build, blonde hair, and perfect vision must have paired perfectly with Samuel's stocky frame, dark hair, and thick-rimmed glasses.

"What are you drinking?" Keith asks, peering into my cup.

Taking another sip, I shrug. "I have no idea. Some fruity drink Matt made."

Keith smiles at that. "I'll make your next one," he says with a wink.

I smile for the sake of being polite and look over my shoulder for Rae. It looks like she and Matt have already wandered off. I look back at Keith and Samuel, suddenly grateful to have them here with me.

"So, do you know whose party this is?" I ask Keith over the sound of the music.

He shakes his head and points to Samuel. "Some kid in one of his classes lives here and told him about it."

Samuel steps closer so he doesn't have to yell but ends up yelling anyway. "The guy in my class said one of his roommates was having a huge party. I think five or six guys live here."

The house is huge, so I wouldn't be surprised. The furniture in the large family room is pushed aside to make room for multiple beer pong tables, and Keith catches my eye as I take everything in.

"Want to play?" he asks.

I'm not sure what else to do, so I go ahead and nod. "Okay."

14
jackson

SPEAKERS in the distance blare a song with an electric beat that I'm sure I won't be able to get out of my head for the rest of the night. Standing outside on the back patio doesn't do much to get away from the noise. With how big this party is, people are spilling out of every cracked doorway and taking over the lawn, too. Spending most of my time with the guys in the band hasn't exactly made it easy to meet people here. I had never really worried about making friends because I had Matt, but now that he's obsessed with Rae, he hasn't been around much.

It's crazy to think in just a few weeks, I'll have gigs booked most Saturday nights. The band took some time off when they hired me. They wanted us to rehearse together before we go on stage, but it didn't take long for them to realize there isn't much for me to rehearse. I know their songs by heart and could play them in my sleep.

I take another swig from the bottle of whiskey I hocked off the kitchen counter and head back inside. Sitting by myself around this many people just feels weird.

As soon as I walk through the sliding glass doors, my eyes

land on Margot. She's easy to spot with her hair, and even though I'd never give her the satisfaction of knowing, she looks incredible tonight. I usually only see her around the dorm, where she wears T-shirts and leggings. Nothing could have prepared me for the wave of stupidity that slapped me in the face as soon as she walked into her room tonight. She might have terrible taste in music and be annoying as hell, but tonight she's prettier than the rest of the girls here by a longshot.

She's about to take her turn in a game of beer pong and smiles at Keith before focusing on the cups in front of her. Her arm goes up and over as she throws the ball, and her shirt rides up enough to show a peek of ivory skin I can't tear my eyes away from. The way her jeans hug her hips has me thinking things I shouldn't be thinking, and when my stare makes its way up her body, I find her eyes locked on me.

God damn it.

She frowns, and I hope she didn't catch me checking her out. The last thing I need is little miss perfect thinking she turns me on. It doesn't matter how good she looks, she's still the last person I want to be around. Without giving much time to register her reaction, I take another sip from the bottle and keep walking.

I nearly bump into Izzy, but I guess that's what I get for walking with a bottle raised. "Oh, good!" she exclaims with too much enthusiasm. "You can be my partner."

"What?" I ask, but she's already taken the bottle of whiskey from my hands and set it down on an end table before dragging me with her.

"I need a partner!" she yells over the music, pulling me back in the direction I came from.

By the time I open my mouth to ask what she's talking about, we've stopped in front of the beer pong table, and I once again find myself in front of Margot and Keith.

Her big, brown eyes jump between Izzy and me. "I thought you were getting Jess?"

Izzy shrugs. "I found him instead."

Margot's eyes jump to me before she settles back on Izzy with the trace of a scowl. "Are you sure you don't want to look harder?"

I scoff. "I don't even want to play."

Her eyes snap to mine, and there's a sharpness to them now. "Let me guess, you're too cool for beer pong, too?" She cocks her eyebrow like she's challenging me, her lips pulled into a smirk.

"You know what? Fuck it." I hold out my hand. "Give me the ball."

She walks around the table before shoving the tiny white ball into my hand, and I try not to react to the jolt of electricity I feel when her fingers graze mine.

What the hell is wrong with me tonight?

That's it. No more whiskey.

Before aiming for the cups, I casually toss the ball up and catch it. "It's nothing against you, Keith." Locking eyes on the cup that's front and center, I shoot the ball across the table. "But Red over there is going down." The ball falls into the cup effortlessly like I knew it would, and I take a little too much pleasure in the crimson flare on Margot's cheeks.

Izzy beams at me, holding up her hand for a high five. "I'm so glad I couldn't find Jess," she says with a laugh.

Still holding Margot's pissed-off gaze, I smack my hand against Izzy's—no electricity.

My shoulders drop, and I look over at Margot as Keith whispers something in her ear, making her smile as she whacks his arm playfully. He puts his arm around her, nodding to my partner as he does. "All right, Izzy, let's see what you've got."

Margot tenses at the gesture and takes another long sip from her drink. She's not interested, but she's trying to be nice.

Izzy takes her shot, missing it completely, and I can't help laughing. "Damn it, Izzy."

She playfully shoots me a glare, her blonde curls bouncing at her shoulders as she says, "Don't you worry. I'm just getting warmed up."

"Let's hope," I answer dryly, and she nudges me with her shoulder. "Let's see what you've got, Red."

Her eyes narrow. "Stop calling me that," she huffs as she grabs the ball off the floor.

"What should I call you, then?" I ask just to piss her off.

She holds the ball up, squinting with one eye as she tries to line it up to the cup. "Oh, I don't know," she says absently. "How about Margot?" She shoots her shot, and the ball goes into the cup. "Drink up, jackass," she mutters, looking pleased with herself.

Holding up both empty hands, I shrug. "Sorry. No drink."

Izzy offers her cup to me. "You can have some of mine."

I take a sip, instantly regretting it. "What the hell is that?" I ask, grimacing.

"Hawaiian Punch and vodka," she says with a laugh, taking it back from me and drinking.

I nod. "Yup. That's what it tastes like."

Keith gives Margot a high five for the point and gears up to throw the ball. "You want me to call you Margot?" I ask. "What's the fun in that?"

I'm still watching her, waiting for her reaction when the white ball lands in the cup in front of me. Fishing it out and pulling the cup to the side, I ask, "Well?" as I take my next shot.

Margot frowns. "How about you don't call me anything? I don't see a reason for you to talk to me, anyway."

She has a point.

Nothing good ever comes from being around Margot. She either pisses me off or distracts me. Even now, all I can think about is the freckle on her bottom lip hidden beneath her makeup. What would she do if I walked over and wiped some of her lipstick away with my thumb so I could see it again?

I blink and try to shake the thought from my mind. Jess makes her way through the crowd, and I reach out to stop her. "Hey," I say, catching her attention. "Play for me."

"Aw! Come on," Izzy complains. "I actually had a shot at winning with you!"

Pointing to her cup, I shake my head. "There's no way I'm taking another sip of that." Before she can say anything else, I walk away, making sure not to look at Margot as I do. I need to clear my head and get the hell away from this girl.

15
margot

KEITH PLACES a hand on the small of my back as he takes his turn, and I try to naturally shift away without making it obvious. I'm glad Jess replaced Jackson, but the longer we play, the more Keith finds reasons to touch me. I don't know him well enough for it to be only a friendly touch, but it's not forward enough for me to shut down, either. The result leaves us in a constant limbo of shoulder shrugs and shifting feet.

When Jess and Izzy lose, I ignore the fact that we're supposed to play again and tell him I'm going to look for Rae.

It's half the truth. As much as I'd like to find Rae, I know she's with Matt, so I'm not worried. The two of them are somewhere around here, and I'm sure I'll bump into them eventually.

The other half of the truth is I don't want to give Keith the wrong idea. I've succeeded at keeping him at arm's length so far, but I've never been around him while he drinks, and the last thing I need is for him to let liquid courage lead the way.

At the edge of the family room are two sliding glass doors, and stepping outside for some air sounds better than anything else right now. My fingers wrap around the handle, opening the door to a screened-in patio. It looks like some people have started a bonfire in the backyard, their silhouettes illuminated by the crackling flames. As I step out and watch everyone through the screen, I finally feel like I'm glad to be here. The energy of everyone having fun is electric, and now that I'm outside, the fire reminds me of home. Maybe I'll even stumble across something noteworthy to write about tonight.

The Parties Outside of Greek.

It has potential, but to do a full write-up on it, I'd probably have to compare it to the parties *within* Greek. I guess I can kiss that post goodbye. I already have my parents doubting my major. They don't see how I'll earn more than five figures as a journalist, so to them, my degree is frivolous. If I'm going to go against their wishes, the one thing I can do is at least commit myself to it and make sure I succeed.

No rushing.

No sororities.

No distractions.

"Hiding from Keith?" an all too familiar voice says behind me.

I whip around to find Jackson sprawled casually in a wicker patio chair. He raises the bottle of whiskey in a sort of greeting, and I suddenly don't feel as happy about being here as I did a moment ago.

I cross my arms. "Why would I hide from Keith?"

Jackson sits forward before taking another sip from the bottle. "Because he's boring."

My lips fall. "He is not. He's a really nice guy."

He forces a laugh. "Yeah, a really nice guy who bores you." I glare at him, and when I don't say anything, he raises both hands, still holding the bottle. "Tell me I'm wrong." He doesn't seem drunk. His steel eyes are clear as he watches me, challenging me. I walk over to him, and his lips quirk as I snatch the bottle from his hand. "I thought so."

Ignoring him, I take a sip and grimace at the taste. It's unsettling how well he can read me. I haven't even told Rae I think Keith is boring. I don't think I realized it myself until he put it out there for me to think about, but he's right. Keith has a way of going on about the details of his day for the sake of having something to talk about. "Why do you care, anyway?"

He beckons for the bottle back, so I hand it over before sitting in the chair next to him.

"I don't." He takes a sip. I expect him to say something more, but he just stares out at the backyard with the bottle resting at his lips.

"Are you hiding from Izzy?" I hold out my hand for him to pass the bottle back. I don't even know if Izzy likes him, but if he's throwing shots at Keith, I might as well throw something back.

My question pulls him from his thoughts, and he quickly takes another sip before handing it over. "No."

I thumb the label as I stare at him a little longer, trying to figure him out. "So, you think she likes you?"

He shrugs. "It doesn't matter if she does or doesn't." Rubbing his hands on his jeans, he adds, "If my goal is to tour, there's no point getting involved with someone here."

"Oh, yeah. I heard you joined a band. Congrats."

He gives me a sideways glance. "Thanks."

"It's sort of bleak though, isn't it?"

He frowns. "What is?"

I finally take a sip and let the warmth spread through me before answering. The taste no longer burns as much as it did before. "Assuming a relationship isn't worth it just because you're hoping your band goes on tour."

Jackson gives me a long, sideways glance. "I don't want a relationship."

Now it's my turn to roll my eyes. "Trust me, if you find a

girl who actually wants to spend time with you, you should jump on it. You're not exactly fun to be around."

He holds out his hand for the bottle, and I pass it to him. "You're spending time with me."

"*Wants to,*" I emphasize.

"Yeah. Well, you're no walk in the park either. Maybe you should give Keith a chance."

"Maybe I will."

He scoffs, putting his foot up on the patio table in front of him. "Let me know how that goes."

I can tell by his tone he's calling my bluff. I hate that he's right, and I hate that he *knows* he's right.

Staring out at the people around the bonfire again, I try to find a sliver of what I was feeling when I first walked out here, but my perspective has already shifted. The energy that felt electric and lively now feels loud and overbearing. Someone throws a fresh pallet onto the fire with a crash, and an explosion of sparks flies up toward the sky, and large speakers carry a techno beat that's bound to give me a headache at some point.

"Hey," I finally say as I look over at him. "What was the name of that song you played for me?"

Rolling his head to look at me, he mutters, "Huh?"

"The song you played before. What was it?"

He shifts to get a better look at me, a slow smile creeping at the corner of his mouth. "You like my music."

"Forget it," I huff. "Give me the bottle."

He sits upright, shaking his head. "No, no, no." He sets down the whiskey and leans his elbows on his knees. "I want to hear this. You liked my music so much you've been thinking about it for weeks?"

"I said forget it." I reach for the bottle at his feet, but he moves it to his other side. "I knew you'd be an asshole about it."

He gapes at me. "I would do no such thing." With a lift of his shoulder, he adds, "If anything, I'm glad I could show you the light."

"Oh, my God." I get to my feet. "I shouldn't have asked."

I'm already walking away when he calls out after me, "Aw, come on, Red. I'll tell you the song." But it only makes me bristle more. No song is worth subjecting myself to that condescending jerk. Let him keep his music.

16
jackson

SHE'S IMPOSSIBLE.

Reaching down, I grab the bottle and take a bigger sip than I have all night. I can go days—weeks—without thinking about her, but as soon as we're in the same room, I'm either agitated or hellbent on pissing her off.

My mouth lingers against the bottle—where hers just was. Pulling back, I run my tongue over my bottom lip at the thought.

"Hey," Matt's voice pulls me back to the present. Looking over, I see his head poking out of the sliding glass door. "Get in here, would you? We're about to play a game."

For a second, I consider telling him no, but he gives me a pleading grin that makes me change my mind. "How'd you know I was out here?" I ask once I'm walking through the open door, whiskey bottle in hand.

He lets out a breath of laughter. "Rae asked Margot where you were, and she said we'd find you miserable and alone on the back porch."

"I wasn't miserable," I mutter, taking another sip from the bottle.

He shakes his head as he leads me through the crowd. "You sure looked it."

I scoff. "Well, I wasn't miserable until . . ." My voice trails because when I think back on the time we spent outside together, I didn't hate it. If anything, I was kind of disappointed when she walked away. Something about tonight has me paying more attention to Margot, and it needs to stop.

Matt just raises his hands in surrender. "Leave me out of it, man."

"Oh, good! Now we can start," Rae says when she sees us. "We're playing Never Have I Ever."

Keith laughs. "The ultimate ice-breaker."

He rests his arm on the back of the couch behind Margot, and she leans forward, avoiding his touch. "Ready to start?" she asks with a smile, her eyes jumping from me to Matt.

She's acting like she didn't just walk out on me—like I have no effect on her whatsoever.

Too bad I can see straight through her act, especially when her knee anxiously bounces and she clasps both hands in her lap. She looks like she wants to bolt for the nearest exit, and even her best smile can't hide that.

Between all of us, we take up both couches in the family room. Matt sits next to Rae, and I take the last open seat next to Izzy with a clear view of Margot.

Rae offers to start since she's at the end of the first couch. "Okay," she says, holding up her hands. "Never have I ever smoked pot."

We all stare at her.

"What?" she asks with a laugh before shrugging. "It's usually a good way to knock some fingers down."

I like Rae—despite her taste in friends. She's bold, and she knows who she is. Not many people here would advertise they've never smoked. Not her, though. She is who she is right out of the gate, and she's not apologetic about it. I can see why Matt likes her.

Everyone puts their fingers down except for Matt, and Izzy laughs. "It's a sign," she says. "You two were made for each other."

All focus is on the couple, but I can't help looking at Margot's hand and noticing she *did* put a finger down.

Interesting.

I don't smoke often, but I will when it's offered. Then again, I usually don't drink this much either, but tonight it's a different story.

Matt says he's never gotten a ticket.

Izzy and Jess have.

Keith says he doesn't like pizza, proving he can't be trusted.

Everyone puts a finger down for that one.

Then it's Margot's turn.

"Never have I ever learned to play a musical instrument."

When my eyes find hers, she just shrugs and mouths, "Sorry," in the least apologetic way possible.

I put down a finger, and so do Samuel and Matt. When I see Matt joined, I can't help laughing. "You went to one piano lesson when you were six. Put your finger back up."

He shakes his head. "I suffered as much as any other musician that day."

Samuel says he's never seen Jurassic Park, and we spend a solid ten minutes telling him how meaningless his life is because of it.

Jess has never left the state of Florida, but the rest of us have.

Izzy has never gotten a tattoo, and surprisingly Samuel is the only one who has.

Then it's my turn. Locking my gaze on Margot, I say, "Never have I ever bought a Taylor Swift album," and the glare she gives me is priceless. As it turns out, Keith loves

Taylor Swift and was equally outraged I think her music is trash, so my question gave the two of them something to bond over.

As the night goes on, and the more we drink, the more we learn about each other. The Never Have I Evers gets more personal, and I could have gone my whole life without knowing Keith is a virgin from West Palm Beach with a third nipple. But on the other hand, I now know Margot has never broken a bone, is extremely passionate about the Netflix show Stranger Things, and has had sex in a car. So that's something.

By the time we're ready to head back, Matt and Samuel are the only two sober enough to drive. Izzy clings to my arm as we walk toward the car, and I have to steady her more than once.

Halfway down the driveway, the two drivers realize they've parked at opposite ends of the street.

"Izzy, Jess, and Keith with me?" Samuel asks.

Izzy stares up at me with bloodshot eyes and a sloppy smile. I may be drunk, but I'm nowhere near as gone as this girl. "I can ride back with Jackson." She looks over at Margot. "Hey, why don't you ride back with Keith and Jess?"

Margot's eyes go wide. "Oh, um . . . I don't know." She looks around for Rae to help her, but Rae's busy laughing at something Matt must have said.

She's squirming under pressure, and as much as I enjoy watching it happen, I open my mouth to put her out of her misery. "No. Margot's riding back with us."

All eyes are on me, and of all the shocked faces, Margot's is probably the most surprised. Hell, I'm surprised, too.

"What?" I ask. "It's not like we aren't going to the same place." I glance around at everyone, but it's Margot who catches my attention. She's watching me curiously, her eyebrows pinched as she tilts her head.

Luckily, no one questions my logic, and we end up parting ways with only a few pouts from Izzy.

Margot and I walk next to each other a few paces behind Rae and Matt. She has her arms wrapped around herself as she walks, the night air leaving goosebumps on her bare arms, and I have to fight the urge to try and warm her up somehow.

It's like no matter how bad Margot and I being around each other may be, something about her is taking root, tightening its hold on me like a damn python. I've seen her at her worst, but if anything, I might like her a little more because of it.

What the hell is happening to me?

17
margot

IZZY WAS PUTTING out all the right signals to let him know she's interested. I'm sure he could have slept with her, but instead, he sent her home in the other car. I know he said he doesn't want a relationship, but after playing Never Have I Ever, I also know he's not a stranger to sleeping around, either.

I glance at him to find him already watching me. Having his undivided attention makes me overlook a crack in the asphalt, and I stumble forward. Quickly catching my footing, I ask, "Why did you do that?" and hope he doesn't insult my inability to walk.

I probably drank too much. My buzz has to be what made me almost fall on my face—not his look. It's the whiskey.

To my surprise, he just shrugs and says, "You didn't want to go with them."

I frown, not sure how he'd know that, but maybe it's just the liquor making my thoughts slow. He can always read me so well. It's unnerving—like the feeling of wondering whether or not you remembered to lock the door. Every time he's a little too intuitive about my overall mental state, I get a flood of panic. How does he know? Did I tell him and forget?

But it's always just Jackson reading something between my lines like they're not even there. At least tonight he used his powers for good.

Before I can say anything, he shoves his hands in his pockets. "The real question is, *why* didn't you want to go with them?"

I bite the inside of my cheek, not sure I want to tell him anything personal. I'm sure he'll use it as ammo against me later. Then again, he learned worse about me during the game. I let out a sigh. "I was afraid Keith might try something. The more he drank, the friendlier he became. I just don't want him to get the wrong idea."

"Have you tried telling him you're not interested?"

I weigh my head from side to side, gripping my arms around my torso a little tighter. "Basically."

A laugh escapes him. "What the hell is that supposed to mean?"

"Well, when the semester started, I told him I wanted to focus on school."

He shakes his head. "Not good enough."

I gape at him. "That's perfectly clear!"

"Not when a guy's got hope, and no one has hope like a virgin."

I roll my eyes. "You're disgusting."

He steps closer, and our arms are almost touching as he leans in to whisper in my ear. "I'm honest." His warm breath against my neck makes my entire body tingle. It has such a strong effect on me, I'm instantly embarrassed like he'll know my insides are melting while every hair on my body stands.

I force myself to keep breathing and step away from him. I even go as far as to push him away from me gently, but as soon as my fingertips make contact with his bicep, it only makes my symptoms worse. It ends up not being a quick, playful shove like I intended. Instead, it turns into this slight graze that has my heart buzzing in my chest. His arm is strong under the sleeve of his button-down, and as soon as we're touching, it's harder for me to pull away.

Jackson and I make eye contact while I'm still touching him, and I swear I catch a subtle lift of his brow like he's loving the mental disconnect I'm suffering from—like he loves it so damn much and finds it funny.

I snatch my hand back—just another thing I can blame on the whiskey. "Sure. If that's what you want to call it," I say as I try to recover from what just came over me, but my reaction only pleases him more. He holds my gaze and one side of his mouth lifts into a smirk. He opens his mouth to speak, and I can already feel the crushing weight of dread because I just *know* he's about to call me out.

"Hey, Matt!" Someone calls from behind us, saving me from certain ridicule. We all stop and turn to find a guy with neat, blond hair jogging toward us.

Matt gives him an easy smile. "Hey, man. We're about to leave."

Blond guy nods. "I was hoping for that. Think I can get a ride back to campus?" His eyes jump to the rest of us, and adds, "Hey, I'm Braden."

Matt nods. "Sure. We've got room for one more."

He's right, but it's a tight fit in the back of Matt's Ford Focus. I end up sandwiched between Jackson and Braden in the middle seat, and I'd give anything to make this drive go by faster.

Because Jackson and I are touching.

My foot rests against the side of his shoe, my knee pressed against the outside of his, my shoulder paired with the same muscular arm my fingers grazed earlier.

It's too much.

I keep trying to shift away from him, but it's like there's a magnetic pull drawing my body back to his with every turn.

Jackson and I are *not* magnetic. The only way we'd be similar to magnets is if we were two like poles, repelling the other with everything we've got.

I shift in my seat again, my arm and knee grazing Braden instead.

I feel nothing.

The realization makes me look at him. He briefly meets my stare and gives me a smile.

He's handsome.

Short hair, blue eyes, well dressed.

Braden looks back out the window, but I can't tear my eyes away. From here, I can't see a single flaw. He looks like he might be everything Jackson isn't—in a good way.

So, why don't I *feel* anything?

Jackson leans toward me, closing the space I've tried so desperately to keep. My breath catches in my throat, and when he whispers in my ear his words run down my spine. "Careful, Red. Stare at him any longer and you might hurt Keith's feelings."

I glare at him, but it only seems to please him. He looks out the window, dismissing me, but his knee presses into mine a little more, taking up any space I had to get away from him. I can't stop staring at where our legs are touching. The slightest movement from him sends a wave of nerves and warmth through me, and there suddenly isn't enough air in the car.

It *has* to be the whiskey.

18
jackson

MATT and I have been in the dorm all day, recovering from the party. I was only hungover for a couple of hours this morning, and considering Matt didn't drink, he's been fine all day. Sundays are usually quiet around the dorm, but everyone must be exhausted after the night we had. It might be because our room is at a dead end, but I haven't seen a single soul other than the guy on the bed across from me.

Our door has been open for most of the day, but Margot and Rae's is shut.

I wonder if Margot woke up hungover.

Probably. She may not have been as sloppy as some of the other people last night, but she was still drunk—drunk and staring at that guy, Braden, the whole drive home. She knew the guy for all of two seconds, and I swear she looked like she was ready to crawl into his lap. I might think her not telling Keith how she feels is annoying, but I'll take that over watching her drool over some guy she's never even talked to. My hand shakes, making it impossible to restring my guitar.

I brush off the feeling and shake out my hand. With the band's first gig coming up this Friday, I need to sound as good as possible. It's a cheap instrument. My mom gave it to me when I was in high school, and I'm not sure if she bought it from a music store or just picked it up at Walmart. I've loved this guitar more than anything, but the idea of playing it on stage as a professional musician ties my stomach into a knot.

Buying a new guitar—especially one that would make a difference—is out of the question with how tight my budget is right now, but I was able to get better-quality strings from a small music shop near campus. I doubt it will help as much as I need it to, but it's the best I can do for now.

Hopefully, the guys won't mind me playing this one until we bring in a little cash flow—if that even happens. I guess this is what it's like when you join an up-and-coming band. A lot of *ifs*. Who knows what will happen? All I know is I need to put away as much money as I can to prepare for whatever repercussions my dad throws my way if I drop out. I may not want to be here, but at least he's footing the bill for whatever I need.

If.

My thoughts are starting to make my head spin, so I look at Matt as I pick at the new strings. "Hey, want to get something to eat?"

He looks up from his laptop. "Sorry. I told Rae we could get dinner soon." Shifting his attention back to the screen, he types away at the keys. "Want to come?"

I shake my head even though my stomach is starting to feel empty. I like Rae, and I like Matt, but for whatever reason, I don't like being around the two of them alone. It feels off balance, the restaurant booth always ends up feeling more like a seesaw with two people on one side, and I end up floating in limbo until it's over. "Nah. I'll get my ass up and go get some food eventually." We've been too lazy to walk to the dining hall and get any real food today. I've been getting by on an untoasted bagel and a microwave cup of noodles.

Like clockwork, the door across the hall opens, and Rae

steps out. Looking past her, I scan the room for Margot. I catch a glimpse of her sitting at her desk on her laptop, her fingers hacking at the keys like she's writing a damn novel.

I stare until the door shuts, and I straighten, bringing my attention back to Rae.

"Want to come with us, Jackson? I think we're getting fajitas."

I cock an eyebrow. "From where?"

Matt sighs. "Don't ask. You already know." He gets to his feet, putting his hand on the small of Rae's back as he moves her out the door.

I let out a low laugh. "Have fun at Chili's."

Even as Rae is being pushed forward, she looks over her shoulder at me. "Want us to bring you back something?"

"No. Thanks, though," I say absently, my eyes still stuck on the shut door with Margot behind it.

"See you later, man," Matt says over his shoulder.

I give a weak nod, but the two have already rounded the corner, their voices softening as they make their way down the hall.

With the last string tightened, I should focus on tuning my guitar, but my hands lay relaxed. Matt and Rae may have left, but I still can't stop staring at Margot's door.

I wonder what she's doing.

Did she eat?

I blink, shaking off the thought. Looking at my guitar, I force my hands to play. My fingers pick at the strings on autopilot, but my head isn't in it. My eyes betray me and glance at her door again.

She's probably writing about something in that blog she has. Izzy told me the name of it, but I can't remember what it's called. Maybe I'll ask Izzy next time I see her.

This is bullshit.

I shouldn't be thinking about Margot. Setting down my

guitar, I carefully lean it up against the side of my desk. I slip on my shoes and head toward the door. I need to get out of this room. My hand runs through my hair, and I turn to lock the door.

There's no reason for me to pause and look at Margot's door before walking down the hall.

So why do I do it?

19
margot

SHOWERED AND READY, I grab my keys from my desk. My Monday morning English class starts soon, so I grab my bag and head toward the door. Turning the lock, I hear a second set of keys doing the same thing behind me.

Looking over my shoulder, I see Jackson standing with his guitar case leaning up against the wall as he locks the door.

"Uh, what are you doing?" I ask.

He stares at me like there might be something wrong with *me* before answering, "Going to class."

Pulling my phone from my back pocket, I look at the time. "But you never leave this early."

"So?"

"So," I say as we start walking in the same direction to the class we share. "It's weird."

We've been going to this class for weeks now, and I never see him. We never even come close to walking to class together because I always leave early, and he's always borderline late.

He points over his shoulder. "Want me to go back?"

"No." I shake my head. "Just—" I falter, glancing at him. "Why are you bringing your guitar to class, anyway?"

A trace of a smirk crosses his lips. "Worried I might embarrass you?"

I scoff. "You'd only embarrass yourself."

"Relax, Red. I'm skipping my afternoon class to go straight to practice and get a few hours in with the band."

If he were anyone else, I'd probably question that. I'd probably worry about him skipping class, but because of who he is, and because of how little I'm willing to invest in him, I just say, "How's that been going? Balancing it all."

"It sucks." The way he sighs out the words makes me think he's been wanting to get that off his chest for a while. "I don't know how long I'll be able to keep it up. The guys are being flexible, but I hate asking them to work their schedules around mine. Sometimes they practice without me, and not being there kills me. They must hate it too, but they know I'm good at showing up and knowing my shit." He glances at me with a trace of uncertainty that probably matches my own.

I'm not sure why he just told me all that either.

Nodding, I just say, "That does suck." I'm not sure what else to say, but we still have a little time before we get to class, and I'd rather not walk in awkward silence. "What do you think you'll do?"

He shrugs, adjusting the guitar strap on his shoulder. "I'm not sure. A lot depends on if we end up touring. I can probably keep this up while we're doing local shows, but the band wants to go on the road. We'd only be opening for someone else, but if that happens, I'll drop out."

This gets my full attention, my feet halting. Living next to Jackson may not be the most enjoyable part of college, but it's become my new normal. It's weird to think of him not being across the hall. "What?"

He's a few steps ahead of me when he realizes I've stopped. Turning to face me, he tilts his head. "Oh, come on. Don't tell me you'll miss me."

"Not likely." My feet move beneath me again. "I just think that's a big decision."

We've reached the door to our classroom, and he surprisingly holds it open for me to walk through first. "I know it is," he says as I walk past him. "But the fact that I have the opportunity to even consider it means I'm doing something right."

I give him a small smile before heading to the front of the room. Jackson hangs back, taking his seat in the last row while I take mine in the front. I try to give the professor my full attention as she writes on the board, but I can't shake the thought of Jackson leaving. Imagining him not living across from me anymore leaves a hollow feeling in my chest. I shouldn't care if Jackson leaves—if anything, I should feel some type of relief at the thought of not having to face off against him every time we step outside our respective spaces.

But I don't.

I don't feel any relief. Instead, the new hollowness makes room for budding anxiety. It creeps in slowly, but as soon as the thought hits me, it feels like an ambush.

What if I never see him again? What if this is where my knowing Jackson starts and ends?

I bite the inside of my lip, desperate to not face what this means. If there's one thing I know, it's that I shouldn't miss Jackson Phillips.

But if he leaves, I think I might.

20
jackson

AS SOON AS CLASS ENDS, I slip out the back and head to my car. The guys are already together and waiting for me.

I don't know why I said all of that to Margot earlier. I haven't even told Matt about the possibility of dropping out. Partly because I haven't seen much of him lately. I'm usually with the band when I'm not in class, and he's with Rae every waking hour. But another part of me is worried he'll be pissed. College was something we were supposed to do together. I may not care about bailing on college or bailing on my dad's dreams, but I don't want to bail on Matt.

Dave's house is only a ten-mile drive from campus, but with traffic full of tourists and retirees, it's painful. The more I think about how nice it would be to practice with the band whenever I want, the more I want to walk away from USF for good.

Dave's garage is open when I get there, and the guys are all drinking beer as they set up. Dave sits on a stool, his legs perched on the pegs as he talks to our drummer, Brady. It's our bass guitarist, Marty, who sees me first, giving me a nod. As I step out of my car, I hear him say, "The puppy's here."

I flip him the bird, and he grins. It's all in good fun, but I hate the nickname.

Dave spins on his stool to greet me. "Hey, man. Ready for the gig Friday?"

I nod. "I feel like I've been waiting for Friday my entire life."

Brady sits behind the drum set, tapping his foot. He's always fidgeting. The guy can't relax. It's no wonder he became a drummer—any excuse to keep his hands moving. "There's nothing like that first gig," he says. "You'll feel sick with nerves, and something will probably go wrong, but you'll remember it forever."

I give him a grateful smile as I pick up my guitar, and Dave jumps to his feet.

"Hey, put that thing away. We've got something for you."

My eyebrows pull together as I slowly set my guitar back in the case. "What?"

Reaching behind the drum set, Dave grabs a different guitar case and hands it to me. "Think of it as a loaner. You can't play your first gig with that guitar. No offense."

"None taken," I say with a bewildered laugh as I take the case from him. Opening it, my jaw nearly drops to the floor. Even with obvious wear and tear, the vintage sunburst mahogany finish still shines. My hand traces over the dark outer edges as I glance at the three guys in front of me. "A Gibson?"

"Don't get too excited," Marty says. "It's my old one, and I bought it used. It's been through some shit, but you're welcome to use it until you can get something a little better."

"Are you kidding?" I grab the guitar and hold it. Letting my fingers strum over the strings. "This is the best thing anyone has ever given me." The three guys I've idolized for years grin, and a sense of calm hits me. This is where I'm supposed to be. I might not have anything in common with these guys outside of music, but this is where I belong. Right now, they feel more like family than anyone I'm related to by blood, and I need to make this work. Friday, I'll make sure I play better than I've ever played before.

The door to Margot and Rae's dorm is open when I get back from practice. It's just after 9:00 p.m. and I steal a glance as I walk by.

Margot is sitting on her bed, her laptop open, and Rae is nowhere in sight. Instead, Keith sits on the other end of her bed with his laptop in front of him.

She sees me looking and goes to give me a tight-lipped smile when her eyes catch on my guitar case. "New guitar?"

My eyebrows furrow as I look down at the case in hand. It's a different case than I had this morning, but they're both black. Dave said he'd hold my old one for me, and I didn't think anyone would notice. "Uh. Yeah."

"Cool," she says with a nod before looking back down at her laptop. Keith gives me a wave I awkwardly return. This poor guy needs to read her signals better. She's practically using her laptop as a barrier to keep them apart, and I have a feeling she left the door open so he wouldn't try anything.

Unlocking the door to my dorm, I leave it open as I go inside. It's too quiet when Matt's gone. Setting the guitar on my bed, I can't help noticing Keith does more of the talking than Margot. She's mostly just answering his many questions.

I don't have much to do tonight. I plan on catching up on my classes tomorrow, so I fall back against my bed. I'd normally put on music, but Keith has just mentioned Taylor Swift for the second time since I got home, and I know he's grasping at straws, desperate to prove he and Margot have something in common. There's no way Margot will go along with this conversation and indulge him. She has to draw the line *somewhere*.

Margot's response is quiet, so I don't make out what she says. It's like she knows I'm trying to listen and she wants to ruin my fun. Letting out a sigh, I get to my feet, not sure why I want to help her but doing it anyway.

"Hey," I say, with a hand on her door frame. "I'm ready to work on that project for English whenever you are."

She stares at me, wide-eyed and clueless until something clicks. "Oh, right!" She looks at Keith. "I'm sorry, I completely forgot. Mind if we call it a night?"

Keith glances between Margot and me before closing his laptop. "Sure. No problem." He forces a smile before turning to Margot, his back facing me like he can cut me out of their moment. "This was great. You're really good at explaining things."

Margot's eyes jump past Keith to me, and I act like I'm about to stick my finger down my throat, making a gagging face. She presses her lips together like she's trying to seal in a laugh. "Yeah, this was great," she says, focusing her eyes back on him.

I walk into my room, leaving them to handle their awkward goodbye and collapse onto my bed again, resting my arm over my head.

I don't expect Margot to come in here when she's done. There's no project for English. She and I both know that, so when she's standing in my doorway, I sit up.

She walks across my room and takes a seat at the foot of my bed, her back resting against the wall as if she's done this a million times. "Thanks for that," she says with a sigh.

I sit against the head of my bed, my back pressed against the other wall. "Just tell him you don't want to study with him."

Her eyes widen as she looks over at me. "I can't do that."

I force a laugh. "Sure, you can."

"I don't want to hurt his feelings. Plus, it might make things weird. We live on the same floor."

I cock an eyebrow. "You don't have a problem hurting my feelings."

"Keith is *nice*. You're . . ." She waves her hand aimlessly in my direction. "You."

"Thanks," I mutter dryly. When she doesn't make a move to leave, I say, "You can go home now."

Her eyes narrow as she crosses her arms. "No."

"No?"

Hiking one leg up, she gets comfortable. "I'm not leaving until you tell me the name of the song."

"I would have told you at the party, but you had to storm off like a child." I expect her to take offense, but she just keeps watching me expectantly, waiting for what she came here for. Sighing, I say, "Song: 'Do I Wanna Know?' Band: Arctic Monkeys, Album: AM."

She smiles. "Thank you." Then she gets to her feet, and without another word, heads toward the door.

"Oh, and Margot?"

She stops and turns.

"Listen to the whole album. I think you'll like it."

Her shoulders relax and she falters. "Oh. Okay, I will."

And she's gone.

21
margot

"I THINK it's right up here!" Rae says as she looks down at the map on her phone. We parked Matt's car in a parking garage, and now the three of us are headed to the small bar where Jackson has his first gig tonight.

The sign above the door reads West End, and we file inside, showing our IDs at the door and getting a black X on each of our hands in exchange. A long bar takes up the left side, and there are a few tables in the back with standing room in front of a small stage.

The place isn't packed, but it looks like the band has a local following. Rae, Matt, and I stand as close as we can to the stage, but we're still about halfway back because we didn't get here early enough to beat the crowd.

"Have you ever seen him play live?" I ask Matt over the sound of excited chatter.

He shakes his head. "Never with a band."

"Wow, big day." I suddenly feel guilty for not wanting to come at first. I didn't see the point. If Rae wasn't dating Matt, I wouldn't be here—that much I know for sure. I told them I didn't want to be the third wheel, but they insisted it wouldn't be like that. They said it would be a great way for us to go out and have a fun night. I tried inviting some people on our floor, but as much as Izzy said she'd *love* to go, they all had other plans to go to a foam party at a frat.

If I had gone to the party with everyone else, maybe I could have written about it. But the last thing I need is to be around Keith while he drinks again. I would have been a little nervous about drinking with them, and the thought of being the only sober one in the group didn't sound like much fun either. Rae is my comfort zone, so as pathetic as it may be, I feel better about following her here.

Who knows, maybe I'll still find something to write about tonight.

I've never cared to know anything about the band Jackson joined. It meant he'd be practicing less around the dorm, and that was good enough for me. I didn't even know the band's name until I saw a sign that said they would start performing at 9:00 p.m.

American Thieves.

The name alone makes me think it won't be my type of music.

"Do you think he's nervous?" I ask Matt for the sake of having something to talk about.

He considers my question but shakes his head. "I don't think so. Jackson doesn't really get nervous, and he's been wanting to do this since middle school." He laughs. "I think the only time I've seen Jackson nervous was when his dad told him he had to go to college, and he wasn't sure if he'd be able to get into the same school as me."

"That'll do it," Rae says with a laugh. "Margot and I were worried about the same thing."

"Yeah, school has never been his thing. It's not because he isn't smart. He just thinks doing the work is stupid and doesn't want to waste his time with it." He shrugs. "He's never failed or anything. He just does the bare minimum."

"Except when it comes to music," I say as I watch the stage. The band walks out, and the people in front cheer at the sight. As I focus on Jackson, it doesn't take long to see Matt was right. He doesn't seem nervous at all. He looks like he does this every weekend—perfectly at home.

The lights dim, casting shadows on Jackson's open dark gray and black flannel rolled up to his forearms. He positions his guitar and looks out over the small audience, his eyes landing on me. His head tilts like he didn't think I'd be here. *I* didn't think I'd be here. His lips pull tight before he laughs to himself and shakes his head like the fact that I actually showed up here is funny to him.

Matt leans in closer so I can hear him over the crowd. "And except when it comes to trying to piss you off apparently."

I give him a heavy-lidded stare as the lead singer yells out, "Are you beautiful motherfuckers ready?" and the small crowd roars in response. All the members of the band have tattoos and look older than Jackson by at least ten years, but that's the only way he stands out. Other than the age difference and the ink, he looks like he belongs.

A small smile comes to my lips. There have been plenty of times when I've wanted to make Jackson miserable, but I can't deny it's nice seeing him in his element—that it's nice seeing him happy.

The first song starts, and I'm surprised when my ears don't immediately bleed. I was expecting a head-banging rock, but it's not. Layered sounds fill my ears, and even though the song is more intense than what I usually listen to, the beats and rhythm are clean.

I want to hate it. The last thing I need is for Jackson to see me enjoying this, but I don't hate it at all.

JUST DON'T CALL ME YOURS

"They're good!" Rae says, her surprise mirroring what I'm feeling.

Matt yells something I can't make out, but he looks enthusiastic like he agrees.

I don't say anything. I'm too busy watching Jackson, standing in the back corner of the stage as he plays his new guitar. He's so focused. He doesn't even glance at the crowd like he doesn't want them to distract him. Aside from occasionally smiling at his bandmates, he hardly notices anyone. It's just him and the music. He doesn't even look like my asshole neighbor right now. Instead, he's just a guy in a band.

A *hot* guy in a band.

My brain trips up over that last thought like maybe the wires got crossed. But when I look at him again, noticing the way the muscles in his arms move as he plays, I can't deny it. Jackson is attractive.

Like *really* attractive.

I noticed it that first day of class, but for the past few months, my mind has done me a solid favor by burying those thoughts. I haven't noticed the way his hair curls at the ends in weeks. Haven't spent a second considering his wide shoulders or the way his eyebrow twitches right before he's about to rip me a new one. I didn't even let the way he bites his lip while he's lost in thought faze me at all.

But I am considering it all now.

As if he can read my mind, his neck jerks up, his gaze landing on me like a magnet. We lock eyes, and I wish I could read his expression better. I expect him to look away, but he doesn't. He holds my stare until heat rises to my cheeks, and I'm forced to lower my gaze.

When I dare to lift it again, he isn't looking at me anymore. Did I imagine it?

The song ends, and the lead singer grins at the crowd like

it's a stadium full of fans and not a dingy dive bar. The band keeps a beat going as he says, "If you're wondering why we sound so good tonight, I'd like to introduce Jackson Phillips!" He holds an outstretched arm toward Jackson, and the crowd cheers.

Jackson fights his smile, shaking his head with a breath of laughter, and I've never seen him look so humble.

It's a good look on him.

They kick off with another song I actually like a little better than the first, and I try to keep my eyes fixed on the lead singer. Matt stands behind Rae with his arms wrapped around her, and I sort of wish I had what they have. When we're around the dorm, I never think about the fact that I'm single. I'm happy with how things are going, and after my breakup with Chris, I didn't want to jump into anything new right away. Even as I smile at my best friend, I'm not sure if I actually want a relationship or if it's just a product of being around a newly in love couple in public that has me feeling a little left out.

Between being alone and trying to avoid looking at the new guitarist at all costs, I shift to taking in the crowd around me. A few people sing along to the words, and it must be such a rush for the band on stage. To have people resonate with the words and melodies you've written, and then see they not only enjoy them but know them by heart.

I've been to concerts, but never in this intimate of a setting, and never when someone I know is in the band. It makes me think about the whole experience in a new light, and I feel like I understand Jackson a little more because of it. When someone comments on something I've posted, it's the best feeling. Knowing someone resonated with something I wrote, makes for a great day. When Jackson is on stage, looking out at the crowd, I imagine it being an amplified, more tangible version of that because his fans are right in front of him. They bought tickets, made time, and showed up—all to support and celebrate the music they love. I can see why he's so passionate about this—I think I would be, too.

22
jackson

WE FINISH OUR SET, and I've never felt more alive. Sweat drips from my hair, and I don't think my heart will ever slow down. As if the rush from playing on stage wasn't enough to keep me on this natural high, a few people ask for pictures with the band after the show. I've been the guy asking for a picture, but being on this end of it feels surreal.

The guys all clap me on the shoulder and tell me how well I played. I know one of the opening riffs was a little sloppy, but I don't think anyone in the crowd noticed. It was toward the beginning of the show, so I think my nerves got to me a little. Dave had looked my way, lowering his open palm slowly at his side to subtly tell me to relax.

Now they're headed for the bar to get a beer before we pack up. Except me. Puppies can't drink, as Marty was kind enough to remind me. Dave offered to try to buy me one, but I told him not to worry about it. I know Matt's probably waiting for me, anyway.

I head to the bathroom before I start looking for Rae and Matt—and Margot. Why she'd come here to listen to music she doesn't like, played by a guy she likes even less, is beyond me. Rae must have dragged her along, and I'm sure she's hating every minute of it. Maybe I shouldn't look for Rae and Matt. The last thing I need is for Margot to tell me we suck and kill the natural buzz coursing through my veins ever since stepping on that stage.

The women's bathroom door swings open, almost hitting me in the face as I walk down the narrow hallway. My arms reach out to stop the force of a woman who's about to crash into me, my hands grabbing her arms.

She yelps, "Sorry!" and when her wide eyes land on me, she freezes. Margot blinks up at me before covering a hand over her mouth in mock disbelief. "Oh, my God. You're the guy who plays guitar!" When I stare at her, she bats her eyelashes and fans herself, but even though she's joking, the sight of her adoring smile makes something inside me crack. My chest warms, and I have to fight the urge to wet my bottom lip with my tongue. Genuine affection from most people doesn't get this much of a physical reaction out of me, so why the hell does Margot faking being starstruck have my pulse racing?

I force myself to snap out of it and give her a taunting grin. "Does seeing me up there make you feel like you're living out a boy-band fantasy?" I tilt my head, the corner of my mouth lifting. "Is this a kink for you, Red?"

Her cheeks flush brighter, and my eyes narrow, scrutinizing her. If I didn't know any better, I'd think . . .

"Are you drunk?" I ask her.

She glares at me, and she suddenly looks more like her usual self.

"Ah, that's better," I say, taunting her. "That's the way your face usually looks—all contorted and pissy."

She scoffs. "Are you always this charming to the people who watch you play?"

Aside from looking pissed off, she's gorgeous. I try not to stare at the way her eyes pop against the color of her shirt.

Or how full her bottom lip is.

Or the way her top dips just enough to break me.

I try not to notice any of those things, but I fucking fail. I fail so hard and end up wondering what she'd do if I pressed her up against the wall and kissed her.

Right here. Right now.

She'd probably slap me—or pepper-spray me. She seems like the type of girl who'd have pepper spray. But in my mind, before she assaults me, she kisses me back.

Margot lowers her head, forcing my gaze back to hers. "Are you having a stroke, or is this what happens when you're out in public?"

"I'm fine." I probably answer too quickly, but right now, I kind of wish I could bang my head against the wall. I don't want to think about her that way. "I appreciate that you're worried, though," I say, trying to recover. "It shows how much you secretly care."

She quirks the side of her mouth into a sort of half-frown. "Damn. So, it's not a stroke?"

"Sorry to disappoint you, Red." Stepping around her, I add, "Now, if you'll excuse me, I need to take a piss."

She scoffs, running her hand through her hair. "Such a way with words. I guess it's a good thing you don't write the songs."

She starts to walk away from me, and I open the bathroom door. Before going inside, I watch her. Her hair almost reaches her lower back, drawing my attention to the way her ass looks in her jeans.

Fucking hell.

Storming into the bathroom and slamming the door behind me, I stand there, trying to get my head on straight.

I can't believe I thought about kissing her.

I can't believe how much I *liked* the thought of kissing her.

Turning on the faucet in the dimly lit bathroom, I run my hands under the cold water before splashing some on my face. Staring down my reflection, I contemplate slapping some sense into me but decide against it when a guy goes to leave, walking behind me. Straightening up, I do what I came here to do and then head out into the crowd to find Rae and Matt. It doesn't take me long to spot them because it doesn't take me long to spot *her*. I try to blame it on her red hair and not the fact that I just thought about pressing her up against the wall and seeing what that smart mouth tastes like. Probably a little like whatever she drank tonight and a lot like the insults she loves to throw my way. I've never kissed anyone with such a sharp tongue. I wonder if she'd tear me a new one just for touching her, or if her tongue would soften against mine, her pretty mouth opening more for me.

Damn it. I need to stop thinking like this.

"There he is!" Matt practically cheers when I walk over to the three of them. He claps his hand on my shoulder, giving it a shake. "You were great up there," he says with a grin. "You're in a fucking band!"

I can't help the smile his excitement pulls from me. I've dreamed of this moment for so long, and now to have him at one of my shows—even if it's a small one—feels unreal.

Rae beams at me. "You guys sound so good! It's crazy to think I know someone in a band," she says with a laugh. "I'm going to buy the next album, and I want you to sign it."

"Deal," is all I can think to say. I'm not used to anyone giving my music this much attention, and as much as I love it, it feels fucking weird.

"Why did the guy you replaced leave?" Rae asks.

I shrug. "His wife had a baby or something a couple of months back. I think it just got to be too much for him." That's one of the downfalls of being in a band where everyone is almost ten years older than you. I have no ties to anything. I could tour the country and never look back, but Dave and Brady have girlfriends they've been with for years. All I can do is hope they put the band first.

I glance at Margot. She's been unusually quiet this entire conversation, and as soon as our eyes meet, she shifts to watching the dwindling crowd. Just as my eyebrows pull together, Matt nudges me and nods toward the stage. "Looks like they're getting ready to pack up."

"That's my cue. You guys will hang around?" Rae and Matt nod, but Margot just rocks back on her heels like she'd rather be anywhere else.

Making my way back up on stage, I try to shake the way Margot has me feeling. Catching a glimpse of her as I put my guitar strap up and over my shoulder, I see her eyes are locked on me, her lips pouting into a subtle frown like she's lost in thought. As soon as she realizes I'm looking, she turns to Rae. I don't know what the hell is wrong with that girl, but she's getting under my skin, and I don't like it.

23
margot

WE WAIT for everyone to file out as Jackson helps the band pack their equipment. Matt can't wipe the goofy grin off his face after watching his best friend on stage, and he hasn't stopped talking about how he wishes he were in a band now.

Rae rolls her eyes, but the corners of her mouth reveal her amusement. "What would you even play?"

His eyebrows lift, offended by the fact that she has to ask. "The drums. Are you kidding?" He then plays the air drums for us.

Holding up a hand to shield herself, Rae looks at me and says, "Okay. Well, luckily it doesn't look like American Thieves needs a drummer."

Matt doesn't stop, and even though he isn't producing any sound, he still looks off-beat.

"What's he doing?" Jackson's smooth voice sounds behind me, making me whip around. His eyes are fixed on Matt with a subtle lift of his eyebrow.

Rae stares at Matt, shaking her head. "He's practicing for your band."

Jackson lets out a breath of laughter. "Right."

"So, what's the plan?" Matt asks now that he's finally done with his epic solo. "Is the band good with you coming with us?"

"Yeah." Jackson nods. "I'm not exactly old enough to get into the places they'll go anyway. I'll work on getting a fake, and they said we'll celebrate another night. I'm starving, though."

"There's a pizza place around the corner." I point in that general direction. "I remember passing it on our way in."

I say it to be helpful, and I say it because I *did* see a pizza place on our way here, but once Jackson gives me his full attention, I wish I would have stayed quiet. All night he's affected me—and not in the way he usually does. My palms sweat under the weight of his full attention.

"I could go for pizza," he says, still looking at me like he's surprised by what I've said even though what I've said wasn't interesting or surprising at all.

Matt puts an arm around Rae and nods toward the exit. "Let's do it."

The two lead the way with Jackson and me trailing behind until a dark-haired woman in a low-cut blouse touches Jackson on the arm to stop him. Her curves make it clear she's older than us. She has a confidence and maturity about her that makes me feel like I'm a middle schooler in comparison.

"You were great up there tonight," she says with stars in her emerald eyes.

He looks mildly uncomfortable by the compliment, and I hate how endearing it is. "Thanks."

"Want to get a drink sometime?" she asks, honey dripping in her voice. I know I should keep walking, but for some reason, I can't tear my eyes away. The woman looks at me and falters. "Oh. Um, are you two together?"

Jackson and I stare at each other. At the same time, we

both remember how to speak, and I say, "Definitely not," while he delivers a resounding, "No."

"Great!" the woman says with an award-winning smile. "Here's my number." She hands Jackson a small paper she already had prepared and gives him a wink before sauntering back to her friends, her hips swinging with each step. Jackson doesn't hide the fact that he watches her ass as she walks away, and when he looks back at me, I don't even realize I'm scowling until he defensively whispers, "What?"

I hold up the back of my hand to showcase the black X. "Maybe you should warn her that she would need to be the one buying the drinks."

The side of his mouth twitches as he slips the small piece of paper into his pocket. "What she doesn't know won't hurt her."

Rolling my eyes, I head after Rae and Matt. "Have fun with that," I say over my shoulder, but even I hear the lack of conviction behind my words. I cross my arms, my nails digging into the palms of my clenched fists. I should go tell her he's underage with dirty clothes all over his floor and plays guitar all night, so she better be ready to sleep with earplugs.

Going out for pizza proves more fun than I thought. Rae and I sit across from each other and catch up on everything happening in our classes lately while Matt and Jackson talk about the band and whether Matt's decided to play for the lacrosse club. The only downside is that I have to sit next to Jackson. Tonight I'm all over the place with him. One minute, I'm thinking about how hot he looks on stage, and the next, I'm tempted to slap him for a stupid comment he makes. Either way, it's safe to say I shouldn't be in close proximity to him for both our sake. At least I don't have to look at him unless I deliberately turn my head now.

By the time we've eaten our fair share of pizza, I'm exhausted. I stifle a yawn, but Rae catches it. "Oh, come on," she says with a faint smile. "We were going to check out this club everyone has been talking about. It's right around the corner."

I'm about to open my mouth to tell her I'll still go—even though I'd rather not—when Jackson's voice cuts me off. "I'm probably heading back after this."

Rae frowns, looking back and forth between us. "You guys are no fun," she says with a pout.

"I'll still go with you," I say with a laugh, but I feel another yawn coming on and do my best to fight it.

She gives me a dubious stare before turning to Jackson. "You might as well take her back with you."

Jackson and I both give each other the same glance before I say with more conviction, "No, really. I'll come to the club. It'll be fun."

Matt looks between the two of us like we're crazy. "Just go home with Jackson," he says like it's the simplest solution.

But nothing about being alone with Jackson feels simple right now. The effect he's having on me tonight is unsettling, and I don't like it. I don't want to be keenly aware of how many inches are between us in the booth. I don't want my body to tense and my heart to race every time his arm accidentally brushes mine. I don't want to feel my pulse throughout my entire body when he turns to face me, our knees grazing briefly under the table.

I swallow hard before looking back at him.

"He's right," Jackson relents. "I'm going to the dorm anyway if you want a ride."

I blink. "You want to give me a ride home?"

He presses his lips together and tilts his head. "I don't think I said that."

His comment dissolves whatever lust just came over me, and I let out a tired breath of resignation. "Okay. Fine."

"You're welcome," he answers, and my eyes narrow.

"Why would I thank you? You're going there anyway."

He takes out his card to pay for his meal. "Yeah, but now I have to deal with your always pleasant company all the way there."

Rae groans, and we both look at her. "Can you two just get along for half a second? This whole back and forth is starting to get annoying."

Matt looks at Jackson and speaks in a calming tone. "Just take her home, and then you can pretend she doesn't live across the hall from us like you usually do."

"Fine," Jackson mutters.

I look at him again. "You pretend I don't live across from you?"

He shrugs. "People cope with their trauma in different ways."

My wide eyes dart to Rae, but she just gets to her feet. "Well, see you later! Drive safe!" she says before grabbing hold of Matt's arm and pulling him after her. Jackson and I are left sitting on the same side of the booth. When I look over at him, he impatiently waves for me to move so he can get out of his seat.

"You're such an asshole." I stand up, crossing my arms as I turn and wait for him.

"And you're a delight," he says as he walks right past me, expecting me to follow.

Rae is right, this constant battle between us is exhausting, but at the same time, I don't know how to stop it. Jackson makes everything more intense, and he makes me feel like I'm not in control of my own emotions. I've never had someone get to me the way he does. It makes me crave peace with him, but those same reasons are what make it impossible to keep the peace, too.

24
jackson

MARGOT'S angry footfalls carry on behind me, and I try to ignore the feeling of her shooting daggers into the back of my head. Opening the door to the pizza shop, I let it fall shut behind me, not bothering to wait for her. If she were anyone else, I would have gladly held the door open, but she's Margot.

She doesn't say a word as we walk—which I should be thankful for, but instead, it leaves me unsettled—like she's plotting something. Once the Mazda is in view, I press the unlock button on the fob.

"This is your car?"

Looking over the roof of the car, I see her stopped in her tracks. "What's the problem?"

"Nothing," she says quickly, her eyes jumping back to my car again. "It's just . . . clean."

Raising an eyebrow, I glance at my car. It is clean. I washed it a few days ago, but I don't know why it's worth talking about. "Thanks?"

She regains her bearings when she says, "I mean, I've seen your room. I just figured your car would be equally uninhabitable."

With a shake of my head, I open the driver's side door. "Get in the car, Red."

She does as I say but doesn't look happy about it. "I thought I told you to stop calling me that."

I put the car in reverse. "You tell me a lot of things. It can be hard to keep track of it all." She rolls her eyes, and it's hard for me to remember why the thought of kissing her was so appealing earlier. I'll blame it on my good mood after playing on that stage. I would have wanted to kiss anyone at that moment.

I plug my phone in and let my speakers jolt with a sudden rush of sound. It's on the Arctic Monkeys' album because I started listening to it again after I told her about it.

Turning the music up a little louder, I focus on the people bar hopping downtown under the glow of the streetlights. Movement catches my eye, and when I glance her way, Margot is staring out the window as she taps her hand on her thigh, her head gently bobbing to the beat.

She likes the song.

Stealing a second glance, I catch her lips moving along to the lyrics.

She *knows* the song.

I've known girls who have liked the same type of music as me. Hell, I've known girls who have listened to music I like with hopes it would mean I'd start to like them, too. But with Margot, this feels . . . different. She isn't trying to impress me, but she trusted me enough to know she'd like the album if I said she would.

Turning down the volume makes her look at me, those big, brown eyes waiting for me to say something.

"I didn't think you'd listen to the album," I say, shifting my eyes back to the road and letting the music stay low as we drive onto the highway.

She shrugs. "I downloaded it as soon as you told me about it."

And the way that one sentence sinks its teeth into me, making me feel things for her I don't want to feel. She shouldn't get to erase all the ways she's annoyed me tonight with one innocent glance and the fact that she bought an album I told her she'd like. "Well, I'm glad you like it."

Margot nods, suddenly looking less comfortable and drumming her hands on her knees. Silence falls between us, and I don't like the way it eats at me.

"You guys sounded good tonight." I must have heard her wrong. When I look at her again, I expect to see sarcasm laced in her features, but she's watching for my reaction. Having her eyes on me like this makes me tighten my grip on the steering wheel. Plenty of people told me the same thing tonight, but it's different coming from her. Margot isn't easy to please, and she wouldn't tell me we sounded good just to be nice. She means it.

I swallow and nod. "Thanks." It's all I trust myself saying, determined to keep my eyes on the road.

I can feel her watching me, analyzing my every move, and I want to know why. I want to know what she sees.

"That's it?" she finally says.

"What's it?"

She lets out a light laugh. "This is your chance. You're not going to gloat or be the cocky asshole you are?"

The corner of my mouth lifts. "Not tonight."

She pulls her head back slightly but doesn't say anything. By the time we reach campus, we've fallen into a comfortable silence. I park in the lot closest to our dorm, and we get out without a word. The air has cooled, and Margot wraps her arms around herself as we walk. For the second time, I'm faced with the feeling of wishing I had a jacket to offer her, and that realization freaks me out.

Margot is not the sweet girl you offer your jacket to.

Margot is the headache who lives across the hall, and I don't know why I keep confusing the two.

When we get to our dorms, she turns to face me. She pauses, her mouth opening but then closing. I want to know what she's thinking, so I just wait.

Her eyes are still bright even though she spent most of the night in a shitty dive bar. The makeup that hides her freckles has worn off a little, leaving more of them visible. She tucks her hair behind one of her ears, and my hand twitches with the impulse to reach out and touch her.

"Thanks for the ride home," she finally says.

I blink, and my hand clenches by my side. "Anytime."

A tiny crease forms between her eyebrows, and I know I've said the wrong thing. But with the way she is right now, wide-eyed, vulnerable . . . *open*, I would gladly give her a ride home whenever she needed. I like the idea of being needed by Margot—I like the idea of a softer side to her.

She lingers, still looking at me, and my heart pounds harder in my chest with every passing second. The dorm is quiet, still empty. Everyone must still be at the party. No voices carry down the hall or fade into the background. No doors opening or closing. There's nothing.

No one would know if I took her bottom lip between my teeth.

"Well, goodnight."

I remember to breathe, my head clearing. "Yeah. Goodnight."

I stand there, waiting for her to finish fiddling with her keys and unlock the door. Once she turns the key, she looks over her shoulder at me. "What are you doing?"

"Uh, just making sure you get inside okay, I guess."

"It's kind of weird," she says, and I don't argue with her. It is weird, but that doesn't mean I don't notice the small smile pulling at her lips as she goes inside, shutting the door behind her.

25
margot

WARM SUNLIGHT SHINES through the window of Matt's Ford Focus as I stare out from the back seat. I'm not really sure how I got here, or how Rae managed to convince me that spending Thanksgiving with Matt's parents would be a good idea. Going home to Indiana for Thanksgiving *and* Christmas wasn't going to happen, so that left us with no family plans. It makes sense for her to spend the holiday with her boyfriend's family, but me? Maybe I should have stayed in the dorm and eaten my last Cup Noodles.

The thought alone is depressing. Maybe it's better that I'll be spending Thanksgiving with someone other than myself. There's a good chance I would have ended up hangry blogging about the lack of Thanksgiving dishes you can make solely with a microwave. I let out a silent sigh as I stare out the window. When Rae and I made a promise to do everything together our first year of college, this isn't what I had in mind.

As if she can feel I need the extra encouragement, she looks over her shoulder from the front seat. Her movement tears me away from the window, and I'm met with her grateful, yet apprehensive, smile.

I do my best to smile back, but I know it looks forced. As much as I appreciate the hospitality, I'm still the third wheel in this scenario. I don't miss Jackson, but at least the scales feel more balanced when he's here. We saw him before we left, but he wasn't in a rush. He was still playing guitar on his bed when he nodded our way and gave us a curt goodbye.

I haven't seen him much since the night he drove me home from his gig. Our constant back and forth may not have been my favorite thing, but at least it was entertaining. Without it, I'm left with only my schoolwork and outlining future blog posts.

I was nice to him that night. I told him I liked his band's music, I thanked him for giving me a ride home, and the sight of him standing by his door, waiting for me to get inside, has been burned into my mind.

I focus on the passing trees. Autumn doesn't exist in Florida. Back home, the leaves are changing colors and the temperatures are dropping, but as I stare out at the flat landscape, it looks the same as it did in August. Everything is green.

We've been in the car for just over two hours when Matt finally turns into a cute suburban neighborhood. We cruise through the winding streets until he parks in front of a house on a dead-end street. The soft green stucco and stone pillars give the outside of the home a sense of comfort, and the blooming flowers out front are just another reminder of how far I am from home.

I don't even think Matt has fully put the car in park before a woman in capris and a maroon blouse comes bounding down the two front steps. Her pixie cut leaves her light brown hair neat like the rest of her, and I can't help wondering if she's the reason Matt never has anything left out of place.

Stepping out of the car, Matt catches his mom in a hug.

"You're here!" she squeals excitedly before stepping back

and putting both hands on his cheeks so she can give him the once-over. "Are you eating enough? You look thin."

Matt laughs and steps out of her grasp. He looks over the top of the car at Rae, who gets out of the passenger side, and his mom follows his gaze.

"Oh my goodness!" She bounds around the front of the car. "You must be Rae!" Taking Rae in a hug, she whispers, "He sent me a picture of you two," like she needs to justify how she was able to recognize her. When she releases her, she adds, "I'm so happy to meet you and have you here with us!"

Slinging my bag over my shoulder, I step out and make my way to the front of the car, unsure about interrupting their moment. Matt's mom still has a hand on each of Rae's shoulders when she looks at me. "Margot!"

I blink, caught off guard by her knowing who I am.

She lets go of Rae and trots over. "Everyone gets a hug here," she says with a laugh, and I can't help doing the same when her arms fling around my shoulders.

"You have a beautiful home." Now that I'm able to get a closer look, even the pine bark around the flowers looks freshly placed.

She pulls back and the warmth in her eyes is almost overwhelming. It's the type of warmth I've longed to see in the reflection of my own mother's eyes, but all I ever got was a lift of a brow and a subtle sense of disapproval.

Matt's mom gives my shoulders a squeeze in thanks before bringing her attention back to her son and Rae. She beams. "Come in. Come in." Waving for us to follow, she bounds back up the steps. "I hope you kids are hungry! We've got plenty of food!"

"Come on," Matt says to Rae and me before he puts his arm around my best friend. "I'll introduce you to my dad." Leaning forward, Matt looks past Rae to me, as if making sure I'm okay.

I smile at him, and I'm relieved the gesture comes naturally. I may be far from home, and I'm definitely the third wheel, but at least I'm surrounded by good people.

Walking through the entryway, each room is perfectly decorated with a combination of traditional décor and family photos sprinkled throughout. The only thing that doesn't match the rest of the house is a dark green leather recliner and the tank of a man sitting in it.

As soon as Matt's dad sees us, he pauses the game and hoists himself out of the chair to introduce himself, but instead of saying his name, he says, "Who's ready to watch some FOOTBALL!" The word football comes out as two separate whoops, and I can't fight my laughter.

Everyone gets introduced and Matt gets pulled away by his dad so he can show him his latest project in the garage.

Unsure of where to set my bag, I tap Matt's mom on the shoulder as she works on getting more of our Thanksgiving meal prepped in the kitchen. "Um, Mrs. . . ." I blank. I don't know Matt's last name.

My eyes dart to Rae for help, but before she can answer, Matt's mom says, "Please, call me Janet."

I nod, but I'm not sure if calling her by her first name feels right either. I guess it's better than calling her *Matt's mom* for the rest of our visit, though. "Where should I set my bag?"

"Oh!" She looks between Rae and me. "Of course! I made up the extra bedroom upstairs for you girls. It's the second room on the right, down the hall." She wipes her hands with a towel. "I can show you."

"That's okay," Rae says with a shake of her head. "You have your hands full. I'm sure we can find it."

I nod. "Second room on the right."

The corners of Janet's mouth lift. "If you're sure."

Rae and I start to head toward the stairs. "Of course!" Rae

says over her shoulder. "And once we set our stuff down, we'll help with anything you need."

Rae and I make our way upstairs and easily find the room Janet was referring to. The bed looks like it's been freshly made and there are clean towels folded on the dresser.

"Hey." I set my bag on the floor under the window. "Feel free to sneak into Matt's room tonight if you want. You don't have to stay here with me."

Rae pauses before setting down her stuff. "Really?"

I look at her expectantly. "Wouldn't you rather stay with him? You and I already share a room every night."

A slow smile pulls at her mouth. "I guess that's true."

"It's settled then." I head back toward the door as she finishes putting her stuff down. "You'll spend the night with your boyfriend, and tomorrow I get to hear all about it."

Rae barks a laugh. "You already know everything we've done."

Pausing in the doorway, I lean into the frame. "Yeah, but my dating life is nonexistent. I'm living vicariously through you."

"You know . . ." Rae says, giving me a sideways glance. "Matt has a brother."

26
jackson

THE DRIVE TO MY PARENTS' house went by too fast. I was lost in the music, playing out a million different scenarios of how this will all go down.

Every hypothetical ended badly.

I guess that's to be expected. I knew this day would come—or at least I hoped it would. All I ever wanted was to be able to look my dad in the eyes and say, *My band is going on tour, so I have to drop out.* I've dreamed for years about telling him I'm finding success in something he thinks is pointless, but as I pull into the driveway of my childhood home, this is the last place I want to be. The typical Florida stucco house looks as pristine as usual—not a blade of grass out of place. But instead of appreciating how perfect my parents keep everything, it just serves as another reminder of how wildly imperfect I am to them in comparison.

My backpack only has a toothbrush and a change of clothes in it, but I sling it over my shoulder. I considered bringing my guitar so I could practice, but that seemed like a surefire way to piss off the old man before I tell him the news. As I slowly approach the house, I feel empty handed without it.

Stopping in front of the front door, I take a deep breath before knocking my knuckles against it in three steady beats.

I don't have long to fight the urge to bolt before my mom opens the door with a wide grin. "Happy Thanksgiving!"

Some of my tension eases, and I let out a breath of laughter. "Happy Thanksgiving."

Ushering me into the house, she asks, "Was the drive okay? When did you eat last? Is your car still running well?" All in a matter of seconds.

"Drive was fine, I had a bagel on the road, and the car runs great."

She smiles over her shoulder at me as she guides me through the house like I've never been here before. It still looks exactly the same as the last time I was here. Cleaner maybe—without my shit everywhere. My dad probably loves that I don't live here anymore. Now there's no one here to mess up his perfectly organized junk drawer.

When we make it to the kitchen in the back of the house, my tension returns at the sight of my father sorting the mail at the counter.

"Jackson," he says without looking up. He still wears his hair like he's a news anchor from three decades ago.

"Dad."

He lifts his gaze and takes off his reading glasses to get a better look at me. I know he's scrutinizing me. That's what he always does. My suspicions are only confirmed when he says, "You need a haircut."

"Okay, Dad." I'm not going to let him get to me this quickly. I haven't even been in the house for all of thirty seconds.

He holds my stare, waiting for me to come back with something more. When I don't, he scoffs and goes back to sorting the mail. "No guitar, I see." He positions his glasses on his face again.

"Nope."

My mother watches our exchange with anxious eyes. This woman would give anything for a happy family, and sometimes I feel like I'm the one fucking it up for her. If I were more like my dad—more like what he wants me to be—maybe she'd have it.

"I hope that means you've finally come to your senses and quit obsessing over music."

My jaw twitches. "Nope." I know I should walk away. I should go put my stuff down in my room. I should give him time to get over his disappointment in my hair before I give him anything else to gripe about.

"Of course not," he drones as he opens an envelope and starts reading its contents.

"Honey, would you like something to drink?" My mother's voice is barely audible like her speaking at a normal volume might detonate the bomb we're all sidestepping.

I shake my head, but my teeth are too busy biting the inside of my cheek to form words.

"Oh, look," my father muses as he continues to read. "The University of South Florida is renovating its library. I guess my tuition dollars aren't going to complete waste."

That one sentence is all it takes for my resolve to slip. The familiar feeling of fist-clenching anger settles into me. He's more interested in the fucking new library than he is in looking at his son he hasn't seen in three months. Everything about this is bullshit. This house is bullshit. His fucking hair is bullshit. He's the last person who has room to talk about me needing a haircut. My blood boils as I stare at the man who has shit on everything I've ever seen as being good in this world. I can't take a whole weekend of this—I won't. I won't stand here and let him vomit his opinion no one fucking asked for while I keep everything I'm feeling locked in a vault.

I briefly look at my mom. After dinner would be a better

time. Hell, as I'm walking out the door to drive back to campus would be a better time. But I forgot what this feels like. I don't get this treatment on the regular anymore, and I forgot how much it stings—how it has the power to strip you of your self-worth. And he's already acting this pissed, so I might as well give him something to be pissed about.

"Don't worry, Dad. Come next semester, you won't have to waste your money on my tuition anymore. I'm not going back after winter break." The words are liberating and scary as hell all at once. My heart feels like it's going to jump out of my chest and the adrenaline coursing through my veins has the blood in my ears pounding.

He tenses. "What?"

When he finally gives me his full attention, the corner of my mouth twitches. "That's right, Dad. No more college for me. My band confirmed an opening slot on tour next year."

He rips his glasses off his face. "Your *band?*" He shakes his head. "Absolutely not. You might be eighteen, but I won't let you throw your life away over some pipe dream!"

"Honey," my mother's voice chimes in, soft and sweet. "Maybe you can tour over the summer, so you can do both."

I run my hand over my face. "That's not how it works." Daring to look back at my dad, I add, "Look, this is all I've ever wanted. This is my dream, and I have a once in a lifetime opportunity to make it happen. It's not like I haven't thought about this. I've wanted it since I was in middle school."

"Dreams," he scoffs and shakes his head. "Dreams don't pay the bills, Jackson. You're staying in school, and this conversation is over."

Determined to look calm even though everything under the surface is going haywire, I say, "I'm not asking. Legally, I'm an adult, and I've already made up my mind. At the end of the semester, I'm dropping out and going on tour."

He looks me up and down, his entire body shaking with

anger. "Okay, big man. You can do what you want, but not under my roof."

"I don't even live here anymore!" I say with a bewildered laugh.

Through gritted teeth, he manages to say, "Not under my roof. Not now. Not ever." He takes a step toward me, his eyes narrowing. "Get out."

"Chuck!" my mother cries, but it's no use.

"He can do as he pleases, but he will *not* do it here. I won't stand for it." He turns to me. "I won't give you another *dime*. If you can make these big decisions on your own, you can pay for them, too. Now, I won't tell you again. Get out."

"You're kicking me out on Thanksgiving?"

"Out!" He points toward the door.

I look between him and my mother. Her eyes well with tears, and I hate him for it. I hate him for doing this to her.

But I kind of hate her for it, too.

She could at least try to put her foot down, but that's never been her strength—or at least she's never done it in front of me. Growing up, sometimes my dad would come to me and apologize, and I knew she was behind it. She's always behind it, but right now, I need her to be front and center. I need her to fight for me, and she's not.

"Fine." Tossing my backpack over my shoulder, I head for the door.

My mother follows me, saying a string of things I know aren't true. That he loves me, and he just needs time, and that he'll come around.

I hug her goodbye, but I can't look at her. I can't see her fall apart. There's nothing for me to say, so I get in my car. I stare at my steering wheel, but out of the corner of my eye, I see my mother still standing in the doorway—probably crying. Without lifting my gaze, I put the car in reverse and back out of the driveway. I only make it a few houses down before I pull over and try to get my bearings. What the hell just happened? Where do I go now?

I run my hands over my face and look up at the street sign in front of me. The name on the sign reads Thompson Drive, and I let out a breath. There's only one place for me to go.

27
margot

MATT'S DAD—WHO insists I call him Drew—has Rae and me laughing so hard we're on the brink of tears.

"I'm serious!" he exclaims. "She wanted nothing to do with me!"

"That is not true!" Janet calls from the kitchen, only making us laugh that much harder.

Matt sits on the couch with his arm around Rae as his attention toggles between the game and the story he's undoubtedly heard before.

I can't believe I was on the fence about coming here. Matt's parents are wonderful, the atmosphere is great, and even though we haven't sat down to eat dinner yet, the food Janet has given us so far has been amazing.

We're still waiting for Matt's brother and grandmother to get here before we sit down at the table. According to Rae, Matt thinks his brother can be "a douche," but she suspects it might stem from your typical sibling rivalry.

Drew pulls me back into his story when he says, "Her mouth was saying 'It's nice to meet you,' but her eyes were saying 'drop dead.'"

Janet pokes her head out of the kitchen. "Have you ever met a more dramatic man?"

My stomach hurts from laughing so hard, and I wipe a stray tear from my eye.

The doorbell rings, and Matt's eyebrows furrow. "Did Emmet say he was on his way?"

Drew turns over his phone that's resting on the armrest of his chair. "Not to me."

Matt gets to his feet to open the wooden front door, but instead of stepping aside, he stands in the doorway, blocking my view. His voice is hushed as he talks to whoever it is, and Drew calls out, "Who is it?"

Matt doesn't answer right away. He continues his hushed conversation before finally answering. "Uh, it's Jackson."

The name makes me pause. It's like just the mention of Jackson can take me from a laughing fit to completely sober in an instant. What is he doing here? Isn't he supposed to be with his family? I look down at myself, suddenly wondering if I'm dressed okay.

Matt finally steps aside, and from where I'm sitting, I have a perfect view of Jackson in the entryway. He goes to rub the back of his neck, and my eyebrows pull together at the sight of his hand shaking.

Drew leans forward in his chair to get a better view of his visitor.

"Jackson!" he cheers as he gets up from his seat. "To what do we owe the pleasure?"

"You know I can't turn down a chance to see Grandma Lois." Jackson's snappy comeback comes out with no hesitation.

Maybe I imagined his hand shaking.

Drew lets out a bellowing laugh. "Good. With you here, maybe she'll leave me alone for once."

Jackson grins. "She does love me, but I wouldn't count on it."

Drew claps him on the shoulder. "Confident last words, my friend."

A breath of laughter leaves Jackson's lips as he passes Drew and nods to Janet in the kitchen. "Happy Thanksgiving."

"Happy Thanksgiving, dear." I can't see Janet, but a hint of uncertainty laces her voice.

Matt hangs behind Jackson, watching him with a hint of apprehension as the two enter the family room. I can't help feeling it, too. There's a storm brewing behind Jackson's steel eyes, and I have no idea what put it there.

He gives a tight-lipped smile to Rae and me before collapsing into the far end of the couch I'm sitting on. "I forgot you'd be here, Red."

"I didn't think you'd be here either."

The corner of his mouth twitches, but he looks away from me to focus on the TV. "I wanted to give you one more thing to be thankful for."

Following his dismissal, I also watch the game. I don't care about football, but if I keep staring at Jackson, I'm going to keep analyzing him. "And yet it has the opposite effect."

Matt eyes Jackson's bag at his feet. "So, you're staying here tonight?"

Jackson looks at Matt. "I don't have to. I might drive back to the dorm."

Matt shakes his head, finally taking his seat next to Rae again. "No way. Just stay here."

Jackson scans the room, taking in the four of us. "Is there room?"

Rae must see something off about him too, because she says, "We'll make room."

Jackson opens his mouth like he's about to insist otherwise, but then pauses. "Thanks."

He turns back to watch the game, but his knee bounces as he does. I think back to before his first gig when Matt said Jackson rarely gets nervous, and it brings a frown to my lips. I stare at his knee and feel the sudden urge to put my hand on it. I want to know what happened. I want to know why he's here. And more than anything, I want to know what could make him more nervous than getting on stage in front of a crowd of people for the first time.

28
jackson

TOURING with a band is all I've ever wanted, and the fact that my dad basically wants to disown me because of it is messing with my head. I'm still excited. I still feel good about my decision to drop out next semester. But, at the same time, there's this crushing feeling of *what if he's right?*

If he's right—if this is really a waste of time that's going to turn into a waste of my life—I'll never live it down. I want to prove him wrong. No, I *need* to prove him wrong. I need to show him I know what I'm doing—even if it feels like I don't.

I also have to tell Matt.

When he answered the door, I kept things vague. I told him my dad was giving me shit, and I needed to get out, but I have a feeling he knows there's more.

I hate feeling like I'm letting everyone down. Matt will be out of a roommate, and it's my fault. I think he always knew this was a possibility, but it's happening sooner than we both expected. The only thing making me feel less guilty is that he has Rae. She's good for him, and I know he's crazy about her.

Janet comes out of the kitchen. She's eyeing me the same way her son has been for the past twenty minutes, but I try not to let it bother me. It's a mix of pity and uncertainty, and it makes me wish I drove back to campus. She knows my dad and I don't always see eye to eye, but we've never had a fight like this. He's never kicked me out of the fucking house. My hands start to shake at the thought, and I quickly wipe them on my jeans.

"So, what?" she asks, the playful tone of her voice not matching her demeanor. "I don't see you for months and then you come here and don't even give me a hug?"

I give her my best smile and get to my feet. When she hugs me, she squeezes a little tighter than she normally would and rubs my back like I've just been benched for the big game.

Well, I guess I sort of have been, but being fired from a shitty job is probably a more accurate comparison.

The kind gesture makes me think of my own mom, and I can't help wondering what she's doing right now. Did she let my dad have a piece of her mind, or did she shut herself in the bedroom and cry?

When she releases me, she looks around the room. "I love having all of you here. We're just waiting on Emmet and Grandma."

Matt and I give each other a knowing glance. Emmet is his older brother, and he's a tool.

"Let me guess," Matt says. "He has an important meeting . . . on Thanksgiving."

Janet straightens and gives Matt a pointed stare. "Your brother works very hard at what he does."

She turns and walks back into the kitchen, and Matt mutters, "Yeah, that's why he lives with Grandma."

I just laugh and shake my head. I think Emmet coins himself as a motivational speaker or something. I don't know. All I know is that he has his whole "business" running off Facebook, where he basically spam messages people until someone is dumb enough to set up a call with him. Those are his important meetings.

Rae laughs as she leans into Matt, and even though I'm happy for him, part of me envies him just a little. There's no one I want to date right now, and I'm about to go on tour with the band, so the last thing I need is a relationship, but he makes it look so easy.

Margot sits on the other end of the couch, her feet tucked underneath her. I'm glad she still gave me shit when I walked in here. It's the only part of my day that has felt normal, and I need any sense of normalcy I can get right now. My whole life is about to change. If the one thing I can count on is Margot giving me the stink eye, so be it.

The front door opens, and in comes Emmet and Grandma Lois. I wish I liked him as much as I like her. Emmet is a prick, but there's a good chance Grandma Lois is the greatest person to have ever lived.

"Hey, fam!" Emmet calls out as he holds the door open for the petite elderly woman with sharp eyes and a giant handbag. She scurries past us, glaring as she does. "You lot should be cooking." She stares us down before spitting out the word "Lazy" with a shake of her head and continuing her trek into the kitchen.

I let out a breath of laughter. That woman never disappoints. Every time she's around, I'm constantly entertained by the shit that comes out of her mouth.

Rae and Margot look at each other with wide eyes before jumping to their feet and hurrying after her.

That's when Emmet walks into the room. He does a double take when Margot passes, and his eyes linger a little too long as he stops her to introduce himself. He's only three years older than us, but he has that sales look in his eyes like she's a deal he needs to close.

She stares up at him with vulnerability in her eyes and a smile that could bring most guys to their knees.

My heel starts to bounce, the all too familiar feeling of anxiety creeping into my chest again. But this time, it has nothing to do with my dad or the band. This time, it has everything to do with the girl who lives across the hall and the guy I don't want her talking to.

29
margot

EMMET IS FRIENDLY, but he's a lot.

And he's talking to me more than anyone else.

Which I guess is fine.

He certainly has more to say to me than Jackson, and Rae has been helping Matt's mom in the kitchen for a little while now. I offered to help, but Emmet called me over, so here we are. It's not the first time it's happened either.

He's already told me about his life coaching business and talked trash about his clients—which must violate some type of confidentiality agreement, but what do I know? Now he's going on about what it's like being a senior at the University of Central Florida and how he can buy beer now that he's twenty-one.

I smile, hoping he'll realize I'm not contributing to the conversation, and take a hint. On second thought, he hasn't exactly asked me anything about myself. So even if I wanted to contribute something, I don't see where I could have.

My eyes scan over the kitchen as Rae, Matt's grandma, and Matt's mom work together to cook our Thanksgiving dinner. I want to be a part of *their* conversation, but now Emmet has moved on to telling me about UCF's superior business program all entrepreneurs should strive to be a part of, and I can't get away.

I don't usually write about personal things in my blog. Sure, I'll share things about music and movies I like, but my personal life is always safely tucked behind the curtain. This conversation with Emmet is giving me plenty of ideas for things to write about, though.

Life Coach or Lost Puppy?

Looking for an escape, my eyes move past Emmet and back into the living room where the guys are watching the half-time show.

I freeze.

Matt and his dad are in the middle of some type of football debate, but Jackson sits comfortably between them, his eyes locked on me. His mouth pulls into a smirk when he sees me looking at him, and I *hate* it. I hate that he knows I'm miserable talking to Emmet, and I hate even more that he finds enjoyment in it. How is it that the guy talking to me can't pick up that I'm not interested, but the guy across the room has no problem reading me like a book?

"Margot," Rae says from the kitchen, pulling my attention away. She waves me over, and I let out a breath of relief. "Sorry, I'll be right back," I lie to Emmet and make a run for it.

Rae cuts the ends off green beans at the kitchen counter, and when I walk over, her eyes flicker to Emmet to make sure he's not watching. "Well, someone seems to like you," she says quietly.

"Yeah," I mutter under my breath. "It would be nice if he didn't."

She lets out a breath of laughter. "That's why I called you

over here. I think Matt was right about his brother being a douche."

I mouth, "Thank you," and she smiles.

"Are we gossiping or cooking?" says a voice behind us, and we both jump at the sound of it.

"What?" Rae asks with wide eyes as we stare back at Matt's grandma.

The woman's sharp, hawk-like eyes scan over the scene, and I kick myself for being empty-handed. She lifts a brow and repeats her question. "Gossiping or cooking?"

"Gossiping," I say with a nod as I make sure to stand up straight. I'm not the one potentially marrying into this family one day. It doesn't matter if she disapproves of me.

Rae bursts into laughter next to me, but Matt's grandma just stares long enough to make me sweat. Eventually, a slow smile creeps across her lips, and I allow myself to exhale.

"Good," she says with a wink. "And just so you know, Matt is right." Her eyes flicker to Emmet. "He kind of is."

Rae and I burst into laughter, not bothering to be quiet about it. On the brink of tears, I wipe my eyes. I look around to scan for Emmet, hoping he didn't hear that he was the brunt of Grandma's joke. Before I spot him, my eyes snag on Jackson watching me with his head tilted. He's still between Matt and his dad, and I can't help wondering if he's been watching me this whole time.

I swallow at the thought.

"Did she just call her grandson a douche?" Rae asks in my ear, making sure to keep her voice low.

Letting out a laugh, I make a point to look away from Jackson as I say, "I think she did."

"Hey," Rae says, bumping me with her shoulder. "Do you want me to stay with you tonight since Jackson is here now?"

Oh, right. I hadn't thought of what Jackson being here meant for our sleeping arrangements. "No," I say with a shake of my head. "I still think you should stay with Matt." Rae and Matt may have time together when they go out to eat, but they rarely have a room to themselves.

Her eyebrows shoot up. "You do know that means you'll be staying with Jackson, right?"

I look at the guy across the room, relieved to see he's finally joined in on whatever the guys are talking about. "Maybe he'll sleep on the couch."

"Maybe . . ." She doesn't sound convinced, though.

"Don't worry about it," I say with a smile. "We'll figure it out."

"Yeah, okay," she answers, but there's still a sense of apprehension in her voice as she looks from Jackson to me. "We'll have to ask him about it."

I nod, and I can only imagine how Jackson will react.

The smell of sweet potatoes and turkey wafts through the house. This is what Thanksgiving should be like. Growing up, it was only ever the three of us, and my parents never wanted to fuss. They saw cooking an elaborate meal for two adults and a child as being illogical, but I always craved this. Any time I'd watch movies with Thanksgiving scenes showing large families and chaos, it made me hate the quiet of my parents' home.

When it comes time to eat, there are two seats for me to choose from—one next to Emmet and the other next to Jackson. I pause at the head of the table for a split second, unsure which side to take. Emmet gives me a flash of white teeth, and Jackson leans his elbows on the table, his hands clasped in front of his mouth to hide his smirk. My knees lock like a deer on a dark road as blinding headlights round the bend. Jackson lets out a breath of laughter and moves to fold his napkin on his lap, pulling me from my petrified state. Before I even consciously make a decision, my feet carry me to the seat next to Jackson like my body knows which is the lesser of two evils.

I instantly regret my decision when he knowingly says, "Hey, Red," with a trace of laughter still in his voice.

"Is something funny?" I ask, my eyes narrowing.

He shrugs innocently. "You tell me."

Opening my napkin and setting it on my lap, I shake my head. "No. Nothing is funny."

He leans toward me, keeping his voice low so only I can hear him, and my entire body tenses, keenly aware of the fact that our arms are almost touching. "Who knew all it took was a day with Emmet for me to rise in the ranks."

I give him a pitying frown. "Oh, I wouldn't say that. If anything, you two are even."

"Even?" He shakes his head. "No." Subtly pointing his fork at Emmet, he adds, "I'm at least three slots above that guy. I have to be. You sat here for a reason."

I shake my head and try to hide my smile. Looking around the table, I know this is the perfect time to warn Jackson about our sleeping arrangement. Everyone is distracted and busy, settling themselves at the table and carrying on the conversations they've been having.

I reach for his arm on the table to get his attention, and his head whips back in my direction. He drops his stare to my hand on him, his eyes flicking up to meet mine. That look is enough to make me snatch my hand back.

I clasp my fingers in my lap. "Before you came here, I told Rae she could sleep with Matt."

He holds my gaze but says nothing.

"So . . . maybe sleep on the couch?"

He cocks an eyebrow. "And why would I do that?"

I swallow, suddenly wishing I wouldn't have brought this up with so many people around. Keeping my voice low, I say, "So we don't have to share the room."

His eyes roam over my face, a slow lift of his lips forming. "Actually, Red, I don't mind sharing a room with you at all."

I blink. "You can't be serious," I say in a harsh whisper.

Jackson takes a sip of water, but even that can't hide his amusement. "Oh, I've never been more serious about anything."

Janet is the last to settle into her seat at the head of the table with her second glass of wine, bringing our conversation to a halt. Her smile is easy as she says, "Please, dig in!"

I dare to look at Jackson one more time, but he's already moved on to having a conversation with Matt's dad across the table.

Why the hell would Jackson want to share a room with me? Is he trying to make me uncomfortable on purpose? That has to be it . . . right? There's no way he would actually want to willingly subject himself to such a thing. My heart races at the thought of being alone with him for hours. He's affected me more than usual lately. Sharing a room with him is probably the last thing I need.

I force myself to strike up a conversation with Matt's grandma to get my mind off things. She seems to have warmed up to me, even smiling a few times as I tell her about my hopes of getting a summer internship at one of the local papers. I thought it would feel weird to spend Thanksgiving with people I don't know, but Matt's parents have this way of making me feel like I've known them forever. Janet has Rae and me laughing as she spills the dirt on Matt and Jackson growing up. Apparently, they were both convinced they could give themselves superpowers if they tried hard enough. Matt worked at mastering invisibility for a solid month, and Jackson was convinced he had super speed.

Drew has already invited us back for Christmas, which we had to politely decline. Although, I did tell him I'd rather spend it here than go home to Indiana and face the cold, which he seemed to appreciate. As much as I'm looking forward to spending Christmas back home with Rae, spending the holidays in Florida wouldn't be bad.

By the end of the evening, I've eaten more food than I have on any Thanksgiving, stolen a few of Janet's recipes, and laughed to the point of tears at least four times.

Even Jackson is having fun.

It's bizarre seeing him in his element like this. These people are obviously just as much his family as they are Matt's. He takes jabs at Emmet with Grandma Lois, jokes with Matt's dad, and goes out of his way to help Matt's mom with whatever she may need.

I wonder why he didn't stay with his parents today. I think he and Matt grew up living close to each other, so his parents' house can't be too far. He was off when he first got here, but the more time he spends with Matt's family, the more he settles into a version of himself that seems happy. Jackson's happiness might not be as open and outward as Matt's, but he doesn't look like he's dwelling on not seeing his family.

His blue-gray eyes catch me staring, and he furrows his brow.

Luckily, just as my cheeks flush enough to make me look guilty, Grandma Lois stands from the table. "It's getting late. Emmet, we'd better get going."

Emmet frowns before leaning across the table toward me. "I've got to get the old lady home, but I want to give you my number."

"Who are you calling old?" Grandma Lois snaps somewhere in the distance, but I can't tear my eyes away from her grandson.

"Oh." I blink. "Um, okay."

With the smile he gives me, you'd think I had responded by jumping for joy. Awkwardly handing him my phone, I let him type in his number. I'm not sure what's happening right now, but I hope it's over soon.

When he gives me my phone back, he winks.

He literally *winks*.

Rae does a poor job of stifling her laugh as Emmet heads toward the door. I look back at Jackson, but he's already gotten up to help clear the table.

30
jackson

JANET GIVES us each a goodnight hug before we head upstairs. "I'm so glad we got to spend the day with all of you." I think she's getting a little teary, but it might be the wine. She quickly wipes her eyes and smiles. "Both bedrooms are made up for you upstairs."

"Okay, goodnight, Mom," Matt says.

"Goodnight, Janet," I add. My eyes flicker to where Margot stands, and I'm surprised to find her already looking at me.

She's been doing that a lot today—looking at me.

I'm not sure what to make of it. She's probably trying to figure out how she can avoid sleeping in the same room as me tonight. Janet and Drew would never knowingly let Matt and Rae share a room, so it would look too suspicious if either of us slept on the couch.

Once we've said goodnight, the four of us head upstairs. Matt's parents' bedroom is downstairs, so there shouldn't be any reason for them to come upstairs tonight, but we still keep our voices low in the hallway to be safe.

"I just have to get my stuff out of the other room," Rae says as she points down the hallway.

Matt's eyes jump from me to Margot. "And you guys are sure you're okay with this?"

"Of course," Margot says with a nod, but she has her arms wrapped around her torso like she's physically trying to shield herself from this situation.

Matt cocks an eyebrow. "If you're sure . . ."

"The things we do for love," I say dryly. Taking a step toward Matt's room, I add, "Come on, I need to get my stuff, too."

We go our separate ways, and Matt and I sit in his old bedroom. Not much has changed since he lived here. The room is clean and neat without him living here, but it was that way when we were in high school, too. Lacrosse trophies line the shelf over his bed, and there's an old LSU calendar from 2022 still hanging on his wall. A few pictures of him from over the years line his dresser in frames, and I'm in most of them. Sometimes it feels like more of my childhood is showcased here than in my own home.

Matt falls back on his bed. "I ate way too much food."

I let out a laugh as I turn and lean my back against his dresser. "You and Rae are both going to pass out as soon as she gets in here."

He shrugs, still staring up at his ceiling. "That's okay." Rolling his head to the side so he's looking at me, he says, "I think I love her."

"Shit," I mutter. I'm not surprised, though. I can see that he does.

He lets out a laugh, staring up at the ceiling again. "Yeah."

"Will you tell her?"

Matt said that to a girl once in high school, but I don't think he meant it. Or maybe he was too young to understand it. They were only sophomores, but they dated for six months. None of my flings ever got anywhere close to that.

His eyes jump to me before he sits up. "Do you think I should?"

We both know I'm the wrong person to ask, but I guess when you're in love with someone, you ask your friend for advice regardless of their take on love and relationships. "I think you should."

He doesn't bother hiding his surprise. "You do?"

I shrug. "There's no time like the present, right?"

He drops his gaze but can't fight the stupid smile that spreads across his face. If I thought she wasn't right for him, or if I thought she didn't feel the same, I'd tell him.

When he looks up at me again, the smile fades from his face. "Was today weird for you? Being here?"

"Are you kidding?" I say with a laugh. "Do you know how many Thanksgivings I've wished I was sitting at a table with you guys?" He gives me a knowing look, and I come clean even though what I've just said isn't a lie. "Kind of," I admit. "Honestly, I just feel bad for my mom. She's trying to calm my dad and not rock the boat." I shake my head. "He can take it out on me, but it pisses me off that he's being selfish and not thinking about how this affects her."

"Yeah," Matt says with a nod. He knows how my dad can be. "Do you want to tell me what happened today, though? You seemed more . . . bothered than usual."

Pressing my lips together, I shake my head. We don't have time to unpack everything that happened today. I thought I'd be so happy about finally touring with a band it wouldn't matter that my dad was pissed. I wouldn't even care because I'd be *doing it*. I'd be proving him wrong.

But I do care.

And even though I'm excited about touring, it sucks that my own family can't share that excitement.

I hope he'll change the subject because thinking about the fact that my mom has probably cried at some point today over her only son not being there for Thanksgiving bums me out.

He senses I'd rather talk about something else because he says, "So, you and Margot tonight," with a wiggle of his eyebrows.

I scoff. "Let's just hope we're both alive tomorrow morning."

Matt lets out a bark of laughter before sitting up and resting his elbows on his knees to level with me. "I know you guys can't stand each other, but it would be awesome if you got together."

I give him a dubious look. "How so?"

"She's my girlfriend's best friend!" He gapes at me. "Do you know how much fun we'd have if you and Margot actually wanted to be around each other?"

I shake my head before walking across the room and patting him on the shoulder. "There are a lot of things I'd do for you, but that's not one of them."

I go to leave, but not before I hear him say, "Just think about it," over his shoulder, still laughing.

I *have* thought about it. The problem? I don't hate the idea as much as I should.

31
margot

"THANKS AGAIN FOR DOING THIS," Rae says as she gathers her things to bring to Matt's room. "I owe you one."

"You do," I agree, even though I'm smiling.

She studies me. "And you're sure about this?"

"Yes. Now, would you get out of here and go have fun with your boyfriend?"

She looks up from grabbing her phone charger out of her bag. "Try not to kill Jackson, okay?"

"No promises."

She shakes her head with a laugh. "He's actually a nice guy, you know. He's not even annoying like Keith can be."

"Or Emmet," I say and make a gagging face.

Her eyes widen in agreement. "Or Emmet." Pointing at me, she adds, "I did save you from him earlier, so maybe we are even."

I sit on the double bed and look around the room. It occurs to me that we're probably in Emmet's old bedroom, and I squirm at the thought. "Yeah, thanks, but that was a few minutes. I'm going to be with Jackson *all night.*"

Like I've somehow summoned the devil, Jackson appears in the bedroom doorway, and I hope he didn't hear me.

He's looking between Rae and me like he may have interrupted something—probably because I clamped my mouth shut as soon as he walked up.

He leans against the door frame, his arms and ankles crossed. "Ready?" he asks Rae.

"Yeah," she says, "Thanks for doing this."

His eyes jump to me before he says, "No problem."

When Rae walks toward the doorway, Jackson moves further into the room to get out of her way. She's only two steps out the door when she turns around and stares at Jackson and me. After a long pause, she says slowly, "I feel like you two shouldn't be left unsupervised."

"We shouldn't be," Jackson says without missing a beat. "If anything happens, the blood is on your hands."

She looks at me, uncertainty in her eyes, but I just mouth the word, "Go," with a wave of my hand. She'd do the same for me, and I can handle Jackson. That much I know. Even though she doesn't look convinced, she turns and heads down the hallway to the other room.

Then it's just us.

I look at Jackson, and he's already fixed on me. "What?" I ask.

He raises his eyebrows with feigned innocence. "Nothing."

Rolling my eyes, I take the pillow next to me and toss it on the floor before getting to my feet and rummaging through the closet.

"Uh, what are you doing?" Jackson asks. My back is turned as I push up on my tiptoes, craning my neck over a stack of old board games. I hear a soft thud and assume he's taken a seat on the bed.

This was definitely Emmet's old bedroom. There are still high school jerseys and shirts hanging in the closet, along with a stack of old comic books and a bunch of other junk. "Looking for an extra blanket."

"Why?"

I look over my shoulder, and he's sitting on the edge of the bed with his elbows on his knees, watching me. My cheeks heat. By the way his eyes just jumped up to meet mine, I have a feeling he was staring at my ass. "For you."

He cocks an eyebrow but says nothing.

I fill in the gaps for him. "So you can sleep on the floor . . ."

Jackson drops his gaze, letting out a breath of laughter. When his eyes meet mine again, there's that familiar challenge brewing behind them. "What makes you think *I'm* the one sleeping on the floor?"

I let out a huff, turning to face him. "It's not like we're actually going to sleep in the bed together."

He gets to his feet. "Fine by me, but it's your ass who's sleeping on Emmet's old carpet. Who knows what happened on these floors."

My eyes fall to the floor. It looks clean, but the image he painted is enough to make me recoil. He walks around to the other side of the bed with the remaining pillow and lies with his back against the headboard, crossing one ankle over the other. Unbelievable.

I huff. "You can't be serious."

He stretches an arm overhead. "Do I look like I'm joking, Red?"

I take in his mussed hair, striking eyes, and chiseled jaw. He's wearing athletic shorts and a black T-shirt, and he looks *good*. "You look delusional," I mutter under my breath as I snatch the pillow off the floor. "You know, this isn't very chivalrous of you." Clutching the pillow to my chest, I wait and hope he'll have a change of heart.

"I never claimed to be anyone's knight in shining armor."

He doesn't even look at me until a moment passes and I still haven't taken a step toward the bed. "Well, what's it going to be, Red? I promise I don't bite." The corner of his mouth lifts and there's a devilish glint in his eye. "Unless I'm asked *very* nicely."

A rush of heat threatens to incinerate the walls I've built to keep the likes of Jackson out. Even as I narrow my eyes and say, "Gross," my body betrays me. The picture he just painted makes it harder to breathe, and I have to force an inhale to get back on track.

His smile only widens, and I hope he can't see what's happening beneath the surface. He pats the bed beside him. "You might as well get comfortable. We've got all night."

I stare at the spot on the mattress next to him, debating if the floor might be a better option. If I do sleep on the floor, he'll know he got to me. He'll know he has power over me, and that's enough to make me step toward him. Everything with Jackson is like a game of chicken, and I refuse to lose.

Getting into bed, I rest my back against the headboard, crossing my arms in defiance. "Just so you know, if I kick you in my sleep, I'm not sorry, and it probably wasn't an accident."

He leans forward, his elbows resting on his bent knees as he carelessly flips his phone with one hand. "It could be worse, you know."

I fixate at his hand, tossing his phone. It's like everything he does annoys me. "Not likely."

A slow smile forms on his lips. "You could be spending the night with Emmet," he says dryly. Then his hand stills and he looks over at me with a gasp. "Or Keith."

I bite the inside of my lip to keep myself from laughing. "I'd take either of them over you."

He holds up his phone. "Want me to call Emmet? He'd probably rush back here in ten minutes if he knew you were interested." His eyes fall to my phone on the bed in front of us.

"Oh wait," he says like he's piecing together a fun puzzle. "He gave you his number. So, why don't *you* let him know you'd rather be in bed with him tonight?"

Snatching up my phone, I snap, "Maybe I will." As I unlock the screen, I have no intention of texting Emmet, but I go to my contacts, anyway. Jackson's stare burns into me. I know I'm being ridiculous, and I know *he* knows I'm being ridiculous. It makes me want to let out a frustrated groan, but instead, I eye him suspiciously. "What are you doing?"

The corner of his mouth teases an amused smile. "Waiting for you to not text Emmet."

Slamming my phone down on the bed, I turn to face him. "How do you do that?"

"Do what?" he asks, unconcerned.

Read my mind. "Know I'm not interested in someone."

He studies me, and it feels like he's peering into the deepest parts of me. My heart pounds as I wait to hear what he has to say. Eventually, he shrugs. "I just see it." He nods to the phone in my hand. "Plus, if you text Emmet, he'll have your number, and that's the last thing you want."

I let out a breath of laughter. "He'd probably start sending me messages about how I can fix my life if I meet with him twice a week." I look over at Jackson. "At a discounted rate, of course."

"Of course," he says with all seriousness. "Until he recruits you."

I laugh, and the sound that comes out of me makes him smile. It's not a smirk. There's no sign of arrogance in his eyes. It's a real smile—one that generates warmth behind those piercing eyes, and the way it makes my stomach whirl should not be happening. Jackson Phillips' smiles should have no effect on me, but this one has me feeling like one of the desperate groupies at his shows.

How am I supposed to spend an entire night with him?

32
jackson

WHEN A GENUINE SMILE spreads across Margot's face, she looks like she could take on the world. Actually, when she's pissed off, she also looks like she could take on the world, but I prefer this.

If she had smiled at me like this when I first met her, we'd definitely be doing more in this bed. She's gorgeous when she doesn't look like she wants you dead.

"This was his bedroom, wasn't it?" she asks in a whisper like she might wake the sleeping ghost of high school Emmet.

I look around the room. Matt and I used to avoid coming in here when we were younger. That had less to do with the room itself and more to do with Emmet being in it, though. It looks like their parents have tried to turn it into a makeshift guest room, but it doesn't look much different than it did back then. Except now all of Emmet's shit is in the closet.

"Why didn't you just tell him to fuck off?" I ask, without thinking.

Her eyes widen like I've caught her off guard. A small frown crosses her lips. "I mean, I figured I'll never see him again, so what does it matter?"

I let out a laugh. "That's the exact reason you should have shut him down. I would have paid good money just to see the look on his face."

She gives me a heavy-lidded stare. "And what about Matt's parents? I insult their son and then sleep at their house? No, thank you."

I roll my eyes at that. "Oh please. Janet and Drew know he's a tool. Why do you think he's living with Grandma Lois instead of here? The houses are five minutes away from each other."

Her lips turn upward into a slight smile as she sees the truth in what I'm saying. "I figured he was helping take care of her."

Now it's my turn to give her a dubious stare. "Do you think that woman needs to be taken care of?"

Margot laughs, and it brings a small smile to my lips. "No," she says, still grinning. "She's a firecracker. I hope I'm like that when I'm older."

Looking her up and down, I mutter, "Oh, I have no doubt you will be. That's probably why she liked you."

She beams, and for a moment, she's not the pain in my ass who lives across the hall. A dimple that's been hiding makes an appearance, and it adds to how adorable she can be. Seeing her this way, in a pink tank top and gray cardigan that falls off her shoulder, makes it impossible not to look at her in a new light. I rake over her, taking in all the details I've somehow overlooked before. Her high ponytail falls over her shoulder, and a few short strands have pulled free near her ears.

She's just a girl.

And I'm just a guy.

A guy who wants to kiss her.

It's the same feeling I had when I saw her at my gig a few weeks ago, but stronger. The fact that we're not in a bar, standing near the men's restroom, makes it feel like more of a possibility.

I would have never kissed her there, and I still think she would have slapped me if I had. Hell, I've even tried to keep my distance since then. I don't need to have feelings for Margot or anyone else. I thought if I could keep my head down and do my own thing, I wouldn't feel this pull toward her still.

"So, when's the next show?" she asks, and I wonder if she was thinking about that night, too.

"We have one in a couple of weeks. Think you'll be there?" I don't know why, but I don't like the thought of looking out at our measly crowd and *not* seeing her. I glance at her out of the corner of my eye to see her shrug.

"Maybe," she says. "If Rae and Matt go, I'll probably go with them." She turns toward me more, making it impossible not to look at her. "You guys sounded great, though. I've been listening to some of their older stuff, and it's good, but I liked the songs you played at the show."

Knowing she went out of her way to listen to more of my band's music makes my palms sweat, and my eyes betray me, dipping to her mouth for a fraction of a second. I spot the tiny freckle on her bottom lip and my tongue wets my own before I can stop it. "You listened to more of our music?"

Her cheeks turn pink, and her eyes dart to the comforter she's sitting on. "I mean, it's not a big deal. I know you, and you're in a band. Of course, I listened to their music."

Her words hit me right in the chest. "Well, considering my own parents choose not to acknowledge what I'm doing, it's . . . surprising." I said it without thinking because it's true. But the way Margot's eyes soften makes me wish I could take it back.

"Are you serious?" she asks, and her defensive tone catches me off guard.

I nod.

She frowns. "Is that why you came here today? Because you had a fight with your parents about the band?"

With a tilt of my head, I give her my full attention. "What makes you think that?"

She shrugs, smoothing her hand over the bedding. "Well, I don't see your guitar . . . you're never without it. And then you showed up here . . ." She shakes her head. "I don't know. You just didn't seem like yourself."

No wonder she's been looking at me all day. I don't think I've ever had someone pay this much attention to me—or care enough to try to figure out what I'm going through. Maybe Matt, but even he's easy to reassure that I'm fine.

Remembering to speak, I say, "Yeah, my dad can be a prick."

Margot hugs her knees to her chest. "I'm sorry."

I scratch the back of my head. "Thanks."

"For the record, he should cut you some slack."

My eyebrows shoot up. "You think?"

She smiles. It's a small, sweet lift of her lips that makes her look more innocent than I know she is. "Yeah. You're doing it all. The band and school. It can't be easy." Her eyes lock on mine. "You're doing great. Don't let anyone else tell you otherwise."

I could tell her I won't be juggling those two things for long, but hearing her say that felt really fucking good, and I don't want to ruin it.

"You said you guys have a new album out soon?" she asks.

All I can do is nod.

"I'm sure it will feel more rewarding once you're actually on the recorded album, but it's still something to be proud of." She smiles. "Being in a band at all is cool enough."

Other than Matt, no one has made me feel like any of this is something to celebrate. If she keeps this going it's going to be fucking hard to want her less. I swallow, determined to push down everything I'm feeling.

She waves her hand. "Hello? Earth to Jackson?" I blink,

but even when I open my mouth, no words come out. Rolling her eyes, she gets under the covers with a huff. "If you didn't want to talk, you could have just said so." She goes to reach for the bedside table lamp. "I don't exactly want to be here with you, but at least I'm trying."

"Why?" I ask before her hand can pull the tiny chain.

She looks over her shoulder at me, dropping her arm. "What?"

"Why are you trying?" I clarify.

Our eyes lock, and a tinge of pink touches her cheeks before she looks away from me again, lying on her side. "I don't know."

She blushed.

Why would she blush if she hates me?

The answer is that she wouldn't.

"Hey." Reaching for her, I gently put my hand on her arm.

Her entire body stills under my touch, but I let my hand linger to see if she pulls away.

She doesn't.

She leans into it.

When I do pull my hand away, she turns over so she's facing me, lying on her other side. "What?" she asks, but she doesn't look annoyed. She looks like she's dying to hear what I'm about to say.

I want to know where she stands . . . what she's thinking—*really* thinking. I want to know if she's thought of me the way I've thought of her. I want to know if I should keep avoiding her, or if I should welcome whatever this is.

Finally, I let out a sigh. Fuck this. I need to know. "I'm going to ask you something, and I want you to be honest."

33
margot

"OKAY . . ." I say slowly, not trusting where he's going with this.

His lips press into a hard line like he's debating whether he should ask his question. "Okay." He moves to lie on his side so we're facing each other, then props himself up on his elbow. "I know we joke, but do me a favor and don't bullshit me, Red."

"Don't worry," I say sweetly. "I'm not afraid to hurt your feelings."

"Yeah." He lets out a breath of laughter. "Not exactly where I'm going with this, but good to know."

I frown, not understanding.

Jackson takes in a breath before speaking slowly. "If you could be here with Emmet, or stay with me, who would you choose?"

I start to laugh but stop when I register how he's looking at me. His eyes are darker, more focused than usual. "You're serious?"

He nods.

My heart rate picks up and my body warms the longer he looks at me. "Why does it matter?"

"Answer the question."

My instinct is to deflect the question in some other way, but he doesn't look like he'll let this go. He wants the truth, and the truth is that I would gladly be here with him over Emmet. The truth is that, after the initial shock, I think a small part of me has been looking forward to spending the night with him. Jackson infuriates me, but I'm comfortable around him. There's something about being in his presence that feels like letting your hair down after a long day.

But there's also excitement.

Like the unknown of what he'll do or say thrills me. Will he make my blood boil, or will he make me laugh? Will he roll his eyes and dismiss something I've said, or will he stare at me with an intensity that feels like he's trying to understand every part of me?

Keeping my voice low, I say, "Probably you."

He raises his eyebrows, surprise etched in his features. "Probably?"

Too afraid to speak, I nod.

I brace myself for some type of ridicule, but he just holds my gaze, studying me. There's no arrogant smirk pulling at his lips. No cocky lift of a brow. There's nothing. He's just watching me with a crease between his brow, deep in thought.

"And Keith?" he asks, his voice low.

Part of me wants to lie. I don't trust what he might do with this information. He knows I'm not interested in Keith—that much he's made perfectly clear, but he's not asking that. He's asking if I'd rather be here with Keith, right now, and the truth is I wouldn't. When the word "You" leaves my lips, all the air in the room goes with it. My breath hitches in my throat as I wait for his reaction, but his furrowed brow just deepens.

His gaze dips to my mouth, lingering a beat longer than it should, and all the heat in my body rises to the surface. I can't deny I'm attracted to him—especially when he's not being an ass.

Especially when he's looking at me like he wants to understand everything about me.

Doing my best to hide my shallow breathing, I say, "Why?" in a voice that's hardly a whisper.

His eyes jump to meet mine. "Because," he says, the fog in his eyes clearing. "I was thinking about kissing you."

My breathing stops. Did he just say what I think he said? Maybe I heard him wrong. I *must* have heard him wrong. I'm frozen, my wide eyes searching his and asking the millions of questions I can't form into words.

His lips—his stupidly perfect lips—pull into a slow smirk at my reaction.

Then nothing.

He doesn't lean toward me.

He doesn't reach for me.

He doesn't even look at my mouth again.

Instead, he rolls onto his back with an arm above his head like he doesn't have a care in the world.

I gape at him, flustered and out of breath. "What are you doing?"

He raises an unconcerned brow and gives me a side-long glance. "Going to sleep?"

I blink, unsure of what just happened. Did I imagine it? "Are you serious? You talk about kissing me, and now you're *going to sleep?*"

He looks over at me. "Was there something else you wanted me to do?"

Glaring at him, I mutter, "No," but it's a lie. And right now, it feels like the biggest lie I've ever told.

Turning toward me again, he asks, "Are you sure?"

I scoff. "You're an asshole. You barely talk to me for weeks and now . . ." I shake my head. "Forget it." I start to roll away from him, but he puts his hand on me, stilling me. His hand is strong, *sure* as he pushes me flat on my back. Before I even realize what's happening, he has me pinned beneath him, expertly keeping space between us other than the light brush of our arms and legs.

But even that light brush is enough for me to feel my pulse throughout my body. He takes up my entire view, and from this angle, he's even more devastatingly good-looking. His tousled hair falls forward, his blue eyes are bright with mischief, but there's a darkness to them, too. A shadow of what might be mistaken for lust if I didn't know better.

"Maybe this is why I've been avoiding you," he croons in my ear. "Maybe you distract me." His breath on my skin alone could make my back arch, but I force myself to hold my ground.

I swallow hard. "I don't think that's true."

He pulls away to look at me with a tilt of his head. "It is. All I can think about lately are the things I'd like to do to you." The pad of his thumb brushes my bottom lip and I suck in a breath. Everything inside me is short-circuiting. I don't understand what the hell is happening, but I know I want more of it. I don't think I've ever wanted someone so badly, and the fact that it's Jackson of all people has me dazed. My chest rises and falls with anticipation, and I hate how obvious it is. He knows how turned on I am right now—he has to. His nose skims mine, his thumb gently parting my lips like he's about to take one between his teeth. "There's only one problem."

I wait. When I don't say anything, the corner of his mouth twitches. "You can't seem to tell a guy when you're not interested." He leans in close, our mouths almost touching. "How do I know you want this, too?"

"Because you always know," I blurt without thinking, hating the truth of it, and hating the heavy heat that settles between my thighs at the thought.

Amusement flares behind his eyes. "But where's the fun in that?"

I squirm underneath him, trying to ease the building ache.

"I'll kiss you," he says as he brushes my hair from my forehead in a surprisingly tender gesture. "Right now." When he looks me in the eyes again, he adds, "I'll do anything you want." A faint whimper leaves my throat, and his wicked smile grows. "But you need to say it. If you want me to kiss you, tell me." Lowering his lips to my ear, he adds, "If you want me to do something else, you can tell me that, too."

But when he pulls back to look at me, I can't speak. I can't do anything. Part of me doesn't want to give him the satisfaction. Because as much as my body wants him right now, his game has me fuming.

"Tell me what you want, Margot."

The fact that he uses my name sends a shot of electricity down my spine. I don't understand what's happening right now. Does he want this? Does he want *me?* My face runs hot—just another way my body has betrayed me tonight.

He moves, and my entire body tenses. I thought he was leaning in to kiss me, but he just tilts his head the other way, leaving me disappointed.

I'm disappointed.

I want him. I want to reach out and touch him. I want to slip my hands under the hem of his shirt and feel the muscles of his back. I want him to press his hips against mine. I want to feel how badly he supposedly wants me.

I want to know if this is real.

Because it feels like a trap.

My mouth opens, but no words come out. If I admit this—if I admit to wanting him at all, I'll never hear the end of it. He'll hold it over my head, and I'll have to face him every day for the rest of the year, knowing he *knows*.

I can't put myself in that position.

But I don't want to tell him I *don't* want him because that's not true either. This would be a lot easier if he'd just kiss me and not have to make it a game. No good can come from playing games with Jackson.

Eventually, he shrugs, accepting my silence for what it is. "Fine, don't say anything," he says casually. Reaching over me, he goes to pull the chain on the lamp but pauses. "But Margot?"

I look up at him, still unable to say a word.

With an unreadable expression, he says, "You should voice what you want—or don't want. You deserve at least that much."

34
jackson

WHEN I WAKE UP, Margot is the first thing that comes to mind. I don't even know why I did it. It's not like she's ever shown an interest in me, but we've been doing this back and forth for months. I think I just wanted to know if she's had the same thoughts.

Once the semester ends, I'll be gone anyway. If anything is weird after this, it will only be three weeks of hell with Margot living across the hall, and I can handle that.

I can handle three weeks.

But what I can't handle is how pretty she looks right now. Her red hair is still up in the bun she slept in, but loose pieces have fallen throughout the night. She looks peaceful—more at peace than I've ever seen her look while she's awake. The way she looks right now, lying next to me in bed, makes me feel like I want to protect her—even if I don't know what I want to protect her from.

But if there's one thing I know, it's that Margot doesn't need protecting. If anything, after last night, I might need protection *from* her. There's a good chance she'll wake up mad as hell after the stunt I pulled.

It sounds like Janet and Drew are already making breakfast downstairs, and I wonder if Matt and Rae are awake yet. I go to move out of bed, but Margot stirs next to me, and I freeze.

Her eyes flutter open and then widen as soon as she registers I'm the one next to her. She shoots up, sitting in the bed and immediately fixing her hair, throwing it up into a new bun.

"Morning," she says with a faint smile, but her eyes never stay on me for more than half a second.

"Morning," I answer, watching her with a pinched brow and waiting for her to actually look at me.

When she does, it's only for a moment.

"How'd you sleep?" I can't read her like this.

She bobs her head a few times and says, "Fine. You?" while she checks her phone.

"Margot." I don't want her to act like this. I can handle her drunk, pissed off, happy, sad—I can handle all of those just fine, but I can't handle her avoiding me and putting up walls because she's embarrassed.

She finally looks at me, those big, brown eyes wide and vulnerable. "Why did you do that?" she demands, even though her voice is soft.

I frown. I didn't think she'd bring it up. "I wanted to kiss you."

Past tense.

It's partially a lie. I still want to kiss her, but at least this way we can move past it.

She opens her mouth but then closes it, clearly caught off guard by my honesty. "Have you ever thought about that before last night?" she asks as she fidgets with her phone.

I know what she's doing. She wants to know if last night was a fluke.

If I were staying at college, I'd probably lie to her. I'd tell her it was a random thought and that I'm over it. It would make things go back to the way they were before—no embarrassment and no hard feelings. But I have nothing to lose, so I just say, "Yeah."

Her eyes snap up to meet mine. "You have?"

I nod.

"When?"

I could tell her everything she wants to know, but I want to save at least a shred of my dignity. "Why do you care? You're not interested."

"I never said that."

"You're right. You never said anything," I say with a laugh.

She frowns, biting her bottom lip, and I'm still close enough to see that damn freckle. "I'm sorry," she finally says. "I didn't know—I thought maybe you were trying to . . ." Her voice trails off.

"What?" I ask. She shrugs, but I prompt her again. "What did you think I was trying to do?"

Some of her usual confidence returns when she says, "I figured you'd be a jerk and use it against me in a week." She shakes her head. "It doesn't matter. It's probably better nothing happened since we live so close to each other."

"Yeah." I get out of bed. "Probably."

"That's it?" she asks, a crease forming between her brows.

I don't know what else she wants from me. I'm the one who put myself out there, not her. She gets to walk away from this as the girl who was almost kissed, and I get left being the guy who wanted to kiss her. "That's it," I say with a nod.

She's sitting on her hands as she stares down at the floor in front of her.

Let her be disappointed.

I take my shirt off and grab the clean one I packed, slipping it over my head. When my head emerges through the top, her eyes dart away.

She gets to her feet. "I'm going to see if Rae and Matt are awake."

I can still hear Janet and Drew happily talking in the kitchen downstairs, so we don't have to worry about them hearing anything. "Okay." It's all I can say because she's already left the room by the time I go to look at her. I'm left alone. I've always been able to read her, but right now, I'm confused. Maybe I only ever saw things clearly because I was watching from a distance. Maybe this is what it's like for guys when they get close to her, unable to see—like standing too close to the sun.

Maybe she's giving me her clear-cut signs, but I'm too distracted by the way her lips quirk when she doesn't want to laugh at something I've said.

Maybe I'm no better than the rest of them.

35
margot

MATT AND RAE'S bedroom door is still closed, but I'm afraid to go back into the room with Jackson after what happened last night. If that means I have to stand here in the hallway with my back against the wall, listening to the sound of Matt's parents talking about Grandma Lois and cooking breakfast downstairs, so be it.

He wanted to kiss me.

I still can't wrap my head around Jackson thinking of me as more than . . . anything. For how long? Why? The questions are reeling in my head. As if last night wasn't weird enough, I didn't think he'd own up to it. He admitted wanting to kiss me simply, casually, like he would admit to being hungry.

Well, I guess he was hungry . . . for *something*.

Sinking my teeth into my bottom lip, I glance back at the door I came from before fixing my gaze on the wall in front of me. My heart pounds just thinking about what it was like having him close to me. The depth behind his eyes as he looked down at me. How he was so sincere at first, but then that devilish smirk came out. He knew how he was affecting me.

He *knew* I wanted him to kiss me. He had to.

"You're just standing out here?"

I jolt at the sound of his voice. Looking down the hall, I see him walking toward me. "I was about to knock," I say, but I'm pretty sure my cheeks betray me.

He lets out a breath of laughter, seeing through my bluff. "You don't have to hide from me, Red. I can take the rejection. Just do me a favor and don't write about this in your blog."

My nails dig into my palms because he's back to calling me Red again. "I wouldn't—wait." My hands unclench. "You read my blog?"

"Sometimes," he says with a shrug as he walks around me and stops in front of Matt's door.

He read my blog? Is that why he wanted to kiss me? Because of what I wrote? I swallow at the thought as every word I've written over these past few months flashes in my mind, and I try to sift through it all in a matter of seconds. Still feeling dazed, I ask, "How do you even know about it?"

He gives me a sideways glance. "It's not a secret blog, Margot." When I don't stop staring at him, he adds, "Izzy mentioned it."

Of course, she did. Izzy interacts with almost all of my posts—even if it's usually just a comment with a row of hearts. "I didn't reject you," I finally say. "I just didn't realize you liked me."

He blinks. "I don't," he says defensively, but then he shakes his head like it doesn't matter. "Not like that, anyway. Look, consider it a moment of weakness. It won't happen again."

I frown. I don't know if I should be offended or flattered. "But you said it wasn't the first time you've thought about me that way."

His mouth opens, but he changes his mind about whatever he was about to say. "I'm going to knock on their door now."

He raises his fist and lightly knocks on the bedroom door where our two best friends are still sleeping.

Matt groans. "Go away!"

"Fat chance," Jackson says, making sure to keep his voice low. "Are you two decent? Because we're coming in."

With that, Jackson opens the door and walks in like he's done it a million times. Rae is already out of bed and unplugging her phone charger while Matt makes his bed. I don't think I've ever seen a guy our age actually make his bed, and I have to admit, I'm impressed.

"Can I wash my face and change before we head downstairs?" Rae asks the guys once she gets her makeup bag.

"Me too," I chime in, perhaps a little too quickly. Rae looks up at me with a quizzical look. "What? You think you're the only one who needs to wash your face?"

She just shrugs. "We'll be back in a few minutes."

Jackson's eyes snag on mine just long enough for my body heat to warm. He's probably wondering if I'll tell Rae what happened last night.

But *nothing* happened.

So, why does it feel like last night changed everything?

When Rae and I are in the hallway, she looks at my empty hands. "Don't you need to get your stuff?"

"Oh, right," I say with a laugh. Ducking into the room, I lean my head against the wall and take a deep breath. I need to get a grip. Not wanting to take too long, I grab my overnight bag and meet Rae in the bathroom.

She's bent over one of the sinks as she washes her face. The oak cabinets look like they're from the 90s, but the room is spotless. Some tiles look slightly crooked in areas, and I wonder if Janet and Drew put it in themselves when they first moved in.

It's crazy to think Matt and Jackson grew up within these

walls. I imagine two young boys making a mess of this bathroom with water guns they aren't supposed to use inside. Maybe Janet once kept superhero Band-Aids in these drawers for when one of them inevitably got hurt. Even though Jackson didn't live here, I can still see how this house—these people—shaped him.

My heart aches.

I should have kissed him last night. Fear of regret is what kept me from doing it, but now that I've done nothing, I regret that, too. At least if I kissed him, I wouldn't be standing here, wondering what would have happened if I had. I wouldn't feel the need to stare at his mouth every time he speaks, studying the curve of his upper lip. If I had just kissed him, I wouldn't be clouded with hypotheticals right now.

"Are you okay?" Rae asks as she dries her face with a towel. I'm still standing in the doorway holding my makeup bag.

I can't bring myself to look at her. She'll know how busy my mind is with a single glance, and I can't put my chaotic thoughts about Jackson into words. Plus, I don't know where he stands. If I tell Rae anything, and then Jackson ignores me, I'll look even more pathetic than I already feel. I nod and walk over to the second sink, setting my bag on the bathroom counter. Reaching for the faucet, I wait for the water to warm, but I can still feel her eyes on me.

"Was Jackson a jerk to you last night or something?"

"No!" I say, but my response only makes the line between her brows deepen. "No," I say again, this time keeping my voice in check. "Surprisingly, he wasn't."

She's still scrutinizing me with a side-long glance, but I splash water on my face and keep my eyes closed as I rub the soap into my skin.

Rae may not be able to read me as well as Jackson, but I've never been able to keep a secret from her. Is this even a secret, though? The logical part of my brain wants to answer that question with a *no*, but something inside me is dying to tell her. I'm dying to know what she'd think. Would she encourage it? Or would she tell me it's a terrible idea and beg me not to see her boyfriend's roommate as anything other than just that?

I don't think I'm ready to know.

36
jackson

DECEMBER ALWAYS STARTS out warm in Florida. If anything, the temperature is finally bearable, and you can sit outside without breaking a sweat. That's why we're all getting ice cream—because now is the time when we can eat some of it before it melts. Imani and Jess sit with Margot and Keith while Matt and I sit with Izzy and Keith's roommate . . . I think his name is Samuel . . . at a second table outside the Ben & Jerry's on campus. Even though she isn't sitting with me, she still looks over here at least seventeen times, and not knowing what she's thinking is making me restless. I thought I could read Margot, but ever since our almost kiss, I've been second-guessing it.

She's been avoiding me since Thanksgiving last week.

Well, she's been avoiding me as much as she can anyway. There isn't much she can do about the fact that we live six feet across from each other.

I guess I shouldn't say she's been avoiding me. It's more that she has gone out of her way to not talk to me.

Her mouth has been avoiding me.

But her eyes have been doing the opposite.

Every time we're in the same place—which let's face it, is more than either of us would probably like at this point—I catch her looking at me. Sometimes she has a small frown on her lips like she's trying to solve some type of complex equation in her head, but whenever I catch her, she quickly finds something else to hold her attention.

I catch her glancing at me again out of the corner of my eye.

Eat your damn ice cream, Red.

Keith briefly touches her on the arm, and my teeth drag over my plastic spoon. I'm not jealous, but this guy has no clue she isn't interested, and it pisses me off that she isn't being upfront with him.

Hell, it pisses me off that she isn't being upfront with me.

He reaches for her hand, and she shifts out of his reach.

I have no idea what he says to her, but her cheeks flush, and she drops her gaze. He must have complimented her because I'm pretty sure I see her mouth form the words *thank you*, and I roll my eyes.

"What's with you?" Matt asks, and I'm brought back to my own table.

"Nothing." I know he can see straight through the lie, but I don't care.

His gaze travels to the next table over, and he frowns. "Did something happen between you two on Thanksgiving or something? You've been acting weird about her ever since we got back."

"No, I haven't." I don't get weird around girls. If they don't like me, I move on. I take another bite of my ice cream and hope this conversation is over.

"Yeah," he says, driving the point home. "You have." He glances in the direction of Margot and Keith before looking back at me. "You both have."

I go to take a bite but lower my spoon. "Wait. You think she's acting weird?"

Izzy watches our back and forth with eager eyes.

Matt practically groans as he grabs his backpack and gets to his feet. "I think something happened on Thanksgiving. I don't know what, but you both are hung up on it." He shakes his head. "I don't know. I have to get to class, but figure it out. This might be more annoying than dealing with you two at each other's throats all the time."

"Yeah," I mutter, glancing at Margot again. "On it."

He lets out a breath of laughter and walks away, leaving me alone at the table with Samuel and Izzy, trying not to stare at the girl I'm apparently hung up on. Matt's right. This past week, I've been distracted. I haven't been as focused on my music, and the classes I go to can't hold my attention for longer than a few minutes. As much as I try to stay on track, thoughts of the redhead across the hall always work their way in.

This meaningless back and forth needs to end. I'm done playing her game. If she wants to side-step around whatever this is, she can, but I'm done. I'm done trying to guess what she is or isn't thinking.

I could have eaten the rest of my ice cream without looking at her, but then I see Keith grab his backpack out of the corner of my eye. He must have a class about to start, too.

Margot doesn't gather her things. She doesn't have a class right now. Her next class isn't until later this afternoon, and it only bothers me a little that I know that.

I mean, we live right next to each other. That's probably why I've accidently memorized her schedule.

Not because I'm in any way hung up on her.

Unable to tear my eyes away from their awkward exchange, I watch as Keith rubs the back of his neck. My knee bounces under the table. I don't know why she won't just tell him to back off, and I don't know why he won't just make a goddamn move so that she can tell him to back off.

His pathetic attempts and her leading him on feel like a car wreck I can't turn away from. It's distracting even though it has nothing to do with me.

It has absolutely nothing to do with me.

Which is why I should stay out of it.

But instead, I get to my feet and head straight for them.

Everyone looks up when I reach the table, but I only see Margot. She's probably wondering what the hell I'm doing, but before she can speak, I reach for her. I tilt her face toward mine, and with my hand still firmly on her cheek, I kiss her.

Just like that.

Her lips part—maybe because she was about to give me a piece of her mind, or maybe because she sucked in a gasp. Regardless of the reason, I take her bottom lip between mine. She tenses, gripping the sides of her chair while my hand grips the back of her neck like a reflex. It feels like forever that she's frozen in place. I wait for some type of reaction—*any* reaction as my heart beats faster in my chest.

Eventually, she sighs into my mouth, and I feel it go straight to my groin. Fuck, she feels good. Being this close to her has a way of stopping time, the only measure coming from the wild thudding in my chest. I could kiss this girl forever. Her body relaxes, and she leans forward. It's probably a fraction of an inch, but it feels like a mile. It feels like the red light she's been flashing for months just turned green, and it's taking everything in me not to go zero to sixty.

She's kissing me back.

She tastes like Cherry Garcia, and she's kissing me back.

My control slips, and my tongue sweeps over hers. Whatever I expected, it wasn't the soft moan that leaves the back of her throat, and it wasn't her tongue slowly dragging over mine like she wants to commit my mouth to memory.

I don't want to stop. I want to pull her into my lap and let her have her way with me. I want to feel her hips writhe against me, and I want to learn what other sounds she might make.

Dropping my hand, I force myself to take a step back. Her head is still tilted up toward me, her eyes shut, lips parted. It isn't until they flutter open and she looks around that she gets her bearings. Her wide eyes snap to me before they turn sharp, and I know I've pissed her off.

Probably more than I ever have.

She looks from Keith to me, her mouth open like she's looking for words that won't come. The only reaction is her cheeks steadily turning a deeper shade of pink.

"I'll see you tonight," I say like we already have plans. Then, I turn and walk toward the dorm.

Four words. That's all I give her. As I walk away, rushed voices break out—she's probably apologizing to Keith, even though she has nothing to be sorry for.

I'm the one who will have to apologize later, but right now, I don't feel sorry about a damn thing.

37
margot

THAT SON OF A BITCH.

I glare after Jackson with my mouth open until he turns out of sight. When I meet the stares of everyone at the table, Keith gives me a similar incredulous look. "Wait," he says, holding up both hands to stop me. "Is something going on between you two? Because I thought you couldn't stand each other."

"We can't!" I say, but then I shake my head because I'm not sure if that's true anymore. "Or we couldn't." Meeting Keith's harsh gaze, I add, "But I have no idea what that was about."

I glance around the table, mortified. Imani and Jess stare at each other wide-eyed. I wish they'd say something. I wish anyone would take some of the heat off me. My eyes find Keith's again, and I wish I could erase the pain written in his expression. He's hurt. He's looking at me like I've betrayed him, and I have to fight the urge to apologize. I didn't ask for this, and the unfairness of it all lights a fire inside me.

With my half-eaten ice cream dripping down the side of the cup, I gather my things. "I have to go."

His eyes widen, and he suddenly looks less angry and more scared. "Wait. Where are you going?"

"I'm going to figure out what the hell that was about." He still has his backpack slung over his shoulder, so I add, "You're going to class, anyway."

Keith frowns, and I don't give him much time to figure out what he needs to say. After a beat of silence falls between us, I shake my head and get to my feet. "I'll see you later."

Keith's voice calls out behind me, but I've already tuned him out and turned in the direction of our dorm.

I'm fuming.

How could he do that? How could he walk up and kiss me in front of everyone without an explanation?

I'll see you tonight.

What the hell is that? Did he think if he kissed me with no warning, I'd look up at him all doe-eyed and do whatever he says?

Jackson Phillips is out of his goddamn mind.

I'm going to march in there and ask—no, *demand*—he tell me what the hell he was thinking. I'm going to let him have it. I want to see him scared. He's going to regret ever messing with me like this. He'll wish he never walked over and put his mouth on mine.

And knotted his fingers in my hair.

And slipped his tongue . . .

Fuck that kiss. It was the type of kiss that somehow had the power to transport me to a different time and place, and he had no business being the one to give it to me. Even as I walk, I can't help brushing my fingers against my lips at the memory. I should have pushed him away—or slapped him.

The walk back to the dorm has me spiraling into a deeper rage. I pick up my pace, determined not to lose focus. The heavy door that leads into the building feels like paper as adrenaline courses through me. I don't bother waiting for the elevator. I don't think I'd be able to stand still right now. Instead, I head for the staircase and let my feet pound out some of what I'm feeling as I take the steps two at a time.

Breathing hard, I enter our familiar hallway. I know he's here. "R U Mine?" by Arctic Monkeys pounds through his stereo speakers. I stomp down the hall until I reach his open door, and the music is loud enough to drown out all of it because he has no idea I'm standing here. He's sitting on the edge of his bed with his elbows on his knees as he stares at the floor between his feet. It isn't until I've slammed the door shut and am standing right in front of him that he finally looks up.

He kissed me in front of everyone as if I were his, but I'm not—and I never will be. How his lips felt on mine may be trying to trick me into thinking Jackson and I have chemistry, but that's only physical. In the real world, Jackson and I don't work.

He doesn't even stand. I should have known he wouldn't be afraid. His gaze just slowly trails up my body like he's been expecting me and has already accepted his fate. When his eyes finally work their way up to meet mine, there's no remorse behind them.

And he doesn't look scared at all.

Sitting up straight, he leans back on his hands, and if anything, those storm-like eyes are full of challenge.

"What the hell, Jackson!" My chest rises and falls as I stare down at him, waiting for a reaction—waiting for *anything*.

He cocks an eyebrow. That's all I get.

"You kissed me!" I blurt.

He tilts his head. "I know. I was there."

"Why?" I demand. "Why did you do that in front of everyone?"

He shakes his head like my question somehow disappoints him. "You mean in front of Keith?" He leans forward, looking up at me, but even though I'm the one towering over him, I still feel like he holds all the power. "I put that guy out of his misery. You should thank me."

I scoff. "I should thank you?"

"Either you or him," he muses, and I roll my eyes. He catches my reaction, and heat flares behind his gaze. "At least now he knows how you feel."

I blink, unable to comprehend the *audacity*. "How I—" I shake my head. "How I *feel?*"

"You know it's not healthy to keep everything bottled up the way you do. You're so worried about everyone else, you put yourself last."

"You don't know me," I snap. I can't believe I followed him here. This is probably what he wanted all along. He wanted me to come in here just so he could act like he knows me better than I know myself. "You are such an asshole," I say under my breath as I go to walk away from him, but his hands catch me on either side of my thighs, stilling me.

He turns me to face him, nodding as his gaze trails down the scope of my body again, and I suddenly wish I had something to hide behind. "Yeah." He pulls me a step closer to him. "I'm the asshole."

"What are you doing?" My traitorous voice shakes, and I clench my jaw.

His thumbs graze the outside of my jeans, lighting tiny fires in their wake, but he says nothing.

I'm completely frozen, each subtle movement made by him sending me further into paralysis. "What are you doing?" I ask again because he's still touching me, and it feels like the wiring to my brain is short-circuiting. I can't think. All I can do is feel —the heat from his hands, the slightest brush of his thumb, my pounding heart.

A faint smile pulls at his lips, and I hate that he knows how he affects me. "I want to do it again." His gaze shifts to the door before settling back on me.

A heavy heat settles at the base of my belly when I follow his gaze to the door, suddenly wondering why I shut it.

"Why did you kiss me?" When I look back at him, my voice comes out breathless.

The corners of his mouth dip as he considers how to answer, his hands slowly sliding up to cup my ass.

I should swat them away and walk out that door.

But I don't.

I *can't.*

No matter how much my brain is screaming *run*, my body is perfectly content being a fly stuck in Jackson's web. He touches me unapologetically with no hesitation. His hands are skilled and steady as he reaches up further, his fingers sliding under my shirt to trace my lower back.

My entire spine tingles.

Letting out a breath of laughter, he says "Why did I kiss you?"

My breath is caught in my throat, but I manage a faint nod.

He answers me in a voice that comes out like a groan. "Margot," he says, and my knees threaten to buckle. His hands move to my hips like he's exploring my every curve, and in a low voice, he says, "If you haven't realized I want you by now, I'm not sure how to help you."

He wants me? The thought alone has my head spinning. When his hands slip fully under my shirt, holding my waist, my lungs stop working. His hands run over my stomach and up the sides. It's too much, but at the same time, not enough.

He says he's not sure how to help me, but I have a feeling he knows *exactly* how to help me. His thumb dips under my bra, grazing the sensitive skin under my left breast, and I fight the urge to clench my thighs together.

I want him. I don't know how much or how little, but right now, I want him to close the space between us. I need him to.

Somehow, between shallow breaths, I say, "Try."

His head snaps up, his pupils blown. Without hesitation, he pulls me onto his lap in one swift movement. My knees hit the mattress on either side of him, and I gasp. Taking full advantage of my open mouth, Jackson's lips crash into mine. Warmth floods my entire body as he expertly claims my mouth with his tongue like it's been his from the start.

Maybe this was inevitable. That's how this feels. Whatever is happening between Jackson and me feels like it couldn't have been stopped. It feels like something outside of our control. Neither of us can fight the desperate need building—at least I know I can't.

My hands are in his hair as I move my mouth over his, and when I slip my tongue between his lips, his hands grip me tighter, pulling me in deeper like he can't get enough. I don't think I've ever been kissed like this—like I'm the air he needs to breathe.

My hips roll, pressing into him and craving friction. I feel him hard beneath me, and the sound that escapes his throat only makes me grind against him again.

How does he feel so good?

Everything happens so fast, neither of us having the patience to take it slow. He pulls my shirt up and over my head, tossing it somewhere on the floor. I unbutton his jeans, pulling them down enough to reveal black boxer briefs stretching tightly over him.

Effortlessly, he flips us so he's holding himself over me, and for a moment, I'm brought back to Thanksgiving night. I'm brought back to what it felt like to want to kiss him and feeling like I couldn't. The memory fades as soon as he presses his hips against me, summoning me back to the present, and my back arches.

I grasp at his shirt, pulling it up, and just like the night of his show, the toned shape of him takes me by surprise. He reaches behind his neck with one hand, pulling his shirt off the rest of the way and his jeans follow shortly after.

Jackson leans over me in just his boxer briefs, and a distinct outline revealing his size is enough to make me swallow hard. His gaze slowly rakes down my body, his hand following close behind. When his feather-light fingertips run over my black lace bra, my head falls back, silently begging him to touch me more. His fingers dip lower, grazing over my bare stomach until they hook into the front waistband of my jeans, and he yanks me toward him.

"These need to go," he says as he unbuttons my pants. I nod, more than agreeing, and work to shimmy my jeans down.

Then there's only one layer left. His mouth finds my neck, his hands cupping my ass, pulling a soft moan from my lips.

"Tell me you want this," he says as his teeth nip at the sensitive skin below my ear. I reach for him, palming him outside his briefs, but even though he sucks in a breath, he shakes his head. Moving his hand to cup my face, he buries his hips against mine, making me gasp. "No." His voice comes out raspy but unwavering. "Say it."

My heart pounds in my chest with our bodies flush together. He holds my gaze for an excruciating moment before leaning in close, his lips brushing against my ear. In a husky whisper, he groans, "Come on, Red. Put me out of my misery." My entire body tenses at the name, and I feel his lips pull into a smile against my skin. "What?" he croons. "Don't want me to call you that?"

Even with the flicker of annoyance, my body is begging for him. I don't know how he can make me want to storm out of here one moment and lose myself in him the next.

"You can call me anything you want," I say through heated breaths. "Just don't call me yours."

38
jackson

I LET OUT A LAUGH, kissing her mouth again. "Finally, something we can agree on." She's not mine, and I don't want her to be. I want her here, sprawled out on my bed underneath me, and anything past that is irrelevant. I meant what I said about putting me out of my misery, though. Having her here like this is torture. I want to be inside her. I want to make her cry out as she comes. But I'm not doing any of that until she admits she wants this.

I want to hear the words.

She moves her lips to my neck, leaving open-mouthed kisses until she runs her tongue up the side of my neck, and I almost lose it. "Fuck," I mutter, trying to regain my bearings. She doesn't want to say it. She'd rather torture me until I crack and fuck her anyway.

But two can play that game.

Even with layers between us, I press my cock against her and feel her writhe beneath me. "Say it."

She whimpers before her mouth is frantically on mine again. Her hands are in my hair and her legs open wider as I lay into her.

"Margot . . ." I groan as she knots her fingers in my hair, tugging it at the roots. "I don't know if I can take this."

"I want you."

"What?" I ask as I stare down at her, thinking maybe I heard her wrong. Burying my hips against her, I groan, and when her fingers weave into my hair, it sends goosebumps down my spine.

"I want you," she says breathlessly before kissing me. I lean into it, taking her bottom lip between my teeth. Hearing her say those words might make me come before I even get to feel her.

"Finally." I pull down her lace underwear and free myself from my damn briefs.

Her eyes drift lower and widen, but I'm too busy reaching into my nightstand drawer for a condom. By the time I grab one, her delicate hand has found me, and she moves with slow, torturous pumps.

Sitting back on my knees, I look down at her. Part of me expects her to stop or look away, but she doesn't. Those brown eyes stay locked on mine as she touches me, and it's the hottest thing I've ever seen.

I lean forward, bracing myself on one hand, and using the other to still her movements. "If you keep looking at me like that, I'm going to come."

She lets out a breath of laughter. "Not yet."

Two words. She said two words, and I love that she's telling me what to do—or not do.

My lips twitch into a trace of a smile, and my fingers reach between her legs. I let out a breath as soon as I touch her because she's fucking perfect. Her head falls back as I slip one finger in and then another. She's warm and tight, and when she urges me with her hips, I give her pressure where she needs it most. She starts to ride my hand, and I curse under my breath. "You're so fucking wet, Margot."

Her eyes flutter shut, her red hair splayed over my pillow as she chases her release. She's always beautiful, but like this, she's breathtaking. I can't help smiling a little, knowing I'm the only one who gets to see her this way.

Not Keith.

Not Emmet.

Me.

My dick hardens more at the thought. Tearing the condom open with my teeth, I sit back to roll it on with one hand, my other hand increasing the building pressure inside her. When I slowly pull my fingers out, she whimpers. I swallow the sound, crashing my lips against hers, and by the time we come up for air, I'm desperate for her.

Pulling her beneath me, I spread her legs with my knee and position myself. I'm about to push into her when she breathes my name.

I pause to meet her stare, and she props herself up on her elbows, breathing hard. "This changes nothing."

Holding her gaze, the corners of my mouth lift. "Good." We stare at each other as I slowly sink into her. She stretches around me until I'm fully inside her, and I curse under my breath.

"Oh, my God." Her head hits the pillow, and I go to move again, pulling out of her. This time, she lets out a soft moan, her hands gripping the sheets as she rolls her hips to meet my next thrust. I curse through gritted teeth and roll my hips into her deeper.

It's like she was fucking made for me. Her legs tighten, and I bend down to claim her mouth again. I can't get enough of her like this. I can't get enough of the way her body moves and reacts to mine. I'm drunk on the way her back arches. I'm high on the way her hands are knotted in my hair. I'm completely under her influence.

I pick up my pace when her legs start to shake. Leaning in

close, our bodies move in perfect rhythm. "I've changed my mind. When you're in my bed, you're mine."

Her nails dig into the skin on my back as her body coils around me, pulsing and shaking. She's close. She's so fucking close, and it's like I can feel everything building inside her. The way she wraps her legs around me tighter. The way her eyes roll back every time I hit deep. The way she's frantic for me to keep going, her hands clawing at my ass, my legs, my back—anything she can get a hold of. Seeing her lose control like this is the biggest turn on. I need to feel her clench around my cock. I need to hear the sound she makes as she falls apart.

"Come for me, Red." I grit my teeth and pound into her.

Margot turns her head to the side and bites down on her palm to stifle her cry. I tear her hand away, and the sound that leaves her lips is cracked and rough. It's a sound I'll never forget and one that makes me come as I bury my face into the curve of her neck. "You're mine when I'm coming inside you," I pant and press a kiss to her neck.

We both stay like that, catching our breath. Eventually, I pull out of her before being close to her like this gets me hard again. I roll onto my back. Looking over at her, I see her just staring at the ceiling, her chest still rapidly rising and falling.

"Are you okay?" I ask, putting an arm overhead, so I can shift toward her.

"Yeah," she says with a nod, only glancing at me briefly before she stares up at the ceiling again. "It's just . . ." She frowns.

"It's just what?"

She looks over at me, her eyes wide and vulnerable. "My ex never made me come during sex like that."

Her words are enough to get me hard again. Letting out a groan, I reach for the drawer in my nightstand and grab another condom. Holding it up, I ask, "Want to be mine for a little longer?"

She bites her bottom lip, looking from me to the condom, then nods.

Positioning myself over her, I roll it on.

Margot's breath catches, her hands gripping my hair. "I'm not yours." She reaches down to guide me into her again. I sink inside her, and her head falls back, a satisfied smile teasing at the corners of her mouth. "But I'll let you pretend."

39
margot

JACKSON MAKES me come undone for a second time, and I collapse on top of him, struggling to catch my breath. "Oh, my God," I groan with my head on his heaving chest, and I barely recognize my own voice.

A throaty laugh leaves him, and the movement of his chest jostles my head, bringing a twinge of a smile to my lips.

I listen to the beats of his heart, unable to bring myself to move. I've only ever slept with my ex from high school, and it was never like this. Never before have I been left with my body loose, my mind blank, and my heart free of obligation. I never thought I'd be the type of person to sleep with someone casually, but with Jackson, it doesn't feel like a random hook-up. Despite wanting to strangle him sometimes, I'm comfortable with him.

His fingers absently comb through my hair. At first, it feels good, sending goosebumps over my skin, but then it feels intimate, like something a boyfriend would do. It almost feels out of character—a side of him I've never seen. It's the touch you give someone you care about, and coming from him, it's too much.

Sitting up, I reach for my clothes and start getting dressed. "I should go."

"Yeah." He rolls off the bed, pulling on his briefs and then his pants. Glancing at me, he adds, "Matt will be back any minute."

"Wow, thanks for the warning." I pull my shirt over my head. "The last thing I need is for Matt and Rae to find out about this."

He lets out a ghost of a laugh. "Worried someone will find out you don't hate me as much as you say you do?"

"I don't hate you." He gives me a dubious look in response, so I add, "I don't—but no one can know about this."

Pulling his shirt over his head, his eyebrows furrow. "Why?"

I gape at him. "Because this doesn't change anything. And if people know about us, it will change *everything*." I'm not looking to be the gossip of the dorm. Everyone already knows we don't get along. If they find out we've slept together, they'll be watching our every move. I'd rather not feel like I'm living under a microscope.

He leans back against his dresser and crosses his ankles. "You're dramatic." As he says the words, I catch his eyes taking me in unapologetically.

I quickly run my fingers through my hair in an attempt to smooth it down before marching up to him with my pinky out. "Promise."

He stares blankly at my outstretched finger before bringing those steel eyes up to meet mine. "Promise what?"

"We tell no one."

He holds my stare. "Fine." He hooks his pinky around mine, but when I go to pull my hand away, he tightens his grip, pulling me back to him. "But let's make one thing clear," he says in a low voice, his eyes never leaving mine. "We're doing that again." His free hand tilts my face toward his, and he presses his lips to mine.

A jolt of heat runs through my veins the moment we kiss, and when he pulls away, I could do it again right now, desire already coiling deep in my core.

Thankfully, the sound of the door swinging open snaps some sense into me, and I take a step away from him just in time.

Matt stops in the doorway, confusion written in the lines of his face. He tilts his head as he studies Jackson and me, and I have to make a conscious effort not to look guilty.

"Uh . . . Hey, Margot." He walks into the room and sets his stuff down on his always pristine bed.

My eyes jump to the mess we made of Jackson's sheets, and I'm suddenly glad he's such a slob. It doesn't look much different than it normally does. "Hey."

Matt's dark eyes jump between his best friend and me. "You guys didn't just have sex in here, did you?"

My eyes jump to Jackson, expecting to see some type of reaction, but he hasn't moved from where he was standing when he last kissed me, and his face reveals nothing. "You caught us," Jackson says, pushing off his dresser to turn his stereo down. "Turns out Red's had it bad for me this whole time."

Matt laughs and pulls out his laptop.

"You wish," I say dismissively before walking out the door. As I leave, I catch a glimpse of his devilish smirk, and it's enough to make my toes curl in my Chucks.

With the door to their dorm shut, I take a moment to lean my head against the wall. The cool surface barely helps me wrap my head around what just happened. As I walk the few steps it takes me to get home, I force a deep breath.

I open the door to find Rae sitting on her bed with her laptop open. She is streaming *Friends*, but as soon as I walk into the room, she slams it shut. "You kissed Jackson?"

I freeze. "What?"

She gapes at me. "Izzy and Jess are freaking out about it! Even *Imani* couldn't stop talking about it, and she never gossips! You two kissed at Ben & Jerry's?"

Oh.

So much had happened since Jackson first kissed me this afternoon, I almost forgot how this whole thing started. "Yeah. He was being dumb."

She's not going to let me brush this off. I can tell by the way she's looking at me. She wants to know more, but I can't tell her I slept with her boyfriend's best friend. I can only imagine all the talk of a double wedding.

And whatever Jackson and I are doing, it isn't that. We're not like Rae and Matt. I don't even know if we'll sleep together again—even if Jackson is confident we will. There are too many unknowns right now, and inviting Rae and Matt into that mess won't be good for any of us.

She's still staring at me, waiting for a better explanation, so I just shrug as I sit on my bed. "First of all, I didn't kiss him. He kissed me, and he only did it to make me mad. What else is new?"

She rolls her eyes. "Why would he kiss you to make you mad?"

I blink. "Uh, because he's Jackson," I say, holding an outstretched arm in the direction of his dorm across the hall. I freeze. "Wait. Why are you here?"

She gives me a funny look. "Um, I'm supposed to be here. You're not. Did your class get canceled?"

I reach for my phone in my back pocket only to find it's not there. I must have left it in Jackson's room—just another thing for me to regret. My eyes jump to Rae's phone face down on the bed, and I hurry over to check the time. My Mass Media class started five minutes ago.

"Shit!"

"Where were you?" Rae asks. There's no accusation in her

voice, just genuine curiosity. This isn't like me. I'm never late to class—school never slips my mind.

But today, it did.

Grabbing my bag off the back of my desk chair, I give a short, "I'll explain later," even though I have no intention of telling Rae where I was or who I was with.

Or what we were doing.

Frantically running out the door, I head to my class across campus with no phone and no idea how to navigate the terrible choices I made today.

40
jackson

ONCE MARGOT LEAVES, Matt looks up from his computer. "Do I even want to know?"

I could tell him. I usually tell Matt everything, but Margot was hell-bent on making sure nothing changed around here, and if I want a repeat of what we did today, I can't piss her off too much. My lips pull downward, and I shake my head. "There's nothing to know."

He looks at me for longer than I'd like. "Yeah, I didn't think Margot would go for your sorry ass anyway."

I collapse onto my bed, and I swear I get a whiff of her strawberry shampoo in my sheets as I do. "Nope."

My phone vibrates in my mess of sheets. Reaching under the blanket, I pull out an iPhone with a mandala case, and when I flip it over to the lit-up screen. The background is a picture of an orange cat curled up on a couch. It has to be Margot's. *Cat person* files into my mind, adding to the random collection of facts I know about this girl.

"Hey, does Margot have a cat?" I ask Matt absently, still staring down at the phone.

"How the hell should I know?"

Fair. "I think she left her phone."

This gets more of his attention. "Seriously, what were you two doing in here?"

"Nothing," I say, still looking down at the phone in my hand. There are three unread messages—all from Keith. "She was just pissed at me because I kissed her."

The kissing her part isn't a secret, but you wouldn't think that by how wide Matt's eyes get. "You what?"

I let out a breath of laughter. "Would you wipe that stupid grin off your face? It didn't mean anything."

He holds up both hands. "Wait. What do you mean you kissed her but it didn't mean anything?"

I turn her phone over in my hand. "Exactly how you said it."

"You like her," he says with a smug look.

I lock eyes with him. "I don't." Leaning back on my bed, I shrug. "Look, she was sending Keith mixed signals. I thought it was annoying. I kissed her, and now she's pissed at me."

"And you like her."

I give him a sideways glance. "And I *don't* like her."

The asshole is still smiling. "It would be great if you two got together."

"Don't get your hopes up. That girl is always mad about something I've done. This isn't any different."

He scoffs. "Well, she'll be even more pissed if she finds out you tried to go through her phone."

"Yeah," I mutter, but I'm not paying attention anymore. I can only see parts of the messages from Keith, but even with that, I'm annoyed.

KEITH:

What was that about? Are you...

Hello?

I need you to tell me what that...

Who knew the third-nippled virgin was so needy? I get that she should have told him she wasn't interested, but I can practically hear him whining through the phone. Our boy Keith needs to take a fucking seat.

And now, as I lie on my bed that still smells like her, I'm not sure what to make of it all. I figured if we ever hooked up, it would be out of my system. I thought that once I had her, I wouldn't want her again. That's how most of my flings usually go. I get bored and move on.

But I'm not bored of Margot.

If anything, she just got a hell of a lot more interesting.

"What's with you lately?" Matt asks.

I've been glaring at Margot's phone for longer than I should. "What do you mean?"

He frowns. "You seem off. Whatever happened with your dad on Thanksgiving, and then Margot . . . I don't know. I just feel like there's stuff you're not telling me."

He's right. The guilt of keeping things from him has been weighing on me lately, and that was before I ever slept with Margot. Sitting up, I rest my elbows on my knees and level with him. "My dad is cutting me off."

Matt's eyes widen for the second time tonight. "What the hell? Why?"

My knee bounces, but I force it to stop. "American Thieves will open for some of Sidecar's shows starting January."

He blinks. "You're going on tour?"

Without saying anything, I nod. Matt knows what this means. I don't have to spell it out for him. I wring my hands together as I brace myself. Will he be disappointed? Will he stress about getting a new roommate? Does he regret living with me?

"Dude!"

Matt's voice nearly makes me jump.

"You're going on tour!" he practically cheers. "You're actually doing this!"

It's impossible to bite back my smile. "Seems like it."

"And your dad . . .?" he adds as a cautionary question.

My smile fades, and I shake my head.

"Shit."

He looks at me for a long moment, and I know he's about to comment on our living arrangement. He has to be piecing together the fact that I'm leaving him in a shitty position with no roommate. The biggest fight Matt and I ever had was when he let me wear his favorite LSU jersey when we were fourteen, and I spilled Spaghetti Os on it.

I'd say this is worse.

"Fuck him."

I force a laugh. "What?"

"Fuck him," Matt says again with a shrug. "You're going on tour! College will always be here if you need it."

Now I'm the one who can't wipe the grin off my face, relief flooding through me. He's not mad. He doesn't even care that I'm leaving him to chase what I want. "Yeah," I say with a laugh. "I guess you're right."

His support only makes me want to tell him about Margot that much more. Partly because I'm curious what he might think about it, but mostly because his unwavering support has my guilt skyrocketing. Why would I keep anything from him?

I'm alone in the common room, trying and failing to write a song when I spot Margot coming out of the elevator. She's getting back from class, I guess.

She looks tired.

And not in the good—I've just had the best sex of my life

—kind of way. She looks exhausted like today has worn her down, bit by bit.

"Hey," she says, plopping down on the other end of the couch.

I'm still holding my guitar, but I stop playing and take a closer look at her. "Are you okay?" I ask, and I'm surprised by how much I want to know the answer.

She blinks, looking over at me with a similar sense of surprise. "Yeah," she says with a nod. "Hey, you have my phone, right?"

I nod, pulling it from the pocket of my hoodie and handing it to her. "You might not want it. Keith is a piece of work."

Her brows furrow as she takes the phone from my hand. Since she's been gone, he's texted her *eight* times. Sometimes he's mad, other times he's apologizing for getting mad. It's an endless cycle of nonsense that no one should have to deal with.

Especially Margot.

I watch her expression carefully as she unlocks her phone and reads the messages, a frown forming on her lips. "Wow," she says quietly to herself.

"Yeah." I start to play the melody I've come up with recently. It's not great, but I think it can be with a little work. I nod toward her phone. "I can give you my number."

She looks at me again like I've somehow surprised her for a second time. With a dubious lift of her brow, she says, "Are you going to start sending me goodnight texts now?"

My hands freeze, the corner of my lips twitching. "Do you want me to?"

Margot laughs. "No."

My mouth quirks at the sound of her laugh, but then my eyebrows furrow. "Wait. You'll have Keith's number in your phone but not mine?"

"To be fair, I didn't want Keith's number in my phone, either."

I nod slowly. "But you wouldn't tell him no because you were afraid you'd hurt his feelings."

She gives me an unapologetic shrug. "But I'm telling you no, so that's progress." I hate that she's cute even when she turns me down. My fingers pick up playing where they left off. I'll get her number before I leave—I have to.

"Hey, that's good." She nods to my guitar.

I cock an eyebrow. "You don't have to be nice to me just because you've seen me naked."

She rolls her eyes, but I catch her cheeks blushing and probably take a little too much pride in it. Maybe I'm not the only one who thinks this shift between us is weird. Not bad. But the air definitely feels different. Maybe we've finally created some type of truce.

"Please," she says with a scoff. "I'd tell you if it was bad."

"So," I say with a suggestive lift of my brow. "It wasn't bad?"

She tries to fight her tight-lipped smile, her mouth twisting. "The song." She laughs as she adds, "The song isn't bad."

I hold her gaze for a beat longer than I should before looking down at my hands as I pick at the strings. "It needs some work—and lyrics."

She gives me a sideways glance. "You know whose lyrics always inspire me?" Without waiting for me to answer, she leans toward me ever so slightly and whispers, "Taylor Swift."

Now it's my turn to roll my eyes. "Yeah, 'Shake it off.' Earth shattering."

Margot shakes her head at me disapprovingly as she reaches into her bag and pulls out her headphones. "No. Here." She hands me an earbud.

My eyes drop to the tiny piece of plastic in her hand. "What?"

"You put it in your ear." She demonstrates by putting half the set in her left ear like I'm an idiot. I'm still staring at her when she holds her phone up and raises her eyebrows, impatiently waiting for me to comply.

"Fine." I put the earbud in. Nodding to her phone, I add, "But I'm only listening to one, so make it a good one."

"They're all good," she says simply.

There's already a song playing. It must have been the last thing she was listening to, and this breathy sigh plays in my ear. "Taylor?" I ask with a hand over my mouth in mock disbelief.

Margot pauses the song, the corners of her mouth lifting. "That's not the one I was going to have you listen to."

"But that's the one I want to listen to. What is it?" Setting my guitar down, I slide closer to her and peer at her phone screen.

Taylor Swift
"Dress"

"Play it from the beginning." I point to the play button.

She gives me an uncertain look.

"What?" I ask. "You wanted me to listen to a Taylor Swift song, and I want to listen to this one."

Giving in, Margot presses play but not without warning. "Just don't make it weird."

The song starts, and even though the intro is softer than what I'd usually listen to, I wouldn't say it's bad. The tempo during the pre-chorus even has my head bobbing. Being this close to Margot while listening to a song about secret hookups playing in my ear might bring back a few memories from this afternoon. My only saving grace is that I've never seen her in a dress. If I had, I might be imagining taking it off her a little too easily.

"Well?" Margot asks when the song ends.

Bringing my lips to her ear, I whisper, "Well, that song is certainly inspiring me to want to do something, but I'm not sure writing is it."

She pushes me away from her, but her cheeks flare. "I knew

you'd make it weird." The next song on her playlist starts, and I immediately recognize the familiar opening guitar rift from "Do I Wanna Know?" by Arctic Monkeys. Now I know I'm screwed. This song already makes me think of her, and listening to it with her sitting here is enough to make my hand wander to her thigh.

"What are you doing?" she breathes, her body tense.

I don't know what I'm doing. It's not like we're going to have sex in the middle of the damn common room, but even though I know that, I still want to be closer to her. I want to feel the way her breath catches when she's turned on. I want to see her lips part from something I've said. Hell, I want her to want me—just a little bit longer.

Unfortunately, I'm not the only one who wants those things, and the other guy looks like he's headed over here to give us a piece of his mind.

41
margot

I SHIFT out of Jackson's reach as Keith approaches, and thankfully, Jackson has the common sense to take his hand off my leg. "Keith, I'm sorry I didn't see your messages all day. I couldn't find my phone."

"Yeah. Sorry, Keith," Jackson adds a little too apologetically. "She left it in my room."

I glare at Jackson before looking back at Keith. His eyes jump between us, and I can only imagine the puzzle he's piecing together.

Keith's gaze finally settles on me, and I feel the weight that comes along with it. "Can we go somewhere and talk?"

I don't want to go somewhere with him alone. The pressure of this conversation already feels suffocating, and I don't think we have anything to talk about.

Both guys are staring at me, each trying to sort out what I'm thinking.

"Um," I finally say. "We're kind of in the middle of something." I look over at Jackson for help.

A slow smile pulls at his perfect lips. "Oh, no. We're done. You are free."

I balk at him, but all I'm met with is the familiar glint of challenge behind his eyes.

My eyes dart to Keith again, and I blurt, "I really need to study." I'm not even sure *I* would believe the words coming out of my mouth, but it's the only thing I can think to say.

Keith's frown deepens, and I feel terrible. But he texted me so many times, and this needs to stop. I knew he might have a crush on me, but he was texting me like I betrayed him.

Jackson picks at his guitar strings. "Maybe you and Keith can discuss things over dinner."

"*What?*" I snap, but he keeps his eyes on his guitar like he never said a thing.

Keith's voice somehow makes it to my ears. "I mean, I'm free later if—"

"No," I say with more force than probably necessary.

Jackson finally looks up from his guitar to meet my gaze, his hands stilling. "No?"

"No," I repeat, giving him a warning look.

Jackson stares at me for a long moment, and I almost falter under the intensity behind his eyes. "I could have sworn you were done studying."

"You," I say, pointing a finger at him. "Stop."

His mouth quirks from being scolded, but he looks back at his guitar and picks up the melody where he left off.

"And you," I say, finally bringing my attention back to Keith standing in front of me. "We have nothing to talk about. I'm sorry, but I don't see you as anything more than a friend."

"I'm sorry for what I said in some of those texts," Keith blurts, kneeling in front of me. You'd think this conversation would be a little less awkward now that he's not towering over me, but the way he's crouching in front of me makes it so much worse.

Jackson's playing slows, so even though I don't look away from Keith, I know he's watching our exchange.

"It's fine," I say, even though it isn't. "But maybe we should stop hanging out for a little while."

"My texts were out of line. I just thought you were ignoring me," he says, his eyes pleading.

I want to melt into the floor. I want to disappear. I want to evaporate into thin air. Anything to get me out of this conversation and anything to get away from him.

I look to Jackson for help again, but he seems content watching this interaction unfold.

Keith pulls my attention back to him when he says, "We can just talk in your room or something. We don't have to go to dinner."

Shaking my head, I squeeze my eyes shut. "No, Keith. I'm sorry, but . . . no."

His mouth presses into a hard line. "Okay, fine." He stands and walks backward toward the common room door but hesitates. "So, I guess just text me later?"

I give him a tight smile, and he nods, seeming to take the hint. I have no intention of texting him later. After seeing how much he was affected by this, I have no plan of reaching out to him at all. It's not fair to him. Turning on his heels, Keith finally leaves, and as soon as he's gone, I'm acutely aware of the fact that Jackson and I are alone again. Taking a deep breath, I finally look at him, expecting him to gloat. This is what he's always wanted—for me to tell Keith it's never going to happen. It made me feel terrible, and it was awkward and uncomfortable, but I have to admit, I can breathe a little easier now.

He doesn't make fun of me, though.

He just stares after Keith with a furrowed brow before saying, "I'll never understand why you're so afraid to hurt that guy's feelings." He looks at me. "You're never worried about hurting mine."

I let out a breath of laughter as my head falls back against the couch. "That's because you can handle it."

42
jackson

SITTING in Dave's garage and practicing with the guys is what I've always wanted, but ever since I kissed her, it's like I can't wait to get back to my dorm and maybe catch a glimpse of Margot before she goes to bed.

It's only happened twice this week. Twice she's been awake when I got back. Twice I saw her, in her leggings and oversized T-shirt. Twice we locked eyes for longer than we should have, and twice I was left wondering what she's thinking as I tried to fall asleep at night.

It's bullshit.

But God, do I want her.

I want to make her laugh.

I want to make her mad.

I want to fuck her like I hate her.

And I want to make love to her like she's the greatest thing to ever happen to me.

Dave looks over his shoulder at me, and my fingers fumble with the strings. Based on the way he's staring me down, it's not the first time I've fucked up during practice today.

He holds up a hand to stop us. "Let's take it from the top."

I look over at Marty only to be met with wide eyes silently asking me what the hell is wrong with me. I shake out my hand and nod to Dave to count us down again. We're practicing one of our newer songs, but I *know* it. I've been practicing it for the past few days on repeat to make sure I wouldn't do shit like this when the band got together.

The opening riff is trickier than most of our other songs, but I was nailing it last night. Dave kicks off the song again, and I focus on every chord. As much as I try to get it right, my hands betray me, making the riff come out sloppy and loose.

"Fuck," I mutter under my breath.

"Let's take a break," Dave calls out to the rest of the band before walking up to me.

"You all right, man?" he asks, and I'm grateful he's so fucking nice. I need this band. This is the road that will take me to where I want to go, and we're about to start touring. I can't piss these guys off or make them think hiring me was a mistake.

"Yeah. Sorry." I shake my head clear. "I don't know what I was thinking. I guess finals are stressing me out."

It's a lie, and from the way he's looking at me, he knows it.

"Finals?" he asks with a furrowed brow. "Aren't you dropping out?"

"Yeah," I say, trying to cover my ass. "But if I ever need to go back, I don't want to have to retake classes."

This seems to ease some of his skepticism, and Marty says, "Let's hope none of us ever have to go back to college," with a laugh.

I don't laugh. I can't believe I'm playing like shit tonight. I'm better than this. They know it. I know it. Hell, even Dave's neighbors probably know it.

Dave's stare is on me as he says, "Let's end things early tonight." I open my mouth to protest, but he cuts me off. "We'll pick this up tomorrow."

Feeling like shit, I get in my car and head back to the dorm. I can't believe I let myself get so distracted. My hands grip the steering wheel, but my fingers move as I commit the riff I ruined to muscle memory. But even as I drive and try to mentally practice the song, thoughts of Margot creep in.

The way she felt.

And moved.

And tasted.

Before I know it, I'm back on campus. I have no idea when my fingers stopped practicing the chords and went back to just driving, but they did. I need to clear this fog from my head and get back on track, but just the thought of Margot has me turned on, and my heart pounds in anticipation as I lock my car and head toward the dorm.

She's sitting on her bed with the door open.

And she looks amazing.

I make sure to only glance at her, giving her a quick nod that she returns with a faint smile before turning to unlock my door. Matt isn't here, so he and Rae must be out doing whatever couples do on a Friday night.

Leaving Margot and me alone.

That's when it hits me. It's ten thirty on a Friday night, and she looks way too good for someone sitting in her dorm watching Netflix alone on her laptop. I've seen Margot when she's about to go to bed. She's usually wearing a T-shirt with leggings, no makeup, and her hair up. She's pretty then, but tonight, she's wearing a tank top with short sleep shorts, and her hair is down, the silky, red strands cascading down her back.

Setting my guitar in the corner of my room, a faint smile pulls at the corner of my mouth.

She wants us to hook up again. She has to. Why else would she have left the door open? Why else would she look the way she does?

Walking across the hall, I lean against her door frame. "So, where's our favorite couple?"

Her head snaps up, and she closes her computer. "They went out with everyone."

"But you didn't go?"

She shrugs. "Keith was going to be there. I didn't want it to be weird." Getting to her feet, she sets her laptop on the corner of her desk before giving me another glance. "Are you going to just stand there?"

"Do you want me to come in?"

A breath of laughter leaves her as she turns, leaning back against the desk. "I don't care what you do. I just think it's weird you're standing in my doorway."

She's cute when she tries to play hardball. With a shrug, I walk further into the room until I'm standing in front of her. As soon as I'm close enough to touch her, I stop, making sure to leave space between us, but that doesn't stop me from noticing her tongue as it quickly dips over her bottom lip.

"You don't care what I do?" I ask.

She stares up at me, those big, brown eyes meeting my challenge. "Nope."

Her answer shoots straight to my cock because I can think of a few things I'd like to do to her, but I'm not playing her game. "Great," I say as I grab her chin and give her a quick kiss. "Goodnight, Red." Then I turn and walk toward the door.

43
margot

JACKSON'S KISS STILL TINGLES on my lips. As he walks away, the panic in my chest tightens. "What are you doing?" I ask, starting after him.

He stops and turns. "What?"

He's infuriating.

"What are you doing?" I say again. The rejection of him walking toward the door already has me feeling pulled to him, like there's a rubber band tethering us together.

Jackson's thumb points over his shoulder as he stands in my doorway. "I thought you don't care what I do," he says slowly like he doesn't understand why I'm questioning him.

He knows *exactly* why I'm questioning him.

I glare at him, my arms crossed, and his only response is a subtle quirk of his mouth. "Is there something else you'd like me to do?"

Torn between telling him what I want and not wanting to give him the satisfaction of making me crack, I hesitate. Finally, I settle on saying, "I want you to close the door."

Without missing a beat, he takes a single step back into my

room and closes the door behind him in one fluid motion. "What else?"

My heart races under the intensity of his stare, and I find myself at a loss for words. "Um—I . . ." A million thoughts cycle through, but I can't settle on one to say out loud.

His brows cinch. "Just say what you want, Margot."

He makes it sound so simple. He doesn't understand what it's like to squirm under the weight of having his full attention. It's always hard for me to say what I want out loud, but with him, it's worse. Finding words feels impossible when he's looking at me like this, let alone words that will articulate how badly I want him. My cheeks warm at the thought.

He takes a step toward me, and I sigh out a breath of relief. "Want to know what I want?"

I swallow hard.

Jackson puts a hand on either side of my face, and I feel the warmth of his fingertips throughout my entire body. He kisses me lightly, his lips teasing. "I want to fuck you like you're mine," he says, his voice low. "I want to taste every part of you, and when I'm done, I want to bury myself so deep inside you that you feel me there for days." His hands slide down until he's gripping the back of my neck, his forehead resting against mine. "I want to fucking consume you, Margot, and I want to be consumed by you."

My chest rises and falls, and the heart-fluttering feeling from moments ago has turned into a heavy heat between my legs. The wires connecting my brain to my mouth must be frayed or flat-out cut because there's no way I can find something coherent to say back to that.

God, someone who looks like him should not be allowed to talk like that. Even with his brows furrowed and his lips pressed in a firm line, he's good-looking. There's no reason for someone to walk through life looking the way he does. It's excessive and unnecessary, but I am also incredibly grateful for it. I'm grateful for the way his captivating eyes hold mine, and the way his tongue instinctively runs over his bottom lip every time he looks at me too long. His thumb lightly brushes my cheek, and I blink, remembering I'm supposed to speak.

Without thinking, my hands find the front of his jeans, unbuttoning them. I look up to find him watching me intently, but he doesn't say a word. Slipping my hand inside, I find him already hard. Jackson practically growls when my hand wraps around him, and I love seeing him react to my touch. He kisses me, his mouth desperate for mine, and I pump my hand. The sounds it pulls from him prompts me to kiss him deeper. It isn't until he says, "Margot, if you don't stop doing that, I'm going to come in my pants," that I remove my hand with a smile tugging at my lips.

Jackson kicks off his jeans, walking me backward until I bump into my desk. Lifting me, he sets me on the cool, wooden surface, parting my legs as he kneels in front of me. Just the sight of him on his knees makes it impossible to think straight. He's quick to maneuver my cotton shorts and underwear down, leaving me completely exposed.

His intense gaze drifts up to meet mine, and I'm left frozen, waiting and wanting. Pulling me to the edge of the desk, he slowly presses his lips to my center. His fingers dig into my thighs as he uses his tongue to part me, and the sensation sends a shudder through my entire body. My head falls back, and an involuntary, "Oh, my God," leaves my lips. With just a few strokes of his tongue, I know I won't last long. Seeing Jackson on his knees may have halted my thoughts, but the way he uses his tongue has completely erased them. My mind is a blank slate, only focused on the building pressure and my aching need for him.

When my legs start to shake, I knot my hands in his hair, urging him closer. I'm silently begging him to give me the release he's been building. "Jackson," I say, and my voice comes out as a desperate plea.

He pauses, his lips pulling into a slow smirk against me. His eyes flick up to meet mine and he holds my stare as he runs over me with a single, slow stroke of his tongue.

Pressing my heel into his back, I urge him to keep going. He's keeping my orgasm just out of reach, and I know he's doing it on purpose. My signal makes him smile wider against my center, but it only lasts a second. A moment later, his expert tongue is licking and sucking, adding and removing pressure where I need it most. I can barely see straight. When my body starts to shatter, I tighten my grip on his hair while my other hand holds the edge of the desk for support. Waves of pleasure more intense than I've ever felt have me crying out. The orgasm lingers, pulsing with every slow and gentle stroke of his tongue.

It isn't until I'm completely spent and catching my breath that Jackson gets to his feet and bends down to check the back pocket of his jeans. "Shit, I don't have a condom." He groans, running a hand over his face.

Still dazed, I ask, "Are you sleeping with anyone else?" If I can count on Jackson for anything, it's honesty.

"Fuck, no," he says with a furrowed brow. "I haven't thought about another girl in months."

Another flutter in my stupid heart. My heart is supposed to stay out of this. This is sex.

I know he could run into his room and grab one, but if he's not inside me soon, I might implode. "I'm on the Pill," I tell him as I hook my leg around him to pull him closer. I glance at my nightstand where my birth control pack sits. "I take it every morning and never miss a day." Jackson's eyes jump from the pack to me, his fingers digging into my skin.

His storm-like eyes search mine. "Are you sleeping with anyone else?"

Letting out a breath of laughter, I slowly shake my head. "No."

He groans like my answer physically does something to him. Hooking his hands behind my knees, he pulls me closer to the edge of the desk, and I can feel him hard against me. A delicious heat radiates off him, and my legs fall open, craving more. He rests his forehead against mine as he weaves his hand through my hair.

"Just us," he says, his voice rough. "We won't do this with anyone else."

I'm breathing hard but manage a faint nod. Before I can say anything, he covers my mouth with his and drops his briefs, positioning himself against me.

My hips tilt, and when he slowly enters me, my nails dig into his shoulder blade. He takes his time, sinking into me, and when he fills me completely his head falls forward. "Fuck, Margot."

All I can do is nod because having him this way leaves me at a loss for words. I can feel every part of him like this, and it's better than I could have imagined. Hooking my leg behind him, I urge him to move, and he does.

Biting his shoulder to avoid crying out, I lose myself a little more every time he thrusts into me.

"No one else comes inside you." It's not a question, and I'm completely at his mercy as he brings me closer and closer to the edge for the second time.

"Okay," I breathe.

His movements keep their dangerous rhythm, but something in his eyes softens. Cradling my face as he holds me close, he says, "No one else." His teeth drag along my bottom lip, pulling a moan from me. Thrusting into me harder, he adds, "Say it."

I gasp, the tension almost too much to bear. "No one else."

Jackson kisses me, and it's surprisingly tender. Gripping me tighter, he pounds into me deeper. With every hit, my eyes cross more. "Only me."

Squeezing around him, my nails dig into the back of his neck. I bring my mouth to his ear, my teeth nipping. "Only you," I breathe, and my second orgasm tears through me at the same time Jackson curses and stiffens, pouring into me. The feeling of him coming inside me, warm and wet, has my head spinning. My teeth drag along his jaw. I nip at his bottom lip. My hands are in his hair. All while he stays inside me, letting me soak up every last drop.

44
jackson

MARGOT IS quick to dress when we're done, so I follow her lead. It's probably for the best. We have no idea when Matt and Rae will be back, and there'd be some explaining to do if they walked in on the two of us naked.

But God, do I love seeing Margot naked.

This isn't how hooking up with a girl usually goes for me. They're usually the ones who want more, and I'm the one keeping them at arm's length. That's not the case with Margot. I know this can only be sex. Starting anything more would be stupid, but if I didn't have that to consider? If I wasn't about to go on my first tour?

I think I'd want to be with her.

The realization leaves an unfamiliar ache in my chest as I look down at her. I'm sitting on her bed with my back against the wall as she rests her head in my lap. She's talking about one of her classes, and she's so animated as she looks up at the ceiling and rambles, her eyes jumping to meet mine every few seconds.

She's adorable.

I'm tempted to brush her cheek with my fingertips, but

every time I move to show affection outside of sex, she tenses and finds a way to shift away from me.

This doesn't change anything.

Maybe it's a good thing I'm leaving. I have no business falling for a girl who doesn't want me. If I stayed across the hall from her all year, I'd only dig myself a deeper grave for the day she finds a guy who wants something real and long-term. I'm sure she'll have no trouble finding him. There are plenty of guys on campus who would jump at the chance to be with her.

"Are you coming to my gig tomorrow night?" I ask, absent-mindedly brushing a strand of hair away from her forehead before I can stop myself.

She sits up, making it abundantly clear she doesn't want that from me, and I mentally kick myself for forgetting what I was literally just thinking about.

"I don't know," she says. "If Rae and Matt go, I'll probably be there."

My chest weighs heavy with disappointment because I already know Rae and Matt won't be there. "I wouldn't count on it," I say as I pull my knees up, resting my elbows on them. "Matt has a lacrosse game tomorrow night." Rae will be at the game for her boyfriend, the same way I wish Margot would come to my gig for me.

But she's not my girlfriend.

I don't know why that's so hard for me to get through my thick skull tonight.

She looks at me with those big, brown eyes. "Oh," she says, a frown pulling at the corners of her mouth.

"You could still come without them, you know." I don't know why I'm pushing this. I need to shut my damn mouth.

She lets out a light laugh. "And do what? Stand by the stage alone, pining after the guy who plays guitar?"

My lips quirk. "I wouldn't mind."

Margot rolls her eyes. "I'm sure you wouldn't."

Our venue tonight might be small, but it's *packed*. Since Sidecar announced us as their opening act for select dates, we've had a surge in exposure. Energy buzzes throughout the entire place, and the guys and I can't wipe the stupid smiles off our faces before we take the stage.

"Holy shit." Dave marvels as he looks out at the crowd from the side of the stage. "We have to be violating some type of fire code."

Marty claps a hand on my shoulder. "You ready for this? Don't space out on us like you did in practice."

"Leave the kid alone," Brady says, his eyes narrowed at Marty as he sits on a nearby stool and taps his drumsticks on his legs, keeping a perfect rhythm.

"Trust me, no distractions tonight," I say as I warm up on my guitar. No one I know will be here, and for the first time, that feels like a good thing. At least I know I'll be able to focus on what's important. Plus, I'm supposed to sing one of our songs for the first time tonight.

I brought Dave the melody I came up with, and to my surprise, he loved it. We sat down together, he helped me with lyrics, and tonight is the night we're testing it out on the crowd.

I figured he'd be the one to sing it, but as we were working on it, he heard me testing out different things and insisted I have the better voice for it.

I'm not sure I believe him, but I'll give it a shot. Singing has never been my thing, and I don't enjoy it as much as I enjoy playing guitar, but I can swallow my pride for one song. My goal at the end of the day is to keep the band happy, so if Dave wants me to sing, I guess I'm singing.

As if he can read my mind, Dave asks, "Are you going to warm up those vocal cords, too?"

I shake my head as I continue to play. "No. I'd hate to put you out of a job."

Dave throws his head back, his booming laughter somehow standing out above the sound of the still growing crowd. "Thanks for looking out," he says as he holds out his fist.

I bump his with mine and get back to playing.

Someone who works for the venue walks up to us, looking stressed. "We've had to start turning people away at the door, so you guys are good to go on whenever you're ready."

"Shit," Dave mutters in disbelief. "All right, boys, let's do it."

We all step onto the stage as the place roars loud enough for me to feel it in my chest. When I look out, I'm met with more lights than faces, but I can still make out the excitement from the crowd, and that alone sends a wave of adrenaline through me.

Dave usually says a few words to the audience before we get started, but tonight, the crowd must be getting to him because he doesn't say a thing. He just looks back at Brady and signals for him to open the first song with one of his iconic drum intros.

And the crowd goes wild.

45
margot

I'M PRESSED against the wall of some tiny venue to watch Jackson and his band play. This place may not be any bigger than the last, but the amount of people who are packed in here tonight is definitely not the same.

The bar in the corner has a line that makes it look like it's serving its own small crowd, but I was able to find some empty wall space between two high-top tables in the very back. They were at capacity by the time I got here, and it wasn't easy getting in.

Being here alone is a little overwhelming, but the fact that Jackson is within eyesight gives me a sense of ease. I'm not completely alone—even if he has no idea I'm here.

I don't even know what compelled me to come tonight. I was about to go to Matt's lacrosse game with Rae but changed my mind at the last minute. Going with her didn't feel right—especially knowing Jackson would be here without Matt or anyone else for support. I never thought I'd turn down time with Rae for time with Jackson. I also never thought I'd drive to downtown Tampa alone to watch a guy in an alternative rock band . . . yet, here we are.

I shift my weight from one foot to the other, suddenly not so sure I should be here. Jackson and I aren't together. What if he doesn't want me here? It's not like he actually invited me. He asked if I was coming, and when I told him I wasn't, he didn't push the topic further.

Oh, my God. He didn't even try to talk me into it.

I glance toward the door, wondering if I can leave without him ever seeing me, when the lead singer puts a standing mic in front of Jackson. He nods to the audience, giving them a small wave. Then he starts to sing, and all my racing thoughts stop.

His voice makes me pause, and a few women around me look like they're in danger of getting drool on the floor. His singing voice has grit to it. It doesn't pass over you, it catches and wraps around you until it's the only thing you can focus on. It's deep and rough, and . . . it's hot. It's really hot.

I can't believe how natural he looks on stage in front of all these people. If I were up there, I'd be shaking. Jackson keeps his composure as he plays and sings, his voice never wavering. It's like standing up there doesn't faze him in the slightest. I guess that's what people mean when they say someone's a natural at something. Jackson is not only a natural when it comes to music, but he's a natural when it comes to performing, too.

The song ends, and I've almost been in a trance. Blinking a few times, I bring my attention back to the lead singer as he holds an outstretched arm toward Jackson. "Ladies and gentlemen, Jackson Phillips!"

The crowd cheers, and Jackson shakes his head with a smile pulling at his lips, bewildered that so many people are clapping for him.

I'm clapping for him.

"And I'm Dave Lutz!" Dave says, "And we've got Mr. Marty Brewer on bass." The other guitarist plays a few chords before falling back into an even tempo. "And on the drums, we have my lifelong friend, Brady!"

The drummer goes into a short drum solo, and Dave adds, "We just want to thank you all for coming out here tonight! We've got one more for you guys!"

The band kicks things up with one of their more popular upbeat hits, and even though Jackson didn't look nervous before he sang, he's looser now. He smiles more easily at the other guys in the band, even laughing when they give him an encouraging nod.

He's beautiful like this.

Seeing him this way, completely in his element, brings out the best parts of him. It warms my heart and leaves an ache in my chest at the same time because seeing him this way has me second-guessing everything.

Maybe it's not just sex.

Maybe a small part of me has feelings for him that go beyond the physical.

Maybe I'm starting to fall for Jackson Philips.

Just a little bit.

The song ends, and some of the crowd starts to clear. Some people stay behind, though, either grabbing drinks or hanging around to speak with the band.

And that's when I realize Jackson has quite the fan club—most of the members being women. Some of them look like middle-aged women, but others are young—young and gorgeous. My chest tightens when he smiles at a stunning blonde who looks to be about our age. Her tight, teal mini dress accentuates all her curves—each one more desirable than the last. He nods to whatever she's saying, agreeing with enthusiasm, and my heart plummets.

I know it's irrational, but the longer she talks to him, the more I'm convinced she is the *worst*.

I could walk over there. I could interrupt, but I'm frozen in place. There's an empty high-top next to me now that the couple sitting there has left, and I slowly take a seat on one of the high-backed chairs, my eyes never leaving him.

No wonder he said he doesn't want a relationship. With the amount of attention he's getting after just one show, I can't imagine why he'd want to commit to one person. He could easily take home the blonde he's still smiling at and do whatever he wants with her. I can tell by the way she touches his arm and the way she plays with her hair as she listens to him talk.

She's probably really nice.

She's definitely nicer to him than I am.

I consider sneaking out and making a run for my car again when he looks past the blonde in front of him, and those piercing eyes catch me. Everything inside me screams to look away, but I can't. His stare pins me in place. He only briefly looks back at the girl to excuse himself before he locks on me again.

My heart pounds in my chest as he cuts across the room, and when he reaches me, he glances around. "Are Rae and Matt here?"

I shake my head.

He studies me. "You came here alone?"

I nod.

Jackson frowns. "You should have come over." He glances over his shoulder where his groupies are watching intently, eagerly waiting for his return. "I had no idea you were here."

I wave away his comment, doing my best to look casual and not like a girl who might be falling for him. "No, that's okay. You were busy." I glance back at the group of girls, and Jackson follows my stare, looking over his shoulder before turning back to me.

He cocks an eyebrow. "Are you jealous, Red?"

I look back at him and find a dangerous smirk playing at

the corner of his mouth. "No," I say with narrowed eyes. "Why would I be jealous?"

His smirk grows. "Because that girl over there gave me her number." He doesn't take his eyes off me, but he nods his head in the direction of the gorgeous blonde.

I gape at him. "She did not."

Jackson laughs, standing up straight so he can reach into his back pocket. "Oh, yes she did." He puts a piece of paper on the small, round table between us, and sure enough, there's a phone number scrawled in perfect handwriting—from Carly.

Seeing the name written with a heart next to it makes my eyes widen, and without thinking, I look up at him and mutter, "I hate her."

Jackson grins. "I know you do." Stepping around to my side of the table, he says, "Here," as he holds my face between his hands.

I tense. "What are you doing?"

"Fuck Carly," he says playfully, and then he full-on kisses me in front of everyone. It's a kiss like you see in the movies. The kind that stops time and makes the room spin, and when he pulls away, my eyes stay shut for a moment until I hear clapping. My eyes fly open to find the other guys in the band responsible for all the noise, and I can't help laughing as an embarrassed smile crosses my lips. At least no one from campus is here.

At least Rae and Matt aren't here.

"Come on," Jackson says, grabbing my hand. "They're going to want to meet you after that."

46
jackson

MARGOT FITS RIGHT in with the guys, and I love watching her with other people. When she's with me, she's challenging and stubborn, and I like that more than I should. But with everyone else, she's this sweeter version of herself that I rarely get to see. I like this version of her, too.

I can't believe she came.

It's not her type of music, and she acts like all I do is piss her off, but she's here. And she was jealous of another girl. It *has* to mean something.

Those girls scattered as soon as I kissed her, and I'm pretty sure Carly isn't expecting a call.

She was cute.

But she's not Margot.

No one is Margot.

Brady laughs at something Margot just said, and I'm brought back to the present. She's standing close enough that we could be mistaken for a couple, but not close enough for us to actually touch.

"So," Brady says, his eyes darting back and forth between

Margot and me before settling on her. "Are you the reason he's been distracted lately?"

Margot looks at me with her eyebrows pinched. "You've been distracted?"

I shrug. "Finals."

The crease between her eyebrows deepens, and I know she can see straight through my lie. Apparently, Brady can read her reaction too and lets out another laugh. "I thought so."

Thankfully, he considers that the end of the conversation and goes to join Marty off to the side.

"Why have you been distracted?" Margot asks again, and this time, she touches my side, letting her hand linger. Her touch isn't sexy, and she's touched me more intimately before, but this time it's in front of people, and that alone has my heart beating harder.

I bring my mouth closer to her ear to answer her. "You, of all people, shouldn't have to ask that."

She turns to face me, and her smile steals the air from my lungs.

I look down at her. "I'm surprised you got here before the doors closed."

Her cheeks flush. "I didn't."

"What?" I ask, pulling back to look at her. "How did you get in?"

The roses blossoming on her cheeks burn brighter. "I lied."

My eyebrows pull together as I study her. "About . . . ?"

She tucks a strand of hair behind her ear, avoiding my gaze. "That you're my boyfriend."

"What?" I ask, unable to stop the smile that comes across my face.

When she looks up at me, she's playfully glaring. "Don't make it weird."

Her lie makes me happier than it should. For years, I've had a one-track mind. Join a band, tour, and make it a career for as long as I can. That's all I've ever cared about. I raise my eyebrows innocently. "I'm not making it weird." Leaning toward her, I ask in a hushed voice, "Is that why you've been so nice to me tonight? You're worried about being found out?"

She rolls her eyes, but when her stare settles back on me, it's unwavering. "No." She shakes her head as she looks out over the trashed venue. "Why were there so many people here tonight? It wasn't like that in October."

"It's probably just hype around the tour and the new album coming out."

I said it casually because it's the truth. It isn't until her eyes widen, and she says, "You're going on tour?" that it hits me, she doesn't know. A small part of me figured she knew already. I've told Matt about the tour and assumed he mentioned it to Rae, and I figured Rae would have told Margot.

But apparently not.

Something inside my gut tightens because if she doesn't know about the tour, there's a good chance she also doesn't know I'm dropping out of college.

Not that it matters.

She's made it clear she doesn't want anything more from me, but at the same time, she's *here*.

Scratching the side of my head, I mutter, "Uh, yeah."

"That's amazing!" She hugs me, filling my senses with her strawberry shampoo, and when she pulls away, she doesn't let go completely. She leaves her arms around my waist as she looks up at me, and it feels so fucking good. "Where will you go?"

I don't know why this topic is making me uneasy. If this were anyone else, I'd gladly talk about my excitement for the tour, but this is Margot.

And as much as I hate to admit it, leaving her makes this once in a lifetime experience bittersweet.

"Sidecar, a band from South Carolina, asked us to open for

them on select dates during their first headlining tour, so we'll be all over." I study her face for any underlying negative feelings about the news, but I've never seen her this radiant.

She's genuinely happy for me.

"Jackson!" she practically squeals. "That's incredible!" She squeezes me a little tighter, and I let out a laugh.

It feels good to have someone view one of my proudest achievements as an actual success. Lord knows I wasn't going to get any approval from my parents. Matt is happy for me, but when it comes to Margot, everything feels different.

More.

I should tell her what this means. I should make it clear that going on tour means I'm dropping out, but a small part of me doesn't want to. What if she has no problem with it? What if she sends me on my way without so much as a backward glance? I don't know why, but I *want* her to care. I want to know I mean something to her.

I kiss her. It's a quick peck on the lips, but it's enough to make those cheeks of hers scarlet, and I take a little too much enjoyment in how much she's affected by it.

Before I know it, it's just the band and Margot left. She's stuck around after most people have gone home, and even though I don't understand it, I'm grateful. I'm grateful to have her by my side all night. I'm grateful for her laugh and her gorgeous smile. I'm grateful for the way she can hold her own with the guys from the band—she even throws a few playful jabs at Marty.

We're not together.

But tonight feels like a glimpse into what it could be like if we were.

And if I'm being honest?

It makes me feel fucking unstoppable.

47
margot

AS I LEAVE my dorm to meet up with Matt and Rae in the common room, my eyes dart to Jackson's door, my chest deflating when I see it's shut. I was hoping he'd be back by now. It's finals week. He should be studying. Well, I guess Jackson doesn't study, but he should at least be here, sitting on his bed and playing guitar.

My temporary disappointment is replaced with another flutter of hope as I walk toward the common room. Maybe he's with Rae and Matt. Instead of going into his dorm, maybe he saw them in the common room on his way back and stopped to sit with them.

I head to our shared space, but it's only Matt and Rae sitting on one of the couches. Everyone else must either be at the library or studying in their rooms.

I let out a disappointed sigh as I flop onto the couch next to them. Reaching for my laptop, I open it and pull up the study guide for my Government exam tomorrow.

The elevator door chimes, and I look up. That same annoying feeling of hope might as well be a hummingbird in my chest.

I think it's safe to say I have feelings for Jackson.

Real feelings.

Because I'm acting like my every waking moment revolves around hopefully running into him. It's borderline pathetic.

Ever since pounding on his door that first night, he's been slowly invading more of my thoughts, and now I struggle to think about anything else. It was supposed to be casual. It wasn't supposed to mean anything to either of us, but somehow everything with Jackson means something to me now.

This time, it's Keith who graces us with his presence. Luckily, he's kept his distance since I talked to him about our friendship needing a break. The most I get from him now are curt nods of acknowledgment. I don't even think I've seen him smile in weeks.

"Glad to see that's not still awkward," Rae says as she looks up from her notes.

I'm still staring at Keith's back, chewing on the end of my pen. "Yeah," I answer flatly.

Matt laughs with a shake of his head. "I still can't believe Jackson kissed you in front of him."

This brings my attention back, and I desperately try to keep my cheeks from flushing. Most mentions of Jackson make my cheeks flush these days. When I was convinced there were no feelings involved, I didn't want Rae and Matt to know. I wanted it to be a secret between Jackson and me. No expectations. No judgment.

But now?

Now I feel like a girl who has a crush on a boy, and all I want to do is gush about it to my best friend.

"Where is he, anyway?" I ask, determined to sound more casual than I feel.

"Where do you think?" Matt asks sarcastically as he

reaches for a different folder on the couch next to him. With finals right around the corner, it's like all we've been doing is studying. "All he does is spend time with the band. I live with the guy, and I probably won't even see him before his going away party."

"His what?" I ask.

Matt looks at me like I should know what he's talking about, but I have no idea where he's going with this.

"Oh!" Rae exclaims, setting her book down. "I keep forgetting to tell you! You'll be happy to know that Jackson is dropping out to focus on the band full-time."

"Really?" My heart skips a beat, and not wanting Rae to notice, I look down at my notes and swallow. What does she mean, dropping out? There's no way. He can't be leaving. She must have misunderstood, and I didn't catch feelings for a guy who's about to leave and didn't even bother to tell me.

There's a consistent hum taking over my ears. I rub my eyes and attempt to smile at Rae. "Really? He—he's leaving?"

"Yup," Matt says with a nod before looking up from his notes. "We're having a going away party for him on Friday. Finals will be over, and then he moves out this weekend." He seems a little unsure as to how he should respond to my wide-eyed stare, so he just gives me an apologetic look. "I told Rae to tell you about it."

Rae shoots him a glare before turning back to me. "We can go together." Her expression shifts to concern as she looks at me. "It will be fun," she says with a reassuring nod. She's probably worried I'm mad at her for not telling me, but that's not where my mind is at all.

"Yeah," I say with a faint smile, trying my best to convince her everything is fine. I knew Jackson dropping out was a possibility, but I had no idea it was actually happening. Why wouldn't he tell me?

She returns the gesture, holding my gaze a second longer before looking down at her notebook and back to studying.

Jackson is leaving.

To tour with his band.

This weekend.

I had one of those pieces already, but when the other two click into place, my heart pounds with an emotion I'm not sure is justified. Jackson and I aren't together. We've never even talked about it. I'm not his. He's not mine. He doesn't owe me anything.

But somehow, this still feels like a punch to the gut.

I try to get back to work, studying for my final, but it's no use. All I can focus on is the sound of blood rushing to my ears, pounding with every thud of my heart.

I should be happy for him—I *am* happy for him. This is all he's ever wanted, and he deserves it. Anyone who has seen him play on stage would agree. That's where he's most comfortable.

That's where he belongs.

And I belong here, in a USF dorm common room with my best friend and her boyfriend.

The sound of the elevator ding snaps me back to the present, and one glance reunites me with the gray-blue eyes I can't stop thinking about. My pulse quickens as he walks toward us, guitar case in hand. It isn't until he pulls up a chair and sets his guitar down that I realize I've been staring. Before he can look over at me, I dart my gaze down to the page and get back to work.

"How was practice?" Matt asks.

I swear I can still feel Jackson looking at me, but I refuse to let him see what I'm feeling right now. He'll read me like he always does, and that's the last thing I need.

Finally, I sense his eyes pulling away from me to answer Matt. "Good. We're taking some time off for the holidays, so it was relaxed today. What have you guys been up to?"

There it is again, the feeling of his eyes on me. I know I can't avoid him forever, but it would have been nice to get the shock out of my system first.

I could probably burn a hole through my keyboard with how hard I'm staring at it.

"Are the guys excited about the tour?" Rae asks, and the heart rate I've been trying to calm comes back with a vengeance.

"Yeah," Jackson says with a laugh. "I think they wish we were going on the whole tour instead of only select dates, but Dave says he's already working on lining up another one after this."

Another tour.

"Seriously?" Matt asks, and it sounds like he's finally set down his notes. "So, this is happening?"

Jackson is quiet for a moment, and I dare to lift my gaze. He's scratching the side of his head as he leans back in his chair, a grin teasing at the corner of his mouth. "That's what I've been trying to tell you."

"Shit," Matt says with his own grin forming. "Remember me when you make it big."

"No promises."

Then Matt turns to Rae. "If only I knew how to play the drums."

Rae laughs. "What? You'd join the band and tour with him?"

"Yeah!" Matt answers like it should be obvious.

"Okay," Rae says dismissively, but there's still a trace of a smile pulling at her lips.

I watch their exchange, and for the first time, I'm jealous of what they have. My eyes flicker to Jackson, and my lips part with the realization that he's watching me. I feel like I should say something, but what can I say? What do you say to someone who has no idea they're breaking your heart? Whatever it is, I couldn't say it even if I wanted to. My mouth has gone dry and needles prick the backs of my eyes, so without even forcing a smile, I focus back on my keyboard and say nothing at all.

48
jackson

MARGOT IS ACTING WEIRD, and I'm trying to figure out if it's just because we're around Rae and Matt.

Or if something is wrong.

She'll barely look at me, and it's making me want to grab her face and kiss her right here. She gets stuck in her head, and she shuts down. I hate seeing her withdraw in on herself.

"I'm starving," Rae says as she closes her notebook.

Matt looks between Margot and me. "Do you guys want to get something to eat?"

Margot shakes her head, still staring at her laptop screen. "No thanks. I have leftover Chipotle."

He looks at me.

"I ate with the band." It's a lie, but if I want to figure out what's going on with this girl, I need the two of them to leave.

Matt shrugs and gets to his feet, stretching his arms overhead. "Fair enough." He turns to Rae. "Where do you want to go?"

She raises an eyebrow at him. "Where do I want to go? Or where do I think we'd both enjoy?"

Matt rolls his eyes. "We can go to Chili's."

Rae smiles up at him and gathers her things. "I don't get why you don't like it. It's great, and it's cheap."

"It's cheap, but I wouldn't say it's great." The two of them say a quick goodbye before heading to the elevator.

I watch their backs until the metal doors close behind them and then look back at Margot, giving her my full attention. "What's up?"

She lifts her gaze, but only for a moment. "Nothing."

I stare at her, waiting for the truth. She chews the cap on her pen as she focuses on her screen. She's anxious.

It takes longer than I want it to, but eventually she glances at me again. When she sees I'm still looking at her, she says, "I hear you're dropping out after the semester ends."

I nod, swallowing hard. By the way she's looking at me now, I know I should have told her at my gig. There's a level of hurt behind her eyes, and I hate knowing I'm the one who put it there. I didn't tell her because I thought she wouldn't care, but as I look at her now, I realize I wasn't afraid she wouldn't care.

I was afraid she *would*.

Because if she asked me to stay, I think I might.

"You're mad," I say, studying her.

This makes her lift her head to look at me, and for the first time today, she looks a little more like herself. "I'm not mad at you." She stares at me for a long moment, and I'm on the edge of my seat, waiting for her to say more.

Part of me wishes I could dismiss whatever she's feeling right now, but I can't. Maybe it's because I want to hear her say I mean something to her.

Or maybe it's because she means something to me.

She wasn't supposed to. I thought this was something fleeting. But as I look at her, waiting to unlock the door she keeps her truth hidden behind, I can't help feeling like I'll be thinking about Margot for a very long time.

Finally, her shoulders drop in defeat. "I'm not. I think it's great you're following your dreams."

"But?"

Her eyes are back to being vulnerable again, and her lips part even though no words come out.

The air shifts between us, and I swear I can feel everything she wants to say but isn't. I know she would want this to turn into something if I wasn't leaving. I know she feels something for me. It was written all over her face this weekend at the gig. I want that Margot back—the one who wasn't hiding.

"Damn it, Margot," I say, leaning toward her with my elbows on my knees. "Would you just say what's on your mind for once?"

Her mouth snaps shut, and that wide-eyed stare turns into an all too familiar glare. "Why? It wouldn't change anything."

"It could." I don't know where I'm going with this. All I know is that I want her—as little or as much of her as she'll give me. We're only touring for a few months. She could come to some of the shows. Even if I don't see her while we're on tour, our best friends are dating, and it doesn't look like they'll break up any time soon. This isn't a goodbye, so why is she putting up walls?

"This"—she gestures between us—"would never work."

"Why?" I demand.

"Jackson," she says, and even when she's pissed, I like the way she says my name. "You don't even want to be with me."

"I didn't want to be with anyone."

She stares at me expectantly. "And now you do?"

"No." I don't want a relationship. I want *her*. "Why are you making this about me? You're the one who insisted us hooking up couldn't change anything."

Her cheeks flare. "I know, and I stand by what I said." She gets up to gather her things, but that doesn't stop her from shooting daggers at me. "This was a mistake. We have nothing to talk about."

I lean back in my seat. "That's how you feel?" It's not how she feels—it can't be.

She throws her bag over her shoulder. "Yeah, that's how I feel."

I stare at her, long and hard, trying to see through any cracks, but she's solid. The girl I could once read so well has figured out how to hide from me. It's a mask, and she wears it well, but I know she'll slip up eventually.

"Fine." I copy her cool tone as I rest my arm on the back of the couch. "Have it your way."

"I will," she snaps. "Good luck with everything," she adds before marching out of the common room.

I'm pissed, and I call bullshit on just about everything she said, but as she walks away, I run a hand through my hair, tugging at the roots. I'll figure out how she feels because whatever front she just put on for me isn't it. If anyone needs luck, it's her.

49
margot

"YOU'RE STILL COMING TONIGHT, RIGHT?" Rae asks as she straightens her hair in our room.

"To what?" I don't bother looking up from my computer. I know what she's referring to, but if I can act like I forgot about it, maybe she won't care that I stay home.

Out of the corner of my eye, I see her stop, pulling the flat iron away from her head. "Jackson's going away party." She says it like I should have marked it on my calendar, but as far as she's concerned Jackson and I are nothing more than neighbors.

"Good riddance," I say with a two-finger salute, still not looking at her. Somehow, I've managed to avoid Jackson for the last few days. I didn't use the gym on campus all semester, but I have used it every day since our conversation in the common room. I wish I could say breaking a sweat helped to clear my head, but it didn't. Instead of studying in the dorm, I've been studying in the library—a place where I definitely won't find him. We had to submit our final paper for English online, so I dodged a bullet there. Other than that, I think he may be avoiding me just as much because I haven't seen a trace of him.

And that somehow feels infuriating and like a relief at the same time. It will be easier once he's gone. At least then I won't be tempted to march over and make more mistakes with him. Even if I haven't seen him, knowing he might be on the other side of that door makes me restless. It's like my body knows he's in close range, and despite my better judgment, it still craves being touched by him.

He tried to tell me it could be different, but I know better. I'm not naïve enough to believe dating a guy in a band will end well. Most of my knowledge about the music industry may come from movies and TV shows, but it's enough to know that temptation and rock and roll go hand in hand. Jackson won't want to be tied down to anything once he's in a new city every night.

Not that he offered to date me. He doesn't want to date anyone.

He wants us to keep up our little friends-with-benefits deal while he's gone, but what's the benefit in that? It's like he expects everyone else's world to stop turning while he's on tour.

I should have known better than to get involved with a musician.

Rae stares at me. "I don't understand you two," she says with a shake of her head. She turns back to the mirror to finish her hair, and I'm grateful for it.

"There's nothing to understand."

"Then there's no reason for you not to come," she snaps, and when I look up, she's glaring at me through the reflection of the mirror.

I blink. "Are you actually mad?"

She shakes her head, grabbing another strand of hair and running it through the straightener. "I just think this is stupid. Nothing *that* terrible ever happened between you two. I know he's not your favorite person, but he's Matt's best friend." She pauses, locking her eyes on me through the reflection of the mirror again. "And you're mine." She huffs. "I just don't see why we can't all do things together without you two being so immature about it."

I bite the inside of my cheek, desperate to keep my secrets locked away. This is what it's come down to. I either have to come clean and tell her everything that's happened between Jackson and me, or I have to swallow my pride.

"Fine. I'll go to the party." If I tell her now, she'll never let this go, and I don't need it. Not when I'm so close to him being gone and forgetting any of this ever happened. I will not look like the girl who was left behind by the wanna-be rockstar. I can do one more party.

She lets out a laugh. "I don't want you to go if you're going to be miserable. I just don't see why it's such a big deal."

Closing my laptop, I gather my makeup bag from my drawer. "You're right. It's not a big deal," I say as I stand next to her to share the mirror. "It'll be fun."

She eyes me suspiciously. "You're sure?"

Not at all, but I hear myself say, "Yeah. I mean, there will be plenty of other people there, right?" Pausing before dabbing a little concealer under my eyes, I add, "And you'll be there, so it will be fine."

Her lips quirk into a smile. "Thank you," she says, and I bump her with my hip in return.

Then I try to make myself believe everything I just said.

"Hey," I say, pulling away from the mirror. "What's Matt going to do once Jackson leaves? Will he get another roommate?" I work hard to make sure my voice doesn't reveal this is a sore subject, and by the time the final word leaves my lips, I'm already depleted.

"He might," she says with a shrug. "I guess it depends on whether they need to house someone here or not. It's the middle of the year, so he'll have the room to himself unless someone transfers in or something."

"You're going to leave me to sleep here all alone, aren't you?" I tease.

Rae scoffs. "Yeah, because both of us stuck on a tiny twin-sized mattress is the dream." Lowering her gaze before putting on her mascara, she says, "I'll be sleeping here."

A sly smile pulls at the corners of my lips. "But you'll be over there to do other things more often?"

"Maybe," she admits with a laugh.

I guess Matt won't be lonely after all. I'll be the one sitting in my dorm alone with no best friend and no . . . whatever Jackson is to me.

Rae's watching me like she can tell I'm sad, so I say, "If anything, the room will look bigger without Jackson's shit everywhere."

It's the truth.

But the thought still leaves an ache in my chest.

"I'm going to miss him," she says, surprising me.

"You will?"

"Yeah." She shrugs. "He's always been around, and he's funny. I'm bummed for Matt, too. It'll be the hardest for him. He finally gets to live with his best friend, and now he's leaving."

"I mean, I'm sure they'll still talk all the time. He's only going on tour for a few months. This isn't goodbye forever." I feel like a hypocrite as soon as the words leave my lips. They're true. I know they're true, but for some reason, applying them to my situation with Jackson doesn't feel the same.

Matt will keep in touch with Jackson because they're childhood best friends.

I won't because I'm just the girl he casually slept with a few times.

Once Rae and I are dressed and ready to go, she looks me up and down. "Damn, for someone who didn't want to go out tonight, you sure did pull out all the stops."

"I did?" I ask, looking down at myself. I'm wearing baggy, ripped jeans, boots, and a button-down sweater that dips at the top.

She nods. "That red lip? You're giving off Jessica Rabbit vibes."

Reaching for my purse, I let out a laugh. "I'm not even wearing red."

"I'm just saying," she says, waving a hand in my direction. "This is very much a look that could break some hearts."

A smile pulls at my lips, but I try to hide it. "I don't want to break anyone's heart."

I just want the guy who's leaving to notice me.

50
jackson

MARGOT JUST GOT HERE, and holy fuck.

I thought about trying to make her jealous. It wouldn't be hard. She admitted to getting jealous at the show. I figured I'd find a girl willing to talk to me and lay it on a little thick. I thought she'd get mad, and I'd be able to call her out on her bluff.

But now?

I nearly choked on my drink as soon as she walked in here, and I'm still not sure if my jaw is lying on the floor at my feet. Forget making her jealous. All I care about is making her look my way.

Because she hasn't yet, and it's killing me.

I finish off my beer and pour myself another from the pitcher. The Irish pub in town is notorious for not checking IDs, so this was the obvious place for a going away party. It doesn't matter that the floors are always sticky and the place reeks of fried food. They give us booze, so we give them money.

It was Izzy's idea to come here. Matt and Rae mentioned throwing me a party, which I told them wasn't necessary. Then

Izzy heard about it and took over completely. For the past three days, she asked me for my favorite color at least twelve times. My only response was, "No balloons."

There are balloons. She went with red, blue, and black. So, now it looks like a Spiderman-themed birthday party for a ten-year-old.

Matt gets up from the table to greet Rae, and I follow because I'm lost, stupid, and three beers in.

And my God, she's pretty.

My knuckles turn white as I grip the glass in my hand. I was relaxed a second ago, but that was before I saw her. I've missed her the past few days, but I've mostly been with the band. With finals out of the way, there wasn't much of a reason to hang around campus—especially with Margot avoiding me like the plague.

Maybe that was better, though. Because as much as I've missed her, nothing compares to the relentless ache seeing her is giving me now. I want to pull her to my side and kiss her. I want her to wrap her arms around me and look up at me with those warm, mahogany eyes like she did at my gig last weekend. I want to make her smile again.

"Hey," she says.

"Hey," I say, trying to recover from staring at her. "You look—"

Her eyes widen, and I catch myself before accidentally complimenting her in front of Rae and Matt. Rae looks like she's already caught on, though. She lifts her brow, and I can't help wondering what she's thinking.

I blink, snapping out of my Margo-induced daze.

Why do I care? Why does it matter if Rae and Matt know I like Margot?

It doesn't.

I'm leaving. After this weekend, Margot won't be the girl

across the hall anymore, and if I want her to be anything at all, I need to do something about it.

"You look incredible," I say with more conviction.

Margot's eyes widen again, but this time it's not a warning. Surprise is written clearly in them before they dart to Rae. When she looks my way again, her cheeks are pink. Her response either means she liked what I said, or she's about to give me hell for it.

Not sure which one yet.

Rae's mouth pulls upward. "She does, doesn't she?" Margot glares at her, but Rae doesn't seem to care. "She wasn't even going to come tonight, but she made sure she looked amazing by the time we left." Her eyebrows lift at Margot, challenging her.

All I can focus on is the first part. "You didn't plan on coming?" I ask, more surprised than I should be. She's pissed at me. I get that. But she means something to me, and I figured I meant something to her. Did she plan on letting me move out this weekend without saying goodbye?

As soon as the thought hits me, I know that's exactly what her plan was.

Margot shrugs—a noncommittal answer to keep her from being honest.

"Give me your phone," I say, holding out my hand.

She stares at me with a furrowed brow. "No."

"Damn it, Margot. Give me your phone." My eyes jump to Rae for help, but she's getting way too much enjoyment out of this. Whatever suspicions she has about Margot and me match what's happening, and from the looks of things, she couldn't be happier.

Matt, on the other hand, watches the three of us—Rae included—with confusion plastered on his face.

"No," Margot says with more conviction, her eyes narrowed.

She can glare at me all she wants, but I'm not leaving without giving her my number. I'm smart enough to know she won't give me hers, so I don't bother asking. I've never needed her number until now. We've seen each other almost every day this semester, and if I ever wanted to get a hold of her, all I had to do was walk across the hall and knock on her door.

That all changes now.

I'll be traveling the country, and she'll be here, probably cursing my name.

"Damn it," I mutter, stepping toward the bar and grabbing a cocktail napkin. I snatch a pen from where someone recently signed for their tab. Looking back at Margot, I say, "You're a real piece of work, you know that?" before scribbling my number on the paper.

"I don't want your number, Jackson," she says through gritted teeth as she stomps over.

Ignoring her, I reach around and tuck the napkin in her back pocket, giving her a pat on the ass when I'm done. "Just in case."

Heat flares on her cheeks, and this time, I know it's definitely because she wants to kick my ass—or worse. She's at a loss for words, just standing in front of me, gaping. She's going to kill me after that. Turning my back on her, I order a whiskey from the bartender. I have a feeling I'll need something stronger than beer tonight.

51
margot

I'M A PIECE OF WORK? He's the one openly flirting with me when we're supposed to make sure Matt and Rae never find out about us. We're supposed to brush whatever happened between us under the rug.

No. Scratch that.

We're supposed to put whatever happened between us into a wooden chest, chain it up, and drop it into the ocean. I clench my fists and glare at the back of his head as he orders a drink from the bar.

For him, maybe it is nothing. He's the one who's leaving. He won't have to answer questions from everyone, but I will. Rae is already eyeing me and mouthing, "What was that?"

Shaking my head, I tell her I'll be back and head for the bathroom. There's a line for the stalls, so I stand near the sink and try to collect myself.

Pulling the paper from my back pocket, I stare down at the number like it has already wronged me. His handwriting is as sloppy as he keeps his room. Should I throw it in the trash or flush it down the toilet?

Then I get a better idea.

Reaching into my cross-body purse, I uncap an old lipstick and start writing on the bathroom mirror.

This asshole

I pause. What the hell am I doing? Is this what Jackson does to me? Can I really let a guy reduce me to defacing public bathrooms? What the hell would I even write? *This asshole made me fall for him* doesn't exactly pack a punch, but that's exactly why I'm angry, isn't it? He made it clear he didn't want anything. His goal was to leave this all behind, but I never thought I'd care. I never thought he'd infiltrate every cell of my body and reprogram them under his control.

The group of girls standing behind me have gone from saying things like, "I love your shoes!" and "Where did you get your necklace? It's the cutest!" to complete silence.

Daring to look over my shoulder, I find four equally stunning sets of eyes staring at me.

"What did he do?" a dark-haired girl asks.

"He . . ."

"Is he one of those pushy assholes who insists on giving you his number?" A blonde standing next to her spits with disgust as she stares at the paper in my hand.

I mean, she's not *totally* wrong. I nod. "Yes. That."

They all shake their heads and roll their eyes as a chorus of phrases like, "Men," and "Do they think we don't know what we want?" spill from their lips.

My eyes dart between them, trying to keep up, until one girl who has had her eyes set on my half-written message says, "Make him spit on cats."

I choke back a laugh. "What?"

She nods toward the mirror with complete confidence. "Seriously, make him spit on cats."

"Make him . . . ?"

She cocks an eyebrow. "Would *you* want to date someone who spits on cats?"

"Of course not," I answer quickly.

"Yeah," the first dark-haired girl next to her agrees. "That will be good."

"Um," I hesitate, "Maybe I should just—" I point my thumb over my shoulder, ready to make my exit.

"No, don't back down!" The blonde practically shrieks.

I stare at these girls I don't know in the slightest, and for whatever reason, the power of the public restroom is making it impossible to let them down. "Okay . . ." I say and turn back to the mirror, finishing my note.

This asshole spits on cats.

Holding the paper in one hand, I copy the number onto the mirror with the other. Stepping back, I look at my work before turning back to the girls, but they already have their phones out, frantically typing a message as they glance up at the number on the mirror.

Leaving the bathroom, I almost crash into someone and stagger backward.

"Whoa!" Rae says, bracing herself against me. Her grip tightens around my arms. "I was looking for you. You have to tell me what that was about."

"What what was about?" I ask.

She purses her lips, unimpressed with my answer. "Jackson."

Forcing a laugh, I push past her. "Nothing." Looking over my shoulder, I add, "I need a drink. Want one?" Without waiting for her to answer, I scan the bar for Jackson. He's talking to Matt where I left him, so I go to the bartender on the opposite end.

I didn't plan on drinking tonight. I don't even have a fake ID, but I wasn't expecting Jackson to tap my ass in front of everyone, either.

My heart pounds as I lean over the bar to be heard above the crowd. "Can I get a rum and Coke?" I ask and wonder if I sound as young as this situation makes me feel.

The way the bartender lets his eyes trail over me means he's either trying to guess my age or he's checking me out. Both possibilities make me regret coming over here.

It isn't until he settles on my chest that I realize it's the latter. It takes everything in me not to pull up the dipping neckline of my sweater, but I leave it.

"Make that two," Rae says as she squeezes into the spot next to me. Turning to face me, she says, "You're not telling me something."

The bartender seems mildly put off that we were interrupted but goes to get our drinks. "It's nothing."

She frowns. "So? Even if it's nothing, since when do you hide things from me?"

My chest aches. I never meant for her to feel like I was hiding things from her. I just didn't want her to get her hopes up. My shoulders sag as I look at her wounded expression. "Nothing is going on between Jackson and me."

"He seemed pretty insistent on giving you his number," she points out.

The bartender sets down our drinks, and I take a sip before instantly pulling back. The burn hits me in the chest, and I have to suppress a cough.

Rae still hasn't touched hers. She's watching me carefully, waiting for me to come clean.

"And he kissed you a few weeks ago," she adds when I don't answer.

"To make me mad," I deflect.

Rae rolls her eyes. "That doesn't make sense. Who does that?" Leveling with me, she says, "He kissed you because he wanted to kiss you, and now he wants you to have his phone number, so what's the holdup?"

I play with the straw in my cup. "He's leaving. He wants to

go on tour with his band." I give her a pointed look. "As he should." My eyes drift back to my drink. "And I . . ." Shaking my head, I shrug. "I don't know what I want."

It's a lie. I know I want him, but I also know that starting a long-distance relationship is stupid. If a couple has been together for a while and then has to part ways, I understand trying to make it work. But trying to establish any type of relationship with someone touring in a rock band—where he'll have new girls at his feet every night—is a different story.

I'm snapped out of my thoughts when Rae slaps the counter playfully. "You should have told me! The four of us could have hung out all semester."

Taking another sip of my drink, I grimace. "That's why I *didn't* tell you."

Her face falls. "What? Why?"

I give her a knowing look. "Come on. You and Matt are a perfect couple, and Jackson and I are . . ." I shrug. "Nothing."

"How many times were you two 'nothing?'" she asks with a lift of her brow.

I wince. "A few."

"Margot!" She gapes at me and shakes her head. "You should have told me!"

"I know," I groan, finally surrendering. "I'm sorry. I just didn't want you to get your hopes up. I didn't want things to be awkward whenever it inevitably ended."

The corner of her mouth lifts, and her eyes settle on something behind me. "Well," she nods to whatever she's looking at. "He looks like he still has a few things he'd like to say to you."

Bracing myself, I look over my shoulder to find Jackson headed straight for us with his phone in hand.

Shit.

52
jackson

"DO you want to tell me why I've gotten six text messages telling me I'm a piece of shit and to leave cats alone?" I lean my forearms on the bar top next to Margot. I know she's behind this—she has to be.

Turning away from Rae, she stares up at me with wide, deceivingly innocent eyes. "No."

My phone lights up in my hand, and I set it on the counter. "Make that seven."

Rae grins at us, which can only mean one thing.

Margot told her.

I don't know how much or how little, but Rae knows something happened between us. Clearing her throat, she says, "It looks like Matt needs me. I'll see you later."

Margot turns to look at her friend, and Rae's eyes bulge at Margot before she steps away.

She seems to take a moment to compose herself before turning to face me, taking a long sip of her drink in the process.

I raise my eyebrows. "Well?"

"I don't know what you're talking about." She takes

another sip. Turning to the bartender, she signals for another, and he calls out, "Sure thing, sweetheart."

I stare at the bartender as he gives her a wink. Jesus. Keith and now this guy?

Shifting my attention back to her, I say, "I think you know exactly what I'm talking about." The pub is packed now, and I'm close enough to smell her strawberry shampoo. It makes me want to reach out and touch her.

Kiss her.

Hell, there are a lot of things I'd like to do to her.

My phone lights up again as another scathing text comes in. "I only see one problem with this," I say, looking down at my phone.

The corners of her lips lift, but she keeps the straw in her mouth, downing her drink. "And what's that?"

She's wearing more makeup than she usually does, but I can still faintly make out her freckles. "None of these numbers are yours."

Her smirk fades, and she pulls the straw from her mouth to look up at me. "I'm not giving you my number, Jackson."

"Why?" I don't understand why she's being like this. Why is she so determined to stay away from me?

A frown pulls at her lips. "Because you don't need it."

"Isn't that up to me?"

The bartender sets a full glass down in front of her, and she quickly moves her straw over and starts sipping. At this rate, she'll be wasted within the hour. Looking down at the drink in her hands, she says, "No," before taking another sip.

She's impossible. Frustration laces my voice when I ask, "Why are you being like this?"

I want her to crack and tell me the truth, but nothing in her expression falters. She's perfected her mask. "Why are *you* being like this? You're about to be on stage every night, and I'll be here. You don't owe me anything just because we slept together. We're both single, and that's the end of it."

"So, what?" I say, the bite in my voice coming out more than I meant. "Why does it have to be all or nothing with you? When I was living across the hall, you were fine with casual, but now that I'm leaving, we can't even have each other's phone numbers? It doesn't make sense."

"You don't get it," she snaps, and I swear half her drink is already missing. "We don't need to stay in touch. It won't be good for either of us. And we don't need to have this conversation. What we did means nothing. *We're* nothing."

My jaw ticks. "You're sure that's what you want?"

"Yes, Jackson. It's what I want." There's so much clarity behind her eyes as she says the words. It's like she hasn't had a drop of alcohol all night, and I can't help feeling like I know she means them.

I don't understand it.

But I know she means it.

I hold her gaze, waiting—*hoping* she'll crack, but she doesn't. She pins me with her unwavering stare. My stomach drops and a sense of hopelessness washes over me. I've given this my best shot, and I don't think I've ever failed so miserably at anything.

My phone lights up two more times on the bar, and I snatch it, jamming it into my pocket. "Okay. Have it your way."

Everyone is getting sloppy around me, but I've been nursing my same drink all night. Margot just started her fifth. Three guys have tried to flirt with her—the bartender and two guys I've never seen. She's still talking to one of them now.

She's drunk.

She's a fun drunk, but she's definitely drunk.

Sometimes we cross paths, but for most of the night, she seems to want to stay as far away from me as possible. I lock eyes with her for the millionth time tonight, and her cheeks flare before she turns and gives her full attention back to her latest admirer.

Figures.

For someone who wants nothing to do with me, she sure knows how to piss me off. Matt takes a seat next to me, but I can't tear my eyes away from her. I can feel him watching me, though. I'm sure I look as pathetic as I feel.

"You'll meet a lot of girls on tour, you know," he says as he scratches the side of his head and sets his beer down on the table in front of us.

So much for a distraction. Margot giggles with Bachelor Number Three about God knows what, and I take a sip of my warm beer. "Yeah."

He's right, but it doesn't make me feel better. Other girls aren't Margot. No one has ever made me feel the way she did at my gig last weekend. Fully accepted and supported. Fuck, she made me feel loved, and even though I know she doesn't love me—not really—I'm not ready to walk away from it yet.

"Want help packing your car?"

This makes me look at him. He's a better friend than I deserve. I should be focused on the people in my life who actually want something to do with me. "Yeah, that would be great. I'm mostly packed, I just have to bring a few things down tomorrow morning."

He squeezes my shoulder. "You're touring in a band. Don't worry about Margot."

A smile comes to my lips, but at the sound of her name, I can't fight the urge to look at her. I bring my eyes back to where I saw her last and freeze.

She's gone.

She and that random guy are fucking gone.

"Where the hell did she go?" I say as I set my drink down.

Matt's still sitting next to me when he asks, "Who?"

Tearing my eyes away from the crowded room, I look back at him long enough to say, "Margot."

Unconcerned, he shrugs. "I don't know. She was just there a second ago. I'm sure she's fine."

He's probably right. And if she didn't have too much to drink tonight, I probably wouldn't look for her. But I walk away without answering, scanning the room for any sign of the redhead who seems to invade my every thought.

"Margot was just talking to that guy over here," I say to Izzy and Jess, interrupting their conversation.

"Yeah?" Jess asks, looking up at me with a furrowed brow.

My phone buzzes in my pocket, and I check it, thinking for some stupid reason it might be Margot, but it's just another pissed-off cat text.

If she wasn't so stubborn and just gave me her phone number, I could text her. I'd ask if she was okay, and she could answer.

Problem solved.

But instead, I'm left with the two girls in front of me. "And where did she go?"

Izzy and Jess look at each other, equally confused. This time Izzy answers, "I think she said that guy was taking her somewhere to talk?"

"Taking her somewhere?" I ask, hoping I heard her wrong.

Jess watches me like I'm having a mental breakdown. Honestly, I might as well be. "Yeah . . . but I don't think she meant leaving the bar. What's the problem?"

I run a hand over my face before ignoring her question and ask, "Where did they go?"

Izzy shrugs. "I don't know." She looks around the bar. "They have to be around here somewhere."

But I look around the bar, too.

And I don't see them.

Pushing past the crowd, I fight my way to the bar. "Hey," I say to the bartender that was gawking at Margot all night. He looks up, and I add, "The gorgeous redhead. Is her tab still open?"

"Oh, Margot?" he asks, and I try to ignore how much it annoys me that he knows her name.

I nod.

"The guy she was with closed the tab for her."

"Damn it," I slam both hands down at the bar before adding a quick "Thanks," as an afterthought and booking it out of the bar.

There aren't many people in the parking lot, so it doesn't take long for me to see them. Some guy walks with Margot as she laughs at whatever he's whispering in her ear.

And before I can think about what I'm doing, I'm headed straight for them.

53
margot

I'M TRYING to reach for the door handle of the car, but I'm buckled over with laughter. I don't think I've ever met someone so funny.

"Whoa," he says, steadying me. "Here. Let me get that."

Turning to look at him, I feign a gasp. "That's so nice of you."

With one hand still around my waist, he pulls back to look at me. "I'm always nice." Opening the door, he starts to help me inside. Maybe this is what I need. I need a fun night with a nice, funny guy to make me forget about all things Jackson.

"Margot!"

I freeze because I know that voice. I try to peer over the shoulder blocking my view, but I can't see him from here.

"You've got to be kidding me." The guy I'm with mutters, and he sounds a little less nice and a little less funny now.

It isn't until Jackson jogs up to the car and pulls me to him that I can see him clearly. The sudden movement makes me fall into him, and I breathe in the familiar scent of his clean clothes. It's like all I have to do is inhale and my entire body hums in approval. I brace my hands on his chest, my fingertips taking advantage of being this close to him and running over the muscles of his torso.

I have no self-control.

Everything inside me wants to climb him. Right here. Right now. God, just *look* at him. The stern line of his jaw, the sharpness behind his eyes, the way his hair curls at the base of his neck. I reach up, tempted to run my fingers through his hair until a tiny voice in the back of my mind scolds me.

We need a clean break.

My hand freezes mid-air, and Jackson gives me a sideways glance. He's looking at me like there's something very wrong with me, and I snatch my hand back.

Yes, something is definitely wrong with me.

Jackson looks at my new friend and demands, "What the hell are you doing?"

"Look at her. She's wasted. I'm taking her home."

"Hey!" I say, taking offense to that.

Jackson shakes his head, gripping me tighter. "Absolutely fucking not."

As he tightens his hold, a soft, "Hmm" leaves my lips and I lean into him. He glances down at me with concern and my cheeks flush.

Damn it. I'm like a cat in heat around him.

"Seriously, man? She obviously needs to go home."

Steadying my shoulders, Jackson turns me to face him and takes my face in his hands. His gray-blue eyes are darker now. It's not just a storm brewing behind them—it's a hurricane. "Margot," he says calmly. "I'm taking you home."

"Hmm," I hum happily, loving how it feels to be this close to him.

Loving how it feels to be touched by him.

So much for holding onto my anger.

"Look, I don't know who you are, but we have plans."

Jackson breaks his gaze from mine to say, "You don't need

to know who I am." Annoyance ripples through him before he focuses his attention back on me. "Let's go home. Okay, Margot?"

"Okay," I answer breathlessly. Between the alcohol and his touch, I can barely think straight, let alone speak. I thought I needed a fun night with a stranger, but now that Jackson is in front of me, all I want is him. It's *always* him.

Without another word, Jackson pulls me to him and walks us toward his car. The guy I was with says something behind us, but Jackson just smooths my hair back and kisses the side of my head. "I leave you alone for five fucking minutes, and you almost get a ride home with some asshole." He shakes his head disapprovingly, but it only makes me smile.

When we reach his car, Jackson helps me into the seat and buckles my seatbelt for me. He's gentle and sweet, and when he shuts the door and walks around the front, my eyes track him the entire way. He gets in and pauses before putting the key in the ignition. "Are you okay?"

I guess my staring wasn't subtle.

Leaning my head back against the seat, a soft, "Mm-hmm," leaves my lips. I am okay. I am beyond okay. Because he's here and being around him somehow makes everything okay—even the fact that he's leaving soon.

Jackson lets out a breath of laughter. "Let's get you home, Red."

The nickname makes a small smile come to my lips. "Okay."

As we drive, Jackson goes on about how he can't believe I almost left, but I just listen. I let the sound of his voice wash over me for the short drive back to campus, finding comfort in all of it.

The dorm is quiet when we get back—everyone is likely asleep or still at the bar. Jackson takes my keys to unlock my door, and as soon as I step inside, I take off my jeans and kick them toward the closet. I can't wear jeans when I'm drunk. They're the most uncomfortable piece of clothing. I consider taking my sweater off too, but it's loose enough. It can stay.

Jackson clears his throat, and I look over my shoulder at him. His eyes jump from my pink lace underwear to my face, and I recognize the flash of hunger in them. "Do you need anything?" His back is against my desk, his hands gripping the edge, and I can't stop myself from looking him up and down.

He's wearing dark jeans, with a gray shirt and a black jacket.

And he looks good.

Really good.

"Are you going back to the party?" I ask, ignoring his question.

He shakes his head. "No. I'll call it a night."

I nod, taking a step toward him. It's probably how many drinks I've had, but, right now, I don't care that he made me angry earlier.

I don't care that he didn't tell me he was leaving sooner.

I don't even care that he's leaving at all.

Right now, all I know is that I want him. The damage is already done, right? We've already slept together. I'll already miss him when he leaves. One more night with him won't change any of that.

"Why didn't you want that guy to drive me?"

He scoffs, but his eyes track my movement as I take a step closer. "Because I didn't trust him."

"And?" I ask, taking another step.

"And I wanted to make sure you were okay," he says, watching me carefully.

By the time I take my third step, I'm standing right in front of him. "Because?" I ask, my voice barely audible.

Jackson's gaze hardens, his eyes dipping to my mouth before meeting my stare again. "You know why."

I let my fingers lightly graze over his T-shirt, feeling the hard lines of the muscles underneath, and he sucks in a breath.

God, I love the way he responds to me.

Pushing myself onto my toes, I press my lips to his neck, leaving a trail of open-mouthed kisses. A low, guttural sound leaves his throat, making me clench his shirt tighter. He says, "We shouldn't," but instead of finishing his thought, he tilts his head to give me more access. Working my way up, my teeth nip at his ear, making him curse my name.

Dropping back onto my heels, I look down at his hands. His knuckles are white as he grips the desk behind him. He hasn't made a move to touch me, but it looks like holding back is taking a toll on him.

I don't want him to hold back.

My eyes trail over his body, and I sink down until I'm kneeling in front of him.

"Margot," he says, his voice strained. I look up at him, but as soon as my eyes lift to meet his, he mutters, "Fuck," and shakes his head like just seeing me on my knees in front of him is too much.

My heart thuds in my chest as I run my fingers over the tight bulge of his jeans.

I want to taste him.

I want him to lose control.

I want to watch him come undone as he grips the back of my head and thrusts into my mouth.

"Margot," he rasps.

Reaching for the button of his jeans, I ask, "Hmm?" as I unclasp and unzip. Moving the denim out of the way, I gently kiss him through his briefs, and his length twitches in response. His reaction brings a twinge of a smile to my lips, and I work my way from his base to the tip, leaving teasing kisses every step of the way.

Peeking up at him, I see his head has fallen forward, those

gray-blue eyes meeting mine. "Fuck, that feels good," he mutters. "But . . ."

"But?" I ask, letting my tongue tease him over his briefs.

He groans before squeezing his eyes shut. "No," he says with a shake of his head.

I sit back on my heels. "No?"

Jackson stares at the ceiling like he's trying to gather his self-control. With another shake of his head, he refastens his pants. "I can't."

I nearly stumble trying to get to my feet too fast. "Seriously?"

He runs a frustrated hand over his face. "You don't want this, Margot. You haven't talked to me in days, you didn't want to come to the party tonight, and you won't even give me your fucking phone number." That last one comes out with an exasperated outstretched arm. "And now . . ." He stares at me with wide eyes before shaking his head in disbelief. "Now you want to—" Pushing off from the desk, he rubs both hands over his face as he steps away from me. "Jesus Christ."

I march after him. "What does it matter? You're leaving!"

Those storm-like eyes settle on me, and I shrink under the intensity of his stare. His voice is a deathly whisper when he says, "What does it matter?" Turning to face me head-on, he takes a step toward me. "It matters because I don't want this for us." He pins me with his stare. "It matters because I care." Grabbing my face in his hands, his eyes search mine as he says, "It matters because even though you have no problem ending this—even though I know you're not mine . . ." His voice trails, his gaze dipping to my mouth before he meets my wide-eyed stare again. With more conviction, he starts over. "Even though I know you're not mine, I've somehow become yours." Brushing his thumb over my cheek, he shakes his head. "I don't know how it happened, and I might not like it, but I am completely and totally yours, Margot." My lips part as I stare up at him, and he tucks a loose strand of hair behind my ear before he goes on to say, "And I can't handle the possibility of you waking up tomorrow morning thinking I took advantage of you." He shakes his head, his eyes never leaving mine. "I won't."

My mouth opens, but I can't find any words.

He's waiting for me to say something. I *want* to say something, but my brain is sluggish, and I feel a little like this might be a dream.

A twinge of a frown crosses his lips, the line between his brows deepening. Opening his mouth, he looks like he's about to say something, but then he changes his mind. Taking a step away from me, he dips his chin. "Goodnight, Margot."

With that, he turns and walks toward the door, and the sight makes it harder to breathe. I try to stay still, but I take an unsure step forward nonetheless. Tears sting my eyes as the panic inside me spikes with every step he takes.

54
jackson

WELL, there it is. I laid all my cards on the table, and she had nothing to say about it. Not a damn word. My hand is on the door handle when I hear her say my name. Letting out a breath, I pause to look back at her.

"I'm scared," she says quietly like it's her biggest secret.

My hand lets go of the door, and I turn to face her. "Of what?"

"Um," she says to buy time as she wrings her hands in front of her. Staring down at her fingers, she says, "You," before quickly adding, "And me." Her eyes jump up to meet mine as she nods to herself. "Mostly me."

With a furrowed brow, I take a step toward her, relieved that she's finally said something. "What do you mean?"

Glancing up at me again, she turns on her heels before taking a hard seat on her bed. "I like you."

She says it like it's a bad thing, but it's probably my favorite thing she's ever said. Tilting my head, I walk to the bed and take a seat next to her, trying to ignore the swollen feeling of hope in my chest. "But?"

Her eyes narrow. "But you're leaving." A moment later her

eyes widen, and she turns to face me. "And you *should* leave. I meant it when I said this is an incredible opportunity." Putting a hand on my arm, she adds, "You're talented, and you deserve this."

My mouth quirks at the compliment. "But?" I ask again, waiting for the other shoe to drop.

Margot sighs, letting her drunken, heavy head fall against my shoulder. I want to smooth down her hair and cradle her face in my hands, but I'm too afraid she'll stop talking. I sit completely still, my heart pounding and chest aching as I wait for her to say more.

She finally groans. "But I know myself, and I don't think I can keep this going while you're gone." Looking up at me, she props her chin on my shoulder and frowns. "I think I'll get jealous and insecure. And in the end, it will probably make me crazy."

My mouth twitches into a smile as I relax and smooth some of her hair away from her face. "Or you might not feel any of those things."

"And *you*," she says, ignoring my comment. "You'll be faced with all sorts of temptation and new things, and you won't want me." She lets out a sigh. "I'll bore you."

A low laugh escapes me. "You could never bore me."

She scoffs as she sits up straight, unimpressed with my answer. Putting her head down on her pillow, she hugs it as she mutters, "Trying to make anything work under these circumstances would be dumb."

So much of what she's saying is right, but I still want to fight her on all of it. I'm not ready to walk away from this. I wish she would at least let me try.

Margot yawns, and I jump to my feet, kneeling in front of her because I know my time is almost up. She'll pass out soon, and I have more I need to say—a lot more.

"Margot."

She lifts her brow, but her eyes are heavy. If I say anything to her, she'll forget it by tomorrow morning. Getting up, I head over to her desk and find paper and a pen. I write my number again since I'm pretty sure she threw the first one away, and then I keep writing.

"Are you writing me a note?" Her groggy voice asks, and I look over my shoulder to find her fighting to stay awake.

"Yes, I'm writing you a note."

"Make sure you include that stuff about you being hopelessly mine," she mumbles, pointing a sleepy finger at the paper.

I let out a breath of laughter as I shake my head. "Go to sleep, Red."

She lets out a light laugh, but that's the last sound she makes. When I've finished writing everything I need to say, I look back to find her completely passed out. Her hair is wild around her perfect face, and I gently brush a strand away from her forehead. She stirs but doesn't wake. Leaning down, I kiss the side of her head. "Bye, Margot."

With each step toward the door, my shoes feel like they're filled with lead. I don't want to leave her. I don't want this to be it between us, but the rest is up to her. I open the door, careful not to make a sound, and before I close it, I look back at her. My chest aches, and when I shut the door behind me, I miss the girl I haven't even left yet.

55
margot

I LET OUT a groan as I roll over. The light pouring into my room might as well be made of shards of glass, and I squint against the glare. I should have picked the bed furthest from the window—or at least invested in some blackout curtains.

My head is *killing* me.

What was the bartender's name last night? Did he even tell me his name? Whoever he is, he's on my list. I've never been this hungover. Bits and pieces of last night flash before my eyes. Everything before the rum comes to me clearly.

Jackson giving me his phone number.

Telling Rae about sleeping with him.

Writing his number on the bathroom mirror.

It's the stuff that happened after the rum that's a little harder to pinpoint. I think I drank enough to last me a lifetime. Even the thought of the stuff makes me nauseous. Foggy pieces of last night's puzzle float in the deepest corners of my mind. Trying to pull them to the forefront, I squint my eyes shut, summoning all of my mental strength.

Izzy and Jess telling me about their plans for the holidays.

Matt making me laugh over a stupid joke I can't remember.

A cute guy flirting with me.

Jackson pulling me away from that cute guy.

Jackson driving me home.

Jackson with his pants unzipped.

Jackson.

Jackson.

Jackson.

Jolting upright, my eyes fly open. The sudden rush of movement makes my head fall into my hands, and I wish the room would stop spinning.

He was here.

Jackson was here, in my room, and I have no idea how much or how little we did.

Why am I so stupid when it comes to this guy?

Half of me wants to remember, but the other half is too afraid of what I'll find. My eyes catch on a piece of paper on my bedside table, and I scramble to reach for it, ignoring the feeling of my head spinning afterward. I squint one eye shut to ease the double-vision and start reading.

> *Margot,*
>
> *Before you overthink everything, we didn't have sex. You tried, but I stopped you from doing anything stupid. You don't have to thank me. The memory of you on your knees in front of me is all the thanks I need.*
>
> *I'm giving you my number again. For the love of God, keep it away from your tribe of cat-loving Taylor Swift fans. I'm still getting messages.*
>
> *Here's what's going to happen.*

You're going to text me.

I'm going to leave a ticket for you. Come to the Orlando show on January 27. I'll put the info below.

Take some Advil.

Jackson

January? Did I agree to go to one of his shows last night? Why would I do that, and what does it mean?

I stare at the page in my hands, reading and rereading the note as I try to make sense of everything. Letting the paper fall to my lap, I drop my head in my hands again. I need to remember what happened last night, but it's all foggy—like watching the night unfold through a clouded lens.

My fingers gently tap against my forehead like they're trying to unlock the code.

Think. Think. Think.

Jackson standing at my desk.

Kissing his neck.

Opening his pants just enough to . . . Oh, God.

I groan and rub the heel of my palm against my forehead like I can wash away the embarrassment.

Telling me no.

Holding my face in his hands.

Those eyes making me feel like they could see into my soul.

He's mine.

He's mine.

He's mine.

Sucking in a breath of air, I lift my head and look around the room. Rae is still asleep in her bed, so I try not to make too much noise as I reach for my phone.

10:17 a.m.

Getting to my feet, I squint my eyes shut when my head

throbs. My hand reaches for my desk to brace myself and stop the room from spinning. Taking another steadying breath, I cross the room, massaging my temple with one hand to try and ease my headache.

I reach for the door handle, careful to unlatch it quietly. The fluorescent lights of the hallway make me want to die, but I try to hide it when I see Matt rounding the corner.

"Hey," I say, my voice rough with sleep. "Rae is still asleep."

He points to his dorm. "I'm about to go back to bed. I was just helping Jackson take some of his stuff down."

I pause. "Where is he?" I'm not sure if I'm ready to face him after last night. My head is still swarming with embarrassment and regret.

"He just left," Matt says, watching for my reaction.

Trying to hide the way those three words hit me because it suddenly feels like I'm free falling into nothing, I swallow. He left, and if he said goodbye, I don't even remember it. My eyes sting, and I bite the inside of my cheek to keep the tears at bay. I nod. "Right. Of course."

Holding up both hands, he says, "He told me you two worked everything out last night."

I force a laugh. "Yeah. We did . . . I think." Nodding toward his dorm, I add, "Get some sleep. I'll see you later."

He rubs the back of his neck as he opens the door. "See you, Margot." As he turns away, the corners of his mouth dip, and I can only imagine how the empty half of his room must make him feel. Before he closes the door, I catch a glimpse. Jackson's usual mess is gone. Even the blue plastic mattress is visible with no sheets. The sight hits me in the chest, and I quickly look away.

He left.

Heading back into my room, I quietly sit back on my bed and pick up the note again. His handwriting is still terrible, but

I love that he left this for me. My eyes run over the page, reading the same words three more times. Hugging my knees to my chest, I set the note on my bed, my eyes locking onto the ten digits at the top of the page. The sight brings a fresh ache to my chest. Because as much as I want to text him, I can't fight the feeling that Jackson and I are a bad idea.

56
jackson

MY CAR'S tires take me in the direction of home, and I try not to think about how much I don't want to go.

Go on tour? Sure.

But home? Home is a different story. I'll have to face my dad for the first time in weeks, and it will only be more awkward since he kicked me out on Thanksgiving. If my dad could have it his way, I'm sure he'd rather I not be there for Christmas. He's not the one who invited me—Mom is. So, I have a feeling this is her way of putting her foot down, which only makes me less eager to go.

The guys said we can get together after the new year. That's just over two weeks. Two weeks with my parents, and I'll be back on track.

My hands grip the steering wheel tighter at the thought.

Things will be easier once Matt is back home with his parents, too. Then I'll at least have somewhere else to go. Matt wants to spend as much time with Rae as possible before they part ways for the holidays, and I don't blame him. If I could have things my way, I'd probably want to spend as much time with Margot. She was still asleep when I left this morning. I thought about waking her, but she needs to sleep off the hangover she's bound to wake up with.

And I'm not sure how much she remembers.

Margot has a way of keeping me on my toes, that's for sure. Even though she told me she likes me, who knows what she's feeling this morning.

That's another reason I wanted to leave. I don't want to give her a chance to tell me no. If she goes back to hating my guts, I'd feel like I ruined something. At least this way, we ended things on good terms. We ended things with an open door, and I'm leaving before she has the chance to shut it.

I barely have my foot on the gas pedal as I coast through my neighborhood. As I inch closer to my parents' house, I wish all four of my tires would just fall off like some type of cartoon.

It isn't until someone drives up behind me that I'm forced to hit the gas. Turning onto the all too familiar dead-end street, I pull into the driveway. I can't delay this any longer. Staring up at the house I grew up in, I try to get a handle on everything I'm feeling. It's a Saturday, so they'll both be home. My mom knows I'm coming home, but even though she swears my dad is on board, I'm not so sure.

The door opens before I make it halfway up the walkway. My mom runs out to greet me, all big smiles and warm hugs, and I wrap my arms around her, not realizing until now how much I've missed her.

She's thin. She's always been that way, but her face is usually round. Even her cheekbones seem more prominent, though. My mind jumps to her not eating because she's stressed, and it makes me more pissed at my dad. He has to see what this is doing to her. Family means everything to her. *I* mean everything to her. His dividing the family will hurt her more than it will hurt anyone else.

Maybe he does see it.

Maybe that's why I'm here.

My stare travels to the front door, where my father stands in the doorway.

Neutral.

There's no emotion as he looks at my mother and me, waiting for us to come into the house. There's nothing. He's a stone of a man, and he's impossible to crack.

"Do you need help bringing anything in?" Mom asks as she peeks over my shoulder at my fully packed car.

Shaking my head, I say, "No. I'll get it later." Her eyes find mine again, a tight-lipped smile forming. She already looks like she's on the verge of tears, so I deflect by saying, "The house looks good," even though I can only see the outside, and it looks the same as it always does.

"Thanks, honey," she says, turning back up the walkway. Over her shoulder, she adds, "Are you hungry? Can I get you something to drink?"

The drive from school takes about two hours, so it's a little after noon, and I didn't eat breakfast. "I could eat," I say behind her.

She steps into the house, but I stop. Looking up at my father in the doorway, I hate that he's a step higher than me. It's only one step. Maybe a few inches, but the fact that he has any leverage over me at all still makes me uncomfortable.

"Hey, Dad," I say out of obligation. He's the parent. He should be the one to step up. He's the one who cast me out and is now begrudgingly letting me come home for the holidays.

"Chuck," my mother warns next to him, and my dad seems to blink, remembering this isn't a shitty dream he's having.

Taking a deep inhale, he mumbles, "You just couldn't wait to leave that fine college your mother and I paid for, huh?"

My grip tightens around the strap of my backpack, but I give him a tight smile. "Yup."

"Chuck!" my mother gasps, but she's the only one surprised here.

My father steps away from the door frame to go back into the house. "What Christine? The boy knows he's making his bed. Whatever happens, he'll lie in it."

Giving me an apologetic glance, my mother trails after him, scolding him with harsh whispers.

Taking a deep breath, I step over the threshold.

Home sweet home.

57
margot

"HAVE YOU TEXTED HIM?" Rae asks as she peers to look at my phone screen.

"No," I say, snatching my phone out of her view as I go back to checking the weather in Indiana. She's been asking me that same question for days, and my answer hasn't changed.

Her head falls back against the seat, and she groans. "We're about to take off. Just text him before you put your phone on airplane mode, and then when we land, we'll have something to look forward to."

Holding up my phone, I give my best frown. "Already in airplane mode."

Her eyes narrow. "You just did that."

Setting my phone down, I lean back in my seat to try and get comfortable for the flight. "I told you. There's nothing to text him about." Okay, there are probably a million things I could text Jackson, but I don't know where to start, and I'm afraid of opening Pandora's box.

Even without looking, I know she's glaring at me. She's been doing it a lot lately. "There are *so many* things you could text him about." She starts listing on her fingers. "Tell him you're going home for Christmas, ask him if he went home for Christmas, ask him if he said goodbye, tell him you can't wait to see him at the show in January."

I give her a knowing look.

"You're going to that show, and if you don't want to mess this up, you're going to text him."

"I will!" That came out a little louder than expected. Checking to make sure I didn't capture unwanted attention, I lower my voice and turn in my seat to face her. "I will text him," I say more calmly. "I just don't know what to say. We left things in a weird place."

She raises her eyebrows. "Him confessing his undying love for you doesn't sound like a weird place. It sounds like the type of place where you should have texted him by now."

I force a laugh. "He did not confess his undying love."

I haven't texted Jackson because I'm afraid of the outcome. If he left me that ticket as some type of olive branch so we can keep casually sleeping together, I've caught too many feelings for that to work. And if he left me that ticket because he wants us to see each other officially? Equally terrifying.

So, I haven't texted him. I've been perfectly content wandering around in this little world of *what if,* and I'm not in a rush to leave.

"You're texting him when we land," Rae says as the pilot announces we're clear for takeoff.

I shake my head at her before looking out the window. "Maybe."

I didn't text him when we landed. In my defense, there was too much going on. Even if I texted Jackson and he answered, what would I do? I can't get into a full-length conversation with him while I'm trying to get my luggage and meet my parents at the airport.

Tonight.

I'll text him tonight.

That's what I told Rae, but she looked at me like I was feeding her bullshit, and honestly, I could be. But as of right now, I have full intentions of texting him tonight.

Rae and I said goodbye at the airport, but I'll see her again while we're home. We only live about fifteen minutes from each other, and her mom has promised to make her signature Texas sheet cake.

Mom cried when she saw me even though she didn't reach out most of the semester, and I don't think I've ever seen my dad smile so big. They grilled me with questions the entire drive home.

How's living with Rae?
Are you making friends?
Have you been eating enough?

Now, alone in my bedroom, I feel like I can finally breathe. Our cat, Peanut, rubs his fluffy orange head against my hand, and I give him a scratch behind the ears. I told my parents I would set my stuff down and be right back, but it's been about twenty minutes, and they haven't come looking for me yet.

My bedroom looks the same as it always has. I didn't grow up in this contemporary home. My parents bought this house when I was a junior in high school, so there are no life-long childhood memories within these walls. Just a handful of nights where Rae and I snuck down to the kitchen to make ourselves amateur cocktails and binge-watch *One Tree Hill*.

A knock on my door frame gets my attention, and I look up to find my father standing there, tall and lean. "Hey, honey," he says, looking at me like I'm more delicate than I am. He didn't always look at me that way. He once treated me like I was fearless, and I can't remember when things shifted between us.

"Are you hungry? We made dinner if you'd like something to eat."

Returning his smile, I say, "That would be great." Getting to my feet, I follow him down the sleek wooden stairs with Peanut following close behind. Even though both parents have concerns about my major, my dad seems to have at least accepted it.

The chicken penne casserole my mother sets on the table still bubbles as we take our seats. Dad is the king of casseroles. He can take a mix of ingredients you'd never put together and turn it into something amazing. Since my mom works such long hours, my dad is usually the one who finds himself in the kitchen.

Mom smiles as she spoons a helping onto my plate and sets it in front of me. "It's nice seeing you at this table again."

"It's nice being here," I say with a smile, and I hope it doesn't come across as forced as it felt. Having a mother who's a shark of a lawyer takes the task of lying to a whole new level.

She takes a seat, eyeing me from across the table. "And your classes are going well, I take it?"

I look down at my food because it's easier than looking at her, and I feel like I'm ten again. "Yes. I have A's in almost all of them."

A light laugh leaves her. "I would hope so."

It's the first backhanded comment of the night, but my eyes still snap up to meet hers before looking at my father and then back down at my food. She thinks my major is easy. She thinks it's a waste of a degree, and more importantly, a waste of tuition.

"Do you think you'll live with Rae again next year?" my dad asks to smooth things over.

"I think so. She said she'll want to live with me for at least another year before she considers moving in with Matt."

Taking another bite, he cocks his head. "It's that serious?"

I push my food around with my fork but still manage a small smile. "I think so. He's great, and he treats her well, so . . ." I shrug as I let my voice trail off.

"And what about you?" my mother asks.

My smile fades, and I repeat, "What about me?"

She stares at me expectantly before circling her fork to urge me to explain. "Are you dating anyone?"

"No," I answer too quickly, but my cheeks heat. Desperate to hide any proof of Jackson, I stuff another bite of casserole into my mouth.

Mom's stare lingers. It's the look I imagine her giving someone during a cross-examination. "Are you sure?"

Rolling my eyes, I mutter, "I think I'd know if I had a boyfriend." I can still feel her eyes on me, so I take another bite, determined to shovel down my food as fast as I can.

"Chris has been asking about you."

My head snaps up, and I almost choke when I force myself to swallow my food too early. "Why?"

Just the thought of my ex-boyfriend still lingering in my life gives me an uneasy feeling. It's a combination of guilt and dread, and I was a lot happier when I didn't have it swirling around in my stomach ten seconds ago.

Guilt for not being as upset about our breakup as he was.

And dreading the possibility of seeing him again while I'm home.

My mother shrugs but still manages to carry her nose in the air as she does. "Why don't you ask him? It might be good for you two to talk things out."

My hand clenches around my fork. "So, what are our plans for Christmas?"

When my mother doesn't answer right away, probably debating whether she should let me get off that easily, my dad fills the silence. "It's going to be small this year. Looks like it will be just the three of us."

I raise my eyebrows. Christmas is usually spent at my grandparents' house an hour away.

"Your grandparents want to visit Uncle Max in Utah this year," Dad says with a shrug. "Max can't make it down, and they want to be fair."

"So, it's just the three of us," I echo, and hopefully, they can't hear the despair in my voice. Being an only child means holidays aren't usually a big affair, but I don't think it's ever been just us. There's always been at least one grandparent and maybe a stray cousin. "Okay," I say with a nod before taking my last bite. As soon as my plate is empty, I jump to my feet. "I'm going to head upstairs. Tired from the flight," I say with a yawn as I pick up my plate and head to the kitchen sink. I don't realize my parents are watching me intently until I've rinsed the plate and put it in the dishwasher.

"You're sure?" my dad asks with mild concern.

"Yeah." I give him my best smile. Turning to head back upstairs, I call out, "Love you guys!" over my shoulder.

Peanut slips in behind me as I close my bedroom door. I flop onto my bed and stare at my ceiling while my hand is met with soft head bumps and loud purrs. As I listen to my parents' hushed conversation about me downstairs, I miss the comfort of my dorm.

Reaching for my phone, I text Rae.

MARGOT:

> Is it just me, or is being home suddenly suffocating?

She answers right away.

RAE:

> Yes. What did Jackson say when you texted him?

My teeth sink into my bottom lip as I stare at her message,

not sure how to respond. Before I have the chance to answer, those three dots appear again.

> **RAE:**
> Because you did text him, right?

My thumbs hover over the keyboard, but I can't bring myself to type anything.

> **RAE:**
> Margot, I'm your best friend, but I am done talking to you until you text him. DONE.

Rolling my eyes, I toss my phone back onto my bed and turn over to find Peanut watching me.

"Should I text him?"

The sleepy orange ball of fluff just winks one eye open.

"I *know* I should text him, but . . ." I stare down at my judgmental feline, but he offers me nothing. Letting out an aggravated sigh, I snatch my phone back and pull up Jackson's name. Even seeing the letters on the screen makes my heart pound.

This is stupid.

The embarrassment of the last time I saw him creeps into the back of my mind, making my hands shake as I type out one word.

> **MARGOT:**
> Hey.

Before I can change my mind, I hastily hit *send* with my thumb and grit my teeth.

I should have said my name.

I should have said *something*.

But there's no going back now, and if I send a second message, it will only look like I sat here overthinking the first.

Nothing happens.

JUST DON'T CALL ME YOURS

No three dots appear to show that he's typing.

He's probably busy. He's probably with his friends from high school, having a great time catching up. Or maybe he's with his family, talking about important holiday plans, and I'm interrupting. They could be eating dinner . . . should I have waited until later? Who texts someone for the first time while they know they're eating dinner?

Appalled at how unknowingly inconsiderate I was, I roll over to bury my face in the pillow, tempted to scream.

My phone chimes next to me, and I push up on my hands, my hair falling in my face as I scramble for the phone. There's one unread message, and it's only one word.

JACKSON:

Margot?

58
jackson

MY GRIP TIGHTENS around my phone as I stare at the screen with unblinking eyes.

It has to be her.

After three days, I was starting to think she wouldn't reach out. I was starting to think I'd have to confront her the next time I visit Matt at school—whenever that is.

I look up at Matt playing Call of Duty. He's sitting on the floor in front of me while I sit on his bed. We were playing together until I got the text. As soon as I saw a message from an unknown number, I put the controller down and walked away.

"What the hell, man?" Matt moves his headset off his ear and glances over his shoulder at me. "You disappeared."

"I'm right here," I answer without looking away from my phone. The three dots haven't appeared yet, but I know she's there. I know she's staring at her phone screen the same way I'm looking at mine.

Or at least I hope she is.

The number appears again with a new message.

> **UNKNOWN NUMBER:**
> Yeah. Sorry it took so long to text you.

Quickly saving her as a contact, I lie back on Matt's bed to answer.

> **JACKSON:**
> It's okay. Are you in Indiana?

Matt finishes the game and throws his headset down. "Damn it. We lost." Glaring at me, he adds, "I wonder why."

Looking over at him, I say, "Margot texted me."

"No shit?" He turns to face me, resting his elbows on his knees. "What'd she say?"

"Hey."

He frowns. "Hey, what?"

My eyes settle back on my phone screen I refuse to let go dark—like letting the phone lock might somehow sever the connection I have with her. "She just said 'Hey.'" I can feel his eyes drilling into me, so I look back at him. "What?"

He drops his gaze. "I don't know, man." Looking up at me, he quickly adds, "Don't get me wrong. She's cool. I like Margot—I like her a lot."

With a lift of my eyebrow, I ask, "But?"

He frowns, debating whether or not he should say anything. He will, though. I can always count on Matt to tell me his honest opinion. We've known each other too long not to be straight with each other. "But I don't know if she's right for you."

I sit up, so I can give him my full attention. "Because?"

"Because you're practically a rockstar, and this girl can't seem to make up her mind. You should date someone who's sure about you—as sure about you as you are about them."

He's right. I know he's right, but I can't help feeling like

Margot *is* sure about her feelings for me . . . she's just trying to fight them.

"Don't take it the wrong way," he adds when I don't answer right away.

I force a breath of laughter. "I'm not taking anything the wrong way." Getting to my feet, I add, "But you're wrong."

He frowns. "Where are you going?"

My phone vibrates in my hand, and it takes all my self-control not to drop this conversation to read whatever text I just got. "I should head home."

The crease between his dark eyebrows deepens. "I can't tell if you're pissed."

I shake my head. "Not pissed. Just tired. See you tomorrow?"

He watches me with untrusting eyes. "Sure . . ." Before I turn to leave, he blurts, "I do really like Margot. If I could see that she likes you as much as you like her, I'd be all for it."

My mouth quirks. "She does. You just don't know her like I do."

Putting both hands up in the air, he says, "All right. Fine. Just know I've got your back, okay? Don't let her play with your head."

I walk to his bedroom door. "No one plays me." I hope I'm right.

As soon as I'm in the hallway outside of Matt's room, I look down at the phone and read the text as I walk through his house.

MARGOT:

Yup. I miss Florida.

My first instinct is to say how much I miss *her,* but I'm not stupid. So instead, I type the next best thing.

> JACKSON:
> Is that all you miss?

Matt and I live close enough to walk to each other's houses. When we first learned how to drive, we'd find any excuse to get in the car and drive the two minutes, but now that the excitement has worn off, we're back to walking.

I don't want to go home, though.

I may have lied to Matt when I said I was tired.

I'm not tired. If anything, getting a text from Margot has me feeling wired.

Taking a seat on a metal electrical box a few houses down, I stare at my phone and wait for her response.

> MARGOT:
> Are you asking if I miss you, Jackson?

My mouth pulls into a smile, and I'm just glad Matt isn't out here. If he saw me smiling down at my phone like an idiot, I'd never hear the end of it. He already knows how much I like this girl. The last thing I need to do is give him more reasons to think I've lost my head.

> JACKSON:
> No. I know you miss me.
> Just figured I'd ask if there was anything else.

My heel bounces against the concrete slab around the box.

> MARGOT:
> No. There's nothing else.

She didn't say she misses me, but she doesn't have to. When it comes to Margot, I know how to read between the lines.

Another text comes in.

> MARGOT:
> I got your note.

My heart pounds in my chest. I could play around. I could flirt. I could say just about anything back to that, but if she's being straightforward enough to bring it up, I'm going to do the same.

> JACKSON:
> I want you at that show in January.

The three dots appear and disappear a few times, and I'm about to send another text when her response finally comes in.

> MARGOT:
> Can I ask why?

My eyebrows pull together. One wrong move and I could scare her away. I want to show her that being with me won't be as hard as she thinks. If she'd just let me prove to her that we can do this, maybe she won't be so desperate to shut me out. Touring is the one thing I've always wanted, but it's also the one thing holding her back. I just want a little time to show her what it could be like.

Taking a deep breath, I send my response.

> JACKSON:
> Because I want to see you, and that show is the closest we'll be to campus.

It takes longer for her to text back this time, but when her message comes in, it brings a smile to my lips.

> MARGOT:
> Are you saying you miss me?

My heart pounds in my chest as I type.

JACKSON:

Too much.

The seconds turn into minutes with no new messages. If she didn't want me to say I missed her, why ask? Rolling my eyes, I get to my feet and start walking toward home.

But not before I call her.

59
margot

WHEN JACKSON'S name flashes on my screen as an incoming call, I drop my phone. It lands on my bed with a soft thud, but all I do is stare at it.

Why is he calling me?

I'm caught between feeling like I've won the lottery and also like I've done something to get myself into trouble. I hesitate like it might shock me if I touch it. But I somehow know Jackson will *know* if I ignore him. The answer bar at the bottom of the screen taunts me with every passing second until I can't take it anymore. Just before the call goes to voicemail, I snatch my phone from my bed and answer, my heart racing. "Jackson?"

My head falls forward. How dumb must I sound? Of course, it's him. His name was literally just staring me in the face.

"Do you think about me?"

My heart stutters. "What?" I ask with a nervous laugh.

"Do you think about me?" he asks again with all seriousness.

My chest tightens, the fear of confessing anything to him gripping me like a vice. "Why are you asking me that?"

"Because I think about you, and I want to know if you think about me, too."

"You think about me?"

A muffled groan comes through the phone, and I can picture him rubbing his hand over his face perfectly. "For fuck's sake, Margot. Yes, I think about you. Every damn day."

How does my entire body get warm just from hearing him say something over the phone? This shouldn't be allowed. He shouldn't be able to affect me the way he does. Especially not when he's hundreds of miles away. I know I should say something meaningful back to that, but the only word that tumbles from my mouth is, "Good."

The bite of his forced laugh cuts through me. "Yeah. Good for who?"

I frown. He doesn't sound like himself. He sounds . . . bothered, and he usually isn't fazed by anything. "What do you mean?"

"I don't know." His words drag out of him like a groan. "I just left Matt's house, and he—I just don't want to waste my time."

My teeth sink into my bottom lip. "So, that's why you called? To ask me if I think about you?"

"Yes," he says in a strained voice that chips away at me.

I can't bear the thought of being the reason he sounds like this. A sigh leaves my lips. "Of course, I think about you."

He sounds like he stops walking. "Yeah?"

I look up at my ceiling and hope I won't regret saying this. "Every damn day." Every minute of every hour would probably have been a more accurate response. I don't think I've stopped thinking about Jackson since I met him. The feelings behind those thoughts may have changed, but he's always been there, in the back of my mind.

A low chuckle leaves him, and it's a sound I can feel in my core. Part of me relaxes with him more at ease, but another part of me is frozen in fear. "But Jackson—"

"I just wanted to know if you think about me, Margot. I'm not asking for anything else."

Holding the phone in the crook of my neck, I fidget with my hands in my lap. "Okay."

"I just got home. I'll text you later, though."

"Has your dad been better?" I blurt before he can hang up. Knowing he's been home for days, and I haven't asked this brings a new wave of guilt. I should have asked him as soon as he was home, but I was too afraid of what texting him might mean *for me*. My chest tightens with regret at the thought.

There's a pause on the other end of the phone, and the silence breaks my heart.

"Jackson." His name is heavy on my lips.

He forces another laugh, but there's no warmth behind it. "I'm not sure 'better' is the word I'd use, but yeah. We've gone from what feels like blatant hate to a beautiful indifference."

I hate that he's going through this at what should be the happiest moment of his life. I grab my phone with my hand and sit up straight. "He'll come around. And if he doesn't, it's his loss."

There's another beat of silence. I wonder if I took things too far with that. I don't know all the ins and outs of his relationship with his dad. Maybe I'm overstepping. After what feels like forever, Jackson's voice comes through the other end of the phone. "I wish you were here."

His words squeeze around my heart. Lying back on my bed, I stare at my ceiling. "Me too," I say quietly, surprised by how much I mean it. How did this happen? How did he become the person my heart both beats and breaks for? "But you probably wouldn't want me there if I'm being honest."

"No?" A ghost of a laugh comes through the phone,

making the hair on the back of my neck stand up. "And why's that?"

A small smile pulls at the corner of my lips. "I don't think I'd be able to fake pleasantries with your dad. He'd hate me."

"He's not allowed to hate you."

Everything inside me aches. I ache to be near him. I ache to make him happy. I ache to stand up for him. Staring at my ceiling, I force myself to take a breath. Jackson isn't just a fling. He's more. He's the type of *more* you can't walk away from. Joining the band and touring might be Jackson's once in a lifetime opportunity that appears like a bolt of lightning, but if I'm being honest with myself, I think he might be mine.

My eyes are hot with the threat of tears, and I quickly wipe one away before it has the chance to fall. "Didn't you say you were home?" I can't let Jackson hear me cry. And over what? The fact that I like him so much? I need to get a grip.

"Yeah. I'm sitting against the garage. I'd rather stay out here with you."

Peanut bumps against my hand, and when I look at him to scratch his head, a rogue tear betrays me, sliding down the corner of my eye. My instinct is to end the call so he can't tell, but I have to stop hiding from him. I have to give him as much as he's given me. It's the right thing to do—it's what I *want* to do. "Okay," I say, wiping my eyes. "I've got nowhere to be."

And for the first time tonight, I can hear the smile in his voice when he says, "So, what are your plans for the holidays?"

Rae and I sit at her kitchen table eating cake. She finally agreed to see me again now that I texted Jackson, and I've been filling her in.

She scrutinizes me, her eyes narrowing. "You like him so much."

I groan and fold my arms onto the table. Letting my head fall, I surrender. "I know."

"Does *he* know?"

Tilting my head to the side to look at her, I say, "I think so?"

Rae shakes her head. "Not good enough."

Smoothing my hair away from my forehead, I sit up straight. "I know. I'm trying, but . . ." My voice trails off.

"But?"

She's looking at me like she knows exactly what the answer is, but she wants to hear me say it. "But he scares the shit out of me."

Rae takes another bite, unfazed by my confession. "I don't understand why."

I bite the inside of my cheek. "What if I'm right about him wanting to be single once he's on the road? What if he breaks up with me for that exact reason?"

She stares at me for a moment. "I don't think he will. And if he does?" She shrugs. "You move on and write about how shitty his band is on your blog."

I let out a breath of laughter. "I'm serious, Rae."

"Why are you so worried about being dumped?" Her eyebrows furrow. "I've never seen anyone handle a breakup as well as you handled yours with Chris."

I push my last few bites of cake around with my fork. "Maybe I like him more than Chris—more than I've liked anyone." I glance at her just long enough to register the surprise in her eyes. Before I can change my mind, I blurt, "Maybe the thought of getting dumped by Chris didn't scare me, but the thought of getting dumped by Jackson *terrifies* me."

I've never said the words out loud, but I know that's what it comes down to. I've never been with someone who could break me.

But with Jackson, I'm not so sure.

Rae leans back in her chair, the weight of my realization dawning on her. "Then you need to give this your all." She leans toward me, dipping her head to make me look at her. "Because if you don't? You'll regret it."

I set my fork down. "I know." She's right. I can't shut Jackson out just because I'm afraid things will end badly. If he's willing to try, the least I can do is meet him halfway. "But I don't know what I can do other than going to that show in Orlando next month."

"That feels so far away, too," Rae says as she takes another bite. She freezes with the fork in her mouth.

"What?" I ask.

Her wide eyes lock on me. "Has Jackson told you where his first show of the tour is?"

I shake my head. "I don't think so. Why?"

She purses her lips. "I could have sworn Matt said something . . . hold on." She reaches for her phone and starts frantically typing.

"Are you texting Matt?"

"No," she says as she continues to scroll and type. "I don't need to. It's on their site." She turns her phone to face me, and I lean forward to get a better look.

"No way," I say with a slow smile pulling at my lips. "Chicago?"

60
jackson

WITH THE HOLIDAYS BEHIND US, the van sits in Dave's driveway with all doors open as we strategically pack it full of equipment and gear. We each get a small bin to store clothes, a toothbrush, and a phone charger. It will be a tight fit all the way to Illinois, but right now, I love the sight of this overpacked van more than anything.

Stuffing my sleeping bag into the small space near my stuff, I curse under my breath when my headphones slip, falling around my neck.

"Yeah," Dave says next to me. Startled, I look over at him. I guess I have my noise-canceling headphones to thank for that. "It's going to be a tight few months," he says with a laugh as he shoves his own sleeping bag next to mine. Standing up straight, he steps back and looks at me funny. "Are you listening to Taylor Swift?"

Now that my headphones are around my neck, "Don't Blame Me" plays loud enough to be heard. "Shit," I mutter as I pause the song on my phone. When I look up again, Dave's watching me carefully with a knowing smile. "Missing a certain redhead?" he asks with a smirk.

There's no point trying to hide it. Just the indirect mention of her makes my mouth turn upward. "Fuck off," I say with a breath of laughter, and Dave only laughs harder.

"Are you two officially a thing yet, or what?" he asks casually as he moves on to organizing some of the equipment.

Leaning against the platform where we'll all sleep for the next few months, I say, "Still working on it."

He looks over his shoulder at me with an interested lift on his eyebrow. "Chasing tail, Phillips?"

"I guess we'll find out." Scratching the side of my head, I wish I had a better answer for him. I don't know if I'm wasting my time with Margot.

I hope not.

"Well," Dave says, turning to face me. "If it doesn't work out, you'll meet plenty of girls to help pick that ego up off the floor."

"Yeah." I scuff my foot against the dingy van floor.

I can still feel his eyes on me, and when I look up again, he has that same knowing smile. "But you don't want other girls."

I shake my head. "Not even a little."

The bark of laughter that comes from Dave's mouth is enough to make me laugh, too.

"What's going on in here?" Marty asks as he pokes his head into the van. He has his guitar slung over his back because we haven't figured out where he should store it yet.

Dave gives me a sideways glance before shrugging and shaking his head. "Don't look at me."

Marty's eyes jump to me instead, and I say, "We were talking about Margot." I don't mind talking to Dave about stuff, but I'm still on the fence about Marty.

He gives me an overly sympathetic look. "Is the puppy feeling a little lovesick?"

And there it is, the reason I don't want to talk to him.

"Hey," Dave says, holding up a hand. "Lay off. If it weren't for that so-called puppy, we never would have nailed this tour."

I frown, my eyebrows furrowing. "I doubt that." The band had already written and recorded most of their songs before I joined. I can't take credit for any of this.

But Dave's eyes bulge, and he enthusiastically nods. "Yeah, man. No shit. Someone at that first gig sent Sidecar's manager an article about you joining the band. He was scouting out some of the bands in the area and said he chose American Thieves because of it." He pauses, waiting for me to understand before continuing. "It wasn't our music, it wasn't our lyrics, it was *you*. He loved our 'new dynamic.'"

"An article?" I ask with a dubious lift of my brow. "Why would anyone write an article about me?" I'm pretty sure Dave's electric energy is what draws people to the stage.

"Here. I'll show you." He pulls out his phone before pointing at Marty over his shoulder. "It's not like this asshole was drawing anyone in. We haven't had such a big turnout until you showed up. They're all Jackson groupies."

Pushing off the platform, I scoff and shake my head. "Sure." Dave holds his phone out for me to take, and I stop breathing when I see the familiar header and formatting of Margot's blog. "Let me see that." I practically snatch the phone from his hands and skim the article.

American Thieves and their refreshing new dynamic.

This local treasure of a band has always found success within the city limits. Anyone can see the dedication shining in their fans' eyes as they line the front of the stage. But tonight, this beloved local group debuted their new guitarist, and it's clear he'll have them crossing state lines in no time.

The article goes on to talk about some of our hits and which songs were her favorite. It's a raving review from the girl I could have sworn hated me back then. How did I never see this? Scrolling back to the top, I check the date. It looks like she posted it a couple of days after the show.

She wrote about me.

This must have happened before I found out about her blog. I only ever looked at her most recent posts, and I definitely never saw this. If I had . . . fuck. I can't even think about how this might have changed things. She supported me . . . she's *always* supported me—even when I was the last person she wanted to be around.

Handing Dave back his phone, I try to hide the fact that the van suddenly feels like it's spinning. "Thanks."

"See!" Dave says with a grin. "We've got you to thank for all of this!"

I give him a weak smile before stepping out of the van. He's wrong. I have Margot to thank for this. She's the reason my dreams are coming true, and she did it all while I was having fun making her life a living hell. I blink, trying to understand how it's even possible. My palms sweat, and I wipe them against my jeans as Dave calls out, "Load up!"

Running a hand through my hair, I let out a breath. It was all her, from the very beginning. I put my headphones back on and let Taylor fucking Swift bring me a little bit closer to the girl who used to be just across the hall.

61
margot

OVER THREE HOURS on a train has given my nerves plenty of time to ramp up. My knee bounces in the back of the car as the driver weaves in and out of bumper-to-bumper traffic. Add driving in Chicago as one of the things I hate most in this world. Holy shit, I've never seen so many cars. Letting out a huff, I say, "Can you just pull over here?" to my Uber driver. I'll walk the rest of the way. It will be faster than dealing with the chaos.

The cold wind whips my hair as I step out of the car and onto the sidewalk. The bustle of the busy streets feels overwhelming at first, but there's also something easing about being one among many. I pull my coat tighter around me, and blend with the rest of the people walking in the same direction.

By the time I reach the venue, there's no one left in line, and I recognize the familiar heavy bass of one of American Thieves' top tracks.

They've already started playing.

I was supposed to get here early. That was the plan. The place has standing room only, so I wanted to be at the front of that stage. I wanted him to see me when he looked out into the crowd. This is the first night of his first tour, *someone* has to show up for him, and I think he'd want that person to be me.

I have no idea how I'll get to him. This may not be a huge venue, but it's big enough to know lying about my boyfriend being in the band won't get me anywhere.

Security scans my ticket, and I head into the large room where I'm instantly hit with a wall of bodies. They're all moving to the beat of the song, and I have to stand on the tips of my toes to get a good look at the stage.

The sight of him steals the breath from my lungs. He might look better than I remember, which I didn't think was possible. His hair is damp with sweat under the glow of the lights, and the muscles in his arms flex and move as he plays.

He's looking down, the way he usually does when he's on stage—like the music is all that matters. He doesn't need to see the crowd. He doesn't need to look up for anyone's approval or check for their reaction. He just plays. The way Jackson looks when he's on stage makes it seem like it's just him and his guitar. That's the beauty of it.

I have to get to the stage.

Slowly, I start to work my way forward as subtly as I can. At least it's just me. Being only one person makes it easier to look like I'm trying to get back to my friends. I only get a few weird looks from people who got here much earlier than I did to secure a better spot.

It takes me four songs, but I get as far as I think I can get. The people in the very front few rows won't leave an inch for anyone to jeopardize their view. Finally feeling like I can take a breath, I stop where I am and watch him. He's wearing dark jeans with a black shirt, and I take my time drinking in the sight of him. Of course, he doesn't look nervous. He doesn't look like this is his first time playing in a bigger venue for a bigger crowd. He looks perfectly at home, and seeing him like this is everything. *He's* everything.

I've missed him. I knew I missed him, but seeing him sends a fresh pang to my chest. There are too many wonderful feelings inside me, all bursting at the seams. The thought of surprising him by being here brings a sense of giddiness over me. I cup my hands around my mouth, and yell "Jackson!" A few heads turn, but I try my best to ignore their burning stares. "Jackson!" It feels ridiculous and wonderful to call his name. I came all the way here. I can't have it be for nothing. He should know someone is here for him. "Jackson!"

After the third time, Dave squints in my direction. His eyes widen, and he beams at me. Dave looks back at Jackson while he's singing and tries to get his attention with an outstretched arm, but Jackson is too zoned in. He doesn't even look up.

It's Marty who catches sight of the movement and looks at Dave with a furrowed brow. Dave nods in the direction of Jackson as he continues to belt into the mic.

Still playing, Marty walks over to Jackson, bumping him on the shoulder.

Jackson looks at Marty, who nods in Dave's direction.

My heart hammers in my chest because I know this is it. He's about to look my way, and I'll see if coming here was a mistake. I can't take it. Not caring if I make people angry, I push myself to the front of the crowd and lean over the metal barricade as Dave points a finger in my direction.

Jackson's head turns. He squints under the glare of the lights, but as soon as his eyes lock on mine, the blood pounding in my ears drowns out the sound of everything else. The crowd and band are muffled, and all I can focus on is the way his lips break into an easy smile.

And the way he takes me in, shamelessly checking me out like he's done so many times before.

And the way he bounces on his toes with child-like excitement as he continues to play.

Marty seems to finally understand what Dave and Jackson's

exchange was about. He grins and copies Jackson's movement, bouncing on his toes, too.

Dave joins in, mimicking Jackson the same way, and the sight of all three guys bouncing on their toes pulls a laugh from me. The relief that fills me almost makes me want to cry. His reaction beats anything I could have hoped for.

He's glad I'm here.

Jackson looks more alive as he plays now. He isn't wrapped up in the music as he stares down at his guitar. He looks like he's having fun, strumming the chords with more enthusiasm as he makes his way over to the lead singer.

As soon as the song ends, Jackson says something in Dave's ear, and Dave just smiles and shakes his head before stepping away from the mic.

I tilt my head when Jackson hands his guitar to Dave, who pulls the strap over his body and gets it into position, ready to play. Leaning toward the mic, Dave says to the crowd, "I hope you don't mind if we switch things up a little." Glancing at me again, his lips quirk. "You see, Jackson here has had it pretty bad for the girl next door." He winks at me before looking back at the crowd. "And ladies and gentlemen, she's here tonight!" The crowd cheers, and I feel my cheeks flush. "We're going to let Jackson have the mic for this next one, and if you know it, feel free to sing along."

Dave steps away from the mic and quickly runs back to Marty and Brady to tell them about the set change.

Jackson's hands rest on either side of the standing mic, and even though he's front and center, his eyes are glued to me in the crowd.

The band picks up the slow and steady tempo of "I Wanna Be Yours" by Arctic Monkeys, and my lips twist into a smile. It's the last song on the album he told me to listen to, and it's one of my favorite songs by them. Playfully, I shake my head at Jackson as he sings the opening lyrics. It amazes me how natural he looks standing in front of all these people. His body's relaxed, his voice steady, and the fact that he doesn't take his eyes off me brings a flush of heat up my neck.

Once the chorus starts to repeat, Jackson flags Dave over and steps away from the mic. Dave takes over the song without missing a beat, and Jackson jumps down off the stage with a mischievous glint in his eye. In one swift movement, he meets me over the metal barrier and cradles the nape of my neck with one hand as his lips crash into mine. He kisses me like no one's watching, and I cling to him. Guiding my face with his hand, he kisses me deeper, stealing the air from my lungs. I don't hear the music or the crowd—I don't even feel the people dancing around me. It's only Jackson, and I grip the metal railing and push up on my toes to lean into the kiss.

When he pulls away, I stare up at him completely breathless. His eyes are soft as he looks at me, the gray mixing with the blue, and I know this is where I'm supposed to be.

It isn't until his mouth quirks into that familiar, arrogant smirk that I register the roar of the crowd.

They're not watching the stage anymore, they're watching us. They're cheering for *us*.

Taking in the countless strangers celebrating, there are couples in the audience kissing everywhere like Jackson spurred a movement, and I cover my face with my hands.

Gently pulling my hands away, Jackson kisses the backs of my knuckles. "You're here," he says in disbelief.

"So are you," I say with a laugh.

He rests his forehead against mine. "Yeah. All thanks to you." I pull back, my eyebrows furrowing, and he shakes his head. "I'll explain later."

His eyes search mine, his slow smile growing bigger. Then he kisses me again. Fisting his shirt in my hands, I cling to him, never wanting this moment to end.

Dave clears his throat into the mic once the song ends, and

Jackson looks back at him and flips him off with a laugh. Turning back to me, he kisses my forehead and holds my face in his hands. "I'm yours, Margot."

Staring up at him, I slowly shake my head, unsure what to make of it all. "Okay," I say with a light laugh as I give in to everything I've felt since meeting him. "I'm yours."

To be continued . . .

I JUST WANT TO BE YOURS

bonus chapter

Scan the code below for a steamy bonus chapter that picks up after the show!

After the Encore

also by heather garvin

Make Your Move

Crossing the Line

Take What You Can

Give Nothing Back

acknowledgments

Wow, where do I even begin? Jackson and Margot's story has been in the works for a LONG TIME, and because of that, I've had the absolute honor of having the help of so many wonderful people. Readers and authors uniquely bring incredible insight to the table when it comes to making a story great.

A huge thank you to Corey Wys, Georgia Lomas, Courtney Grifo, Gabby Spiller, Cat Broomell, and Katie Moye. I am lucky to call each of you my friend and appreciate you taking the time to read this book more than I could ever express in a few sentences. Your reactions and critiques are what give these characters new life, and you always know how to improve the story.

Authors Letizia Lorini, Tisa Matthews, Dani Keen, and Sarah Hill have also dedicated their time to reading Jackson and Margot's story early. As indie authors, I know we all have a million things on our to-do list when it comes to publishing, so the fact that you take time out of your own projects to help with mine means the world to me. I couldn't have done it without you!

This time around, I also owe a huge THANK YOU to Kristina Haahr. I truly lucked out with finding such a kind, considerate, thorough, and talented editor. I feel so proud of this story, and a lot of that is thanks to you!

As always, I would like to thank Ava Rogers who has become my go-to proofreader for each of my books. Thank you for indulging in a little romance when I need you!

Last, but certainly not least, I would like to thank Trey and

Danielle Schexnayder for being the perfect couple and perfect character inspiration for Rae and Matt. I love you both dearly, and this book will always have a special place in my heart because of the characters inspired by you.

With each book, I am blown away by the support from friends and loved ones. I can't even wrap my head around all of you taking the time to read my silly love stories. You all mean the world to me. If it weren't for your help and friendship, none of this would be possible.

THANK YOU.

about the author

Heather Garvin works as a nationally certified sign language interpreter by day and writes a variety of romances in her spare time.

Aside from working and writing, she's also a wife, mom, and a fur mama to two dogs, two cats, and Tuskan: the horse who inspired her publishing company, Tuskan Publishing LLC.

There's nothing Heather loves more than hearing from readers. Connect with her @heathergarvinbooks